undone

undone

brooke taylor

WALKER & COMPANY
New York

First published in the United States of America in 2008 by
Walker Publishing Company, Inc.
Distributed to the trade by Macmillan

For information about permission to reproduce selections from this book, write to
Permissions, Walker & Company, 175 Fifth Avenue, New York, New York 10010

Library of Congress Cataloging-in-Publication Data
Taylor, Brooke.
Undone / Brooke Taylor.
        p. cm.
Summary: Sixteen-year-olds Serena and Kori look alike but have opposite
personalities and live very different lives in Kismet, Colorado, but when tragedy
strikes, Serena decides to complete Kori's list of "5 Secret Things" and uncovers,
in the process, the mystery that has bound them together.
ISBN-13: 978-0-8027-9763-6 • ISBN-10: 0-8027-9763-6
[1. Best friends—Fiction. 2. Friendship—Fiction. 3. Family life—Colorado—Fiction.
4. Single-parent families—Fiction. 5. High schools—Fiction. 6. Schools—Fiction.
7. Death—Fiction. 8. Colorado—Fiction.] I. Title.
PZ7.T212135Und 2008   [Fic]—dc22   2007037144

Visit Walker & Company's Web site at www.walkeryoungreaders.com

Book design by Nicole Gastonguay
Typeset by Westchester Book Composition
Printed in the U.S.A. by Quebecor World Fairfield
        2   4   6   8   10   9   7   5   3   1

All papers used by Walker & Company are natural, recyclable products
made from wood grown in well-managed forests. The manufacturing processes
conform to the environmental regulations of the country of origin.

To Dad, for your support and enthusiasm in all my many endeavors but particularly in this one—I know you are cheering me on still. XOXO

undone

The Beginning

Kori came with a warning label—a black T-shirt that read: DON'T BELIEVE EVERYTHING YOU HEAR ABOUT ME. On the day we became best friends, I was staring. Gaping. Gawking my geeky little eighth-grade eyes out. I'd expected the bathroom to be empty when I charged in with blue dye from an ill-fated lab experiment soaking through my Ruby Gloom T-shirt. I never expected Kori Kitzler to be standing there, tapping a cigarette out of a red-and-white box and asking me if I had a light.

My mouth dropped wide open. I don't know which startled me more—that she really thought *I* smoked (*at school!*) or that *she* was actually speaking to *me*. From the moment Kori had transformed herself from squeaky-clean cheerleader-wannabe seventh grader to I-puke-cheerleaders-for-breakfast eighth grader, I was fascinated by her beyond any sane boundary.

I looked down, my eyes stalling on the warning stretched across her larger-than-most chest. I'd heard a lot of things about her. I'd heard that before school even started, she'd already had oral with half the junior high football team. I'd heard she dropped E with high school boys and had a three-way with two college guys. I'd heard she cracked a Tiffany lamp over Chelsea Westad's brother's skull just because he told her she couldn't smoke pot in their house. I'd heard she threw up on the arresting officer and had lesbian sex while in the holding tank. I'd heard

1

that while the rest of our class was singing "Kumbaya" and making really crappy jewelry at summer camp, she was pretending to dry out while in rehab. And I believed it all.

In response to her smirk, I braved direct eye contact. In the almost black of her eyes—like two shots of espresso, just as dark and just as deceptively calm—I expected to see my fascination for her spat back at me. But I didn't. Under lazy, half-moon lids, her eyes were soothing, almost hypnotic. And in them, a serrated edge offering both protection and danger glinted.

"You don't know it now." She paused to take a drag (she had a light after all). "But you and I are connected." She held the cigarette out for me. As I took it, a seductive curl of smoke rose up like a ghost between us. "We're more alike than you think."

Discretion is knowing how to hide that which we cannot remedy.

—Spanish proverb

one

There they were—the worst words in all of the English language, scribbled in my mother's perky handwriting. "Let's talk."

I snatched the Post-it off the refrigerator door and glared at it. Heh. It didn't matter who said them—parent, teacher, or police officer—nothing good ever came of those words.

I returned to my bedroom to stick it with all her other "Let's talk" notes. They'd curiously begun appearing two years ago. The day I came home smelling of cigarette smoke with a new best friend.

The look on her face when I brought Kori Kitzler—fallen angel of the eighth grade—home with me was just like those credit card commercials: priceless.

And I could tell exactly what Mom was thinking behind the fake smile she'd scrambled to plaster on: *My daughter's going to hell. What will people think of me?*

Yes, if the growing mosaic on my wall was any indication, my mother believed the slope to hell was paved in yellow, blue, and pink—but mostly yellow—"Let's talk" Post-its.

Who was she kidding? There was no "let's" about it.

Perched on the toes of my boots, I reached over my desk to

add this latest addition and accidentally bumped into my keyboard. The distinctive sparking whoosh of my ancient CRT monitor coming to life pierced the air. Soon the smell of burning dust would rise through the plastic vents at the back. I'd asked for a Sony StylePro 20.1-inch flat panel for Christmas last year; under the tree I found a Conair Pro Style 2-inch flat iron. It probably would have been a good time for me to give my mom a "Let's talk" Post-it.

I moved to power off the monitor, but stopped when an instant message blipped on the screen.

shaym: Kori?

If I wasn't so late already, I would have responded. I would've asked who "shame" was, because I knew everyone Kori did. Would've asked why he thought my screen name was hers. Instead, I shut down my PC. The message disappeared from my monitor, but not from my thoughts.

Kori keeping someone from me meant one thing. She was using the hard stuff again. I wonder if she ever really stopped.

When I spotted the school, I sprinted. Only two weeks into my sophomore year and already I couldn't afford another *"Buenas tardes"* in first-period Spanish. Maybe that's what Mom's note was for, I thought, and right as I did I ran smack into Josh Krivvy, computer gaming geek. Not to be confused with just any computer geek. Thanks to the Japanese-Version-Only gamers, it's become a world divided. For the record, I'm a gaming geek of the development variety—a hacker, a code addict, a "sourceress"—but I play it down big-time at school, so I don't end up like poor Josh.

Poor Josh!

I released the door handle and wheeled back to find him sprawled on the pavement with my boot prints across his back. Quickly, I ran down the stairs toward him, skidding to a stop and dropping my bag with a force that spilled its contents onto the grass alongside his.

Josh clutched at the ballistic nylon and ripcord pulleys of his backpack, salvaging out his PC notebook from its padded-by-NASA slipcase. With a desperate push of his finger, he attempted to power the notebook up. My heart fisted.

I couldn't stomach the waiting. In an unguarded moment of panic, I wailed, "Is it okay?!"

I pulled in deep breaths; Josh held his. We both waited. And watched. And prayed. Then out of the silence, it beeped.

Josh exhaled. I collapsed to my knees in relief.

Normally, I wouldn't have shown that kind of emotion over an electronic device within a hundred-foot radius of school, but seriously, that's one damn fine gaming laptop he's got.

The sound of the first bell shattered my relief.

I scrambled to help him with his books and papers, all of which had gone flying because—*rolls eyes*—his backpack is reserved for electronics and games *only*.

As I glanced guiltily over at him, I couldn't help but think how easily I could've been just like poor Josh—faded into the background, immersed in my own little cyberworld, hiding behind my subnet mask—if not for Kori swooping in on her dark wings and changing everything.

"I'm so sorry, Josh. I didn't even see you."

Josh wheezed, taking a quick hit off his inhaler.

I really didn't think I'd hit him that hard.

God, I hope I didn't bruise him.

"Oh, um . . . uh . . . huh," he stammered, scraping together loose papers. His major crush on me explained, but didn't excuse, his repeated attempts at brushing hands with mine while collecting the last of the papers.

My other friends think his crush on me is cute, but Kori, who always refers to him as my "crushy stalker boy," says it's pathetic. What's pathetic is that last year Principal Teasley busted him ogling the Pixilated Women of *Playboy*. Accusations of him warming his worm to the sex scenes in *Team America World Police* soon spread.

Yes, gamer boy isn't into any RL women except me. Aren't I the lucky one?

Not that he actually speaks to me in "Real Life" or anything. At least not in the two years since his chemistry experiment prematurely ejaculated blue dye on me. But we do have decent IM chats whenever he stalks me online. In real life, he just sort of stares at me and drools. Okay, it's not like he actually dribbles spit or anything, but his lips get freakishly moist.

"S-S-Serena?"

Stunned, I gaped back at him. He speaks! Josh actually broke the seal of silence and spoke words to me? I must have loosened something when I smacked into him.

"Um . . . your . . . um, n-necklace?"

My fingers touched the key that hung around my neck.

"Yes! The um, k-key? Oh, um, y-yes, what's it . . . um . . . t-t-to?"

It was hard to believe this was the same guy who wrote witty IM repartee with me under the egotistical yet well-earned pseudonym King-O-Ding.

Before I could answer, Kori was suddenly standing in front of me. "Yeah, Serena. What *is* the key to?" I jerked at the sound of her throaty voice, bolting to my feet as if Josh and I had been doing something illicit in the grass.

If anyone had something to hide, it was her, I thought watching Parker Walsh's blue Mazda peel out. Parker Walsh, whose crowning achievement is coming up with 360 different ways to smoke a bowl, was the last person I wanted to see her catching a ride—of any kind—with.

Kori circled behind me and tucked her chin onto my shoulder. "Is it the key to your heart?" she asked in a husky whisper—like she was the one in love.

Poor Josh's cheeks turned all blotchy like raw sausage, an interesting complement to his pork chop sideburns.

Even though his crush annoys the hell out of me, I wasn't at all cool with Kori embarrassing him. Probably because I felt guilty about knocking him down. I tried to deflect the embarrassment of crushdom with an evil cackle: "*Muuaaahh*. It's the key to the gates of hell."

Kori lifted her chin off my shoulder and mimicked my evil tone. "It's the key to the crypt."

"It's the key to my cage." I liked that; a puppy kenneled while the master was away.

Josh was too busy staring at the point where my bare thighs emerged out of my plaid kilt mini to come up with anything of his own, but managed to make a strange sound I hoped was laughter.

Luckily Kori didn't capitalize on it but instead exclaimed, rather loudly, "The key to success!"

"Yeah! There are ten of them!" It was kind of an inside joke.

The Ten Keys to Success is one of my mother's self-help books. It sits alongside many, many others, like the entire Chicken Soup collection—including but not limited to *Chicken Soup for the Single Mother's Soul, Chicken Soup for the Teenager's Soul* (and no, I haven't read it, much to my mother's dismay), *Chicken Soup for the Pet Owner's Soul* (never mind that we don't have a pet. Thanks to me, because I was too irresponsible at eight years old to care for the 100-gallon saltwater aquarium Father Hillman had given me. Hello?). And then there was my personal favorite— *Alien Nation: Understanding Today's Teenagers.* Kori and I had a good laugh when we discovered that one. We went to the school's Halloween party as—you guessed it—aliens. When people asked us about our costumes, we said we were dressed as our true selves and it was the rest of the year that we wore costumes.

So when Kori exclaimed, "It's the key to the universe and beyond!" I cracked up. Josh started laughing too, but since he had no idea why it was so funny, Kori and I laughed even louder.

"Come on, we're going to be late," Kori said, taking hold of my wrist.

I grimaced down at Josh. Well, more down at my vintage burgundy Docs. They might as well have been red with his blood; in fact there probably was some on the soles. "I'm *really* sorry."

Then I ran. Up the stairs, through the doors, past my locker, and into Señora Rosa's classroom. I slid into my chair as the second bell hit its last note. Josh wasn't so lucky.

"So, check it." Kori handed me a laminated card as she slid into the seat next to mine two periods later. Supervised study was the only class we actually had together. It was "taught" by Coach Kent, who spent the majority of the hour reading the paper—in the men's room. So there was minimal supervision. And even less studying.

"A license?" I asked.

"Correction: *my* license."

"But, you're not . . ." I held it up, turned it over. "It looks so real."

"Should be. It *is* real. The guy at the DMV did it. All me. Well, except for the messed-up birth date."

I eyed her, wondering if maybe this was the guy who was IM'ing her. I didn't really want to hear, but I asked anyway. "And *why* would he do that?"

She returned my narrow-eyed stare, more playful than angry. "I didn't do anything *sexual* with him, if that's what you're insinuating. Although he is pretty cute."

"So why'd he do it, Kor?"

"Kieren gave him a clean urine sample."

"Gross. So, wait—Kieren's clean now?"

Kieren is Kori's older brother—he's a senior. She has two—Kyle, who is perfect; and Kieren, who pretends to be perfect. Kori, who doesn't give a shit about perfection, is the black sheep of the family despite all her mother's bleaching efforts.

"Yeah," Kori said as she rolled her eyes. "He wants to take his skateboarding to a"—she made finger quotes—"whole new level. Anyway, now I can go down to that club in LoDo I was telling you about."

"The karaoke thing?"

"It's not karaoke, it's a real club, real band, actual singing. Bleeder Valve? Remember, the band I told you about? Kieren's going to drive me. Mom would shit a brick if she knew."

I glanced at the fake ID in my hand. "Well, since you have a license and all, you could actually drive yourself, couldn't you?"

"True. I'd have to get a car, though. The only one I could jack would be Park's. It would be easy; he'd be too stoned to even notice." She thought about it for a moment. "No. I couldn't do that. Wouldn't be fair."

I snorted. "Honor among thieves?"

Her burgundy lip curled in a smirk. "Yeah. Something like that." Then: "You know, Parker thinks the ID looks more like you than me."

"Really?" I looked again at the ID. Now that I'd dyed my hair black and flattened it out with the Pro Style, Kori and I looked identical.

Lexi Devlin (my friend *and yet also my mother's biggest advocate*—go figure) thinks I dyed my hair to upset my mom. But really, I did it to be different from her.

See, the thing with my mom—she was just seventeen when she got pregnant with me. So she's got this chip on her shoulder. Like she has to prove to everyone that she isn't the slutty, white-trash girl they think she is. She totally overcompensates. Like the way she always wears panty hose and pumps even though she's on her feet all day, and all her how-to and self-help books so she can be an expert on everything—oh, perfect example—the Baked Alaska. Okay, so, she asked me what I wanted served for my tenth birthday. My reply—hamburgers and ice cream.

In the living room—full-on Martha Stewart decorations and not a speck of dust, and for dinner these bizarrely exotic vegetarian "hamburgers" with ciabattá-like buns. The whole spread could have made the cover of *Bon Appétit*.

In our kitchen—half a wall burnt to a crisp, because who else besides my mother would even *think* about putting a blowtorch to ice cream?

It's all about the illusion. And my mom would love nothing more than for me to appear, if not actually be, just like her—sunshine, white light, daisies, and doves.

And I wanted to be dark. Like Kori.

She's got this sort of Lisa Marie Presley vibe going on, or a pre-sobriety Drew Barrymore thing. Those great lips, sleepy eyes, and haunting voice.

She's got true darkness about her.

When I told her I envied her that, she told me, *"You'll never be the night, Serena, you've got so much warm light inside of you. You're burning bright."*

She said it like it was a blessing, like she was the one who envied me.

Then she sang Shinedown's "Burning Bright" like a lullaby. God, it sounded so cool drawn out of her ethereal throat. So poetic and perfect, just like Kori herself. The first time I heard her sing, it was pure, flesh-chilling awe, like hearing The Sundays' version of "Wild Horses" after years of the Stones.

"You could use it, you know . . . if you ever have need," Kori said as I handed her fake ID back. "If anyone questions you on it, just remember it has my address and we were born in '87." Kori and I have the same birth date. Twins separated at conception. That's my theory at least.

She scrutinized me. "And, of course, you'd have to remember that you're me."

Ever since Kori and I became friends, ever since she'd spoken those simple words—*"We're more alike than you think"*—I'd been trying to find anything inside of me, anything at all, that resembled her.

Even with her fake ID, I don't think I could ever forget that I was not her.

After all, she was the kind of girl who could get a fake ID, get up in front of a club full of people and sing, and I was so *not* that girl.

In fact, today I was the girl whose mother couldn't even bother to have a verbal conversation with her. The girl who had to crack Da Sticky Note Code.

In my experience with things like this, I've found it's a good idea to have a defense strategy already in place. First I needed to figure out exactly what she knew. In English class, when Mrs. Talaber and her Aqua Nest hair started in on part five of her thirty-part series on sonnets, I decided to make a list of all the possibilities. Not that I'm all that big on lists or anything, but I'm not big on sonnets either.

I decided to classify my crimes into three categories: Petty Offenses, Misdemeanors, and Felonies.

With pen poised as if hanging on Mrs. Talaber's every overly enunciated word, I gave it some thought.

Obviously it was something big enough to warrant a Post-it note parental conference. Since truly heinous crimes usually skipped the request for face time and went straight to an all-out in-your-face trial with immediate conviction, I could rule them out. So, logistically speaking, I was working with a casual sin. The type of crime that generally had a weeklong statute of limitations, because if I didn't hear about it within a week, I considered it gotten away with and forgotten. That should have narrowed it down. It didn't.

Thanks to having Kori Kitzler as a best friend, a lot could happen in one week.

"Miss Serena Moore?"

I glanced up at the expectant Mrs. Talaber and her permanently pursed lips. I hadn't heard a single syllable of her lecture.

I slid my elbow over "Felonies" as she approached. "Yes?"

I felt the sudden pressure of everyone's eyes on me, a feeling

I never enjoyed. Which is why I could never be a cheerleader. Well, that and I can't do a herkie. Whatever the hell that is.

"What strikes you as different when reading this sonnet by Shakespeare?"

Time to fake it. I glanced down at the text in front of me and skimmed the poem, hoping that we hadn't flipped pages while I wasn't paying attention. I'm guessing she didn't want my revelation on Shakespeare's sexual orientation, so I hedged. "His obsession with immortalizing his lover's youth." Wasn't that what all of his were about?

"Yes. Well, that is a very good analysis. Let's give it some more thought, shall we? Miss Mancini, how about you?" We both turned to find Marci positively glowing—as any good cheerleader would—from the attention. "What strikes you as unique about this *type* of sonnet—as it pertains to today's lecture?"

"The rhythm. It's not a-b-b-a; it's a-b-a-b."

"Very good. Exactly."

Whatever. At least I knew she wouldn't be calling on me again, which was all the more reason to continue what I was doing. My brain scoured the past week, while I jotted down all of the possibilities. When I exhausted every potential crime, I categorized and tallied them.

I tapped my pen on "Petty Offenses." These consisted of things that could easily be defended with a simple yet effective, "Give me a break." This week those included countless acts of illegal music downloads, six counts of looking at explicit photographs and lewd jokes online, lost effing count of using profanity (but, damn it, I'm trying), and one count of hacking into various JV cheerleader blogs to slam on the varsity cheerleaders, thereby creating a Kismet High civil war. (Although "hacking" is probably too strong a word, seeing as how they all had the same predictable password: Adrian17. What is it with cheerleaders and quarterbacks anyway?)

For the week's misdemeanors I compiled one count of stealing a Twix from the Mini Mart, multiple counts of stealing beer from Kieren (let the record state—I was merely an accomplice), one count of changing the school's motto on their master e-mail signature from "Achieving Excellence" to "Achieving Ecstasy" after *The Rocky Mountain News* did an exposé on the French club's summer trip to Paris, four counts of allowing Kori to cheat off my Spanish homework, one count of ditching supervised study in conjunction with one count of Menstruation Fabrication so I could watch Maury Povich on Nurse Zimmerman's couch, lost count of smoking cigarettes, and three counts of sneaking out after curfew and drinking aforementioned stolen beer. With cases of this nature, my defense strategy was a combination of repent and trivialize. Something along the lines of: "I'm really sorry, I shouldn't have done it. This was the only time, I won't do it again, I promise."

And just in case it might appear like I use my computer hacking skills only for evil, I'd like the record to reflect that I personally shut down two perverted seniors' attempt at an "Up-Skirt" Web site by redirecting their URL to a site catering to a slightly different clientele—urm . . . I believe they call themselves Chubby Chasers.

Felonies have no real defense strategy; generally I just wing it. And by winging it, I mean a lot of yelling, usually something retro and eighties, like "It's *my* body!" Since felonies tend to elicit an immediate reaction, I could rule them out of cracking Da Sticky Note Code. But for the record, this week there had been only one: the tongue piercing.

I still can't believe I went through with it. I hate painful things. Hate pain. Detest pain. But Kori was giving me shit for always wussing out on her with stuff like this, told me it wasn't actually pain I hate but the fear of pain and that it was about time I got over that crap.

Then she reminded me how pissed off my mother would be. So I did it. And it hurt. Confirming that yes, I do hate pain. Actual pain.

I haven't blatantly flashed it at my mom, but I don't see how she can't know about it. The first two days I sounded like Marlee Matlin whenever I spoke, and Random Acts of Blindness were not something she regularly practiced. Something had to be distracting her.

I glanced over my list. Something was missing.

Oh. Add one count of hacking into the Peak County Medical database. I do this at least once a week, sometimes more. I don't know what category it would fall under or if I even consider it an offense. Yeah, yeah, yeah, I shouldn't be scaling over their piss-poor firewalls, but it's not like I'm looking at other people's records, just my own. Specifically the record regarding my birth, and I wouldn't have to do that if my mom weren't so freaking evasive about it. I don't know why I keep pulling the stupid record up anyway; it's not like it has any of the information I need. But I'm determined to find out exactly who "unknown" is and why my mother has kept him a secret from me.

two

I'm actually surprised my mom has been able to keep my paternity a secret, considering the small community we live in. People usually say Kismet is "nestled" in the foothills of the Rocky Mountains. One of those best-of-both-worlds kind of places—small-town morals, city conveniences less than an hour away, property values that ensure a certain class of neighbors. The scenery is a breathtaking mix of pine and aspen, and the air is fresh. Wives stay at home (*mostly*), kids stay out of trouble (*ahem*), and husbands stay happy (*yeah, right*). The buffalo roam . . . *and deer and antelope play.* During the week, most (people, not deer or antelope) commute into Denver for work. Some go so far as to buy expensive loft apartments in the trendy lower downtown area known as LoDo, so they can have easy access to the hippest bars, best restaurants, and all the major league sports. On the weekend people play golf, mountain bike, ski, and kayak. It's the dream life.

But not everyone in Kismet is living the dream.

Unless you count real estate, there is no industry in Kismet, so the only jobs are low paying—fast food, police, teachers—stuff like that. Or you work at Peak County Medical, like my mom does. Before the developers came and put in the gated subdivisions and golf courses, most people were able to afford a nice house. Now the property values are too high. So, like many, we live in a town house.

It's not, like, "a thing." But for the record, all of my best friends—Kori, Lexi, and Cole Blakely—live behind the gates.

After school Kori and I went outside to have a smoke. From where we were sitting we could see everything—the parking lot, the boys playing football, the girls playing cheerleader, the stands of aspens high on the mountain slopes. We were waiting for Mrs. Blakely to pick up Cole so we could bum a ride, but we weren't optimistic. We hadn't seen Cole at her locker, and her mom's Mercedes SUV wasn't waiting in front of the school. Not surprising, since Cole's mom is a complete diva. If Mrs. B. has an appointment—nails, hair, Botox, colonic—she picks Cole up early, excusing her from supervised study. So the probability of our walking was always high.

Our backs were pressed against the massive river rock wall of what would soon be the new performing arts auditorium. Kori's parents generously donated the funds to build it, which is a little insane, since Kori's mother would never attend an event that didn't require season tickets, ensuring her the best seats and a no-popcorn policy. And as for Kori's father, seeing it among his tax deductions would be as close as he would ever be to it. He showed love with very large buildings that doubled as tax write-offs.

In fact, without him, Peak County Medical would be a mere regional clinic and not a full-service facility. I doubt my mother would even have a job. A lot of people wouldn't. I think Mr. Kitzler likes to have that kind of power. It's probably good that he's more concerned about what the community thinks about him than what his own children do. Because with his latest donation, the community thought he was the most supportive father in all of Kismet. Maybe even the world.

It's no wonder Kori so adamantly dismisses my father fetish— to her it's all a crock. In a way, neither one of us had a father.

Maybe she was right that day in eighth grade. Maybe we were connected in ways I didn't understand. And I may never know why she chose to become friends with me. But now our lives were so intertwined I didn't know where I began or where she ended. I only knew that together we were both whole.

But even as close as we were, she had her secrets. She'd been acting odd all day and I was pretty sure it wasn't drugs. I wondered again about the IM from the mysterious shaym. Wondered who would think I was her. But I wasn't ready to ask her about it. Not yet.

Realizing how quiet Kori'd been, I looked over at her and caught her watching the cheerleaders. Her ex middle-school friends.

She stabbed out her cigarette on the wall behind us, dropping the butt. Then she brought her hand back down, raining her black fingernails through my hair. Little tingles scattered all up and down the nape of my neck.

She's lavish with affection. It doesn't mean we're gay or anything. Kick-ass, Nine Inch Nails girls can be affectionate just like the little Blond Bitch cheerleaders are.

Speaking of the BBs, Chelsea Westad, the mayor's daughter, head cheerleader, and all-around dingbat, was making quite the production of showing off her new car. We watched in rapture as Chelsea dragged two junior girls over to it, pointing to her vanity plate and laughing. Kori narrated the scene for me:

"Look at me! I'm clever! I have a vanity plate! Look at me.

I made a funny! Bar B. Get it? Barbie. I'm blond. I'm cool. That's hot."

Then Kori captures beautifully the Blond Bitches' self-esteem-pumping ritual as it is so annoyingly played out in front of us. "Shu-tup! *No, you shut up!* You, shuddup. *Ohmagawd, we can't shut up!* Ahhh-hahahah."

"Can somebody shove Napoleon Dynamite up her skinny butt, please?" I muttered.

Kori flashed her wrist at me, changing the subject. "Think I should get this for real?"

She'd been drawing tattoos on her arm when I found her after school. She's always doodling—on herself, in her notebooks. She creates some amazing things. I wish I had her creativity, but game coding is the only thing I have that resembles artistry, and if you knew the truth you'd know it was really just a bunch of code—math, syntax, logic—brainiac stuff.

"Wow, Kor, that's amazing," I said, taking a moment to study it. The black ink formed perfect tribal waves in a cuff bracelet. Chinese symbols dangled like charms around it. "But don't you think it's kind of hypocritical, since you're anti cosmetic surgery and all?"

"I'm a vegetarian who loves cheeseburgers and a smoker who despises big business. I hate how my father tries to buy everyone's love but would love it if he would buy me a car when I turn sixteen. What do you want from me? I'm a complicated person."

I was too busy studying her wrist, marveling at her talent, to notice the BBs' approach.

"Uh-oh. Here come Britney Duff and Mary-Kate-and-Ashley Simpson. I wonder what they want," Kori said under her breath.

Marci Mancini jogged toward us, her black-and-blue cheerleader skirt flouncing. Leave it to Kismet High to have a bruise as its school colors. Chelsea followed, less enthusiastically.

"Hey, Kori, can I borrow your pen for like a millisecond-point-five?" That *point-five* thing is the BBs' latest superannoying catch phrase. *"I've got two-point-five gazillion hours of homework . . ." "I've got one-point-five boyfriends . . ."* Surprisingly, Kori didn't try to wing her pen at Marci's face when she flicked it to her.

When Marci returned "ten-point-five" seconds later, she did a double take at Kori's tattoo. I fully expected some lame-ass jab, not: "That's cool, does it mean anything special?"

Before Kori could answer, Chelsea glided up closer to see what the fuss was all about because Chelsea is all about fuss. She twirled the keys to her car, the silver Tiffany key chain shooting off sunrays with each revolution.

Kori glanced up at Marci, as surprised as I was that they were talking to us. Surely Marci wasn't seriously interested in Kori's tattoo. Chelsea definitely wasn't, and her judgmental grunt proved it.

"It's an ancient Chinese proverb."

"Really?" Chelsea said, wrinkling her nose. "You mean like— an ounce of heroin is worth a pound of pot?" She tried to sound disgusted, but she was too excited by her own cleverness that she started snorting.

One look at Kori's smirk and I knew in her head she was continuing to narrate for Chelsea. *Look at me! I'm witty! I'm blond! I made a funny!* But aloud, Kori countered with, "It's Chinese for: Hilary Duff can eat my muff."

Oooh! Smack down! That obliterated the smile off Chelsea's face.

I glimpsed a quirk at the corner of Marci's lips, but Chelsea huffed in revulsion and whatever humor Marci had found in the situation was well masked.

"Well, that was a quick battle of Yo Momma," I said, faking a pout.

Chelsea treated us to one of her perfected ice queen laser stares. Her best one yet. Brava! "Come on, Mar, you don't want to get a contact high off dragon lady here."

"Now, now, let's not be hypocritical. Heath was asking where he could score some *exx-tee-see* for you."

Heath is "the one" of Chelsea's one-point-five boyfriends.

I'm not sure if it's truly to aid her sex life so much as it's a drug with a label. (She'd shoot up if Prada came out with a line of needles. She does love her labels.) But, in a stage whisper to me, loud enough for the rapidly-departing-in-a-huffing-fit Chelsea to hear, Kori added, "I hear it turns the Ice Queen into a hyena in heat."

"Ooh, you mean she's a frosty slut?" I said, and then jerked around, my face flushing at the sound of someone laughing—a deep, throaty, masculine rumble.

"Who was that?" I asked Kori while motioning toward the only guy in the parking lot.

"You mean Becks?"

"Who?"

"Anthony Beck. You remember him. Total rock star."

I looked back toward the parking lot, but he was nowhere to be found. There was just Chelsea sneering back at us. As she whipped her hair over her shoulder, she caught Marci stifling a smile, and practically shouted, "Are you, like, gaining weight? That skirt can't be let out any more, you know!" I dropped my eyes to avoid the hurt look on Marci's face as she slid into Chelsea's car.

As we watched Chelsea's Bar B mobile speed past, Principal Teasley shouted at her to slow down.

Kori laughed. "Park got the Mazda up to seventy-five this morning. Cool, huh?"

I didn't want to talk about Parker Walsh. Certainly didn't feel like congratulating him on breaking the speed record on "The Strip"—the long, straight stretch of Kismet High's driveway.

"What's that look for?" she asked, seeing the scowl on my face. "God, you're such a hater."

"He's a bad influence on you."

That made her laugh. "Kinda like how I'm a bad influence on you?"

Touché.

"Why *are* you friends with him?"

"Why am I friends with you?" she countered, then winked.

Sometimes I wonder, I thought. But what I said was, "Speaking of bizarro friends, I can't believe you used to be best friends with Chelsea Westad. She's such a BBFBBM."

"Is that one of your geeky anachronisms?"

"One of my geeky acronyms actually. Translation: body by Fisher, brains by Mattel."

"Careful, that's a compliment for her."

"So, did you guys like have sleepovers and everything? Shudder."

Kori's eyes darkened a shade. We haven't talked about her old affiliations in forever, and doing so, even casually, is like poking at a bruise—which sometimes you need to do just to gauge how it's healing or to know if it's really gone.

It wasn't.

The circumstances of Kori's defection from the in crowd aren't something she ever talks about. And thinking back, I don't remember much about those days toward the end of seventh grade right before Kori spent the summer at camp, or rehab if you believe everything you've heard about her, which I don't anymore. I was naive and stupid back then. But I do know that when Kori came back, she was the slut of the school. And all I really know is whatever happened between her and Chelsea must've been pretty big if Kori won't talk about it.

I wasn't sure if Kori was angry or hurt or betrayed; anything she'd ever said on the subject was covered with sarcasm. "Oh, bestest buds we were. Our Barbies even had lesbian sex once in college, but then Skipper got between them and Ken got jealous, 'cuz he wanted to be gay first. So he divorced her, took the 'Vette, the beach house, and all of her best dresses. It's been awkward ever since. But our families still exchange Christmas cards."

"Isn't Skipper like Barbie's cousin? I'm sooo calling Maury Povich."

"You do love you some Maury, doncha."

Heat rose up my neck as I remembered requesting to be on his show. I may have even suggested having every man in Kismet DNA-tested to see if any were my father. Kori had to sit on me to get the show application out of my hands, so I really didn't feel like bringing it all up again and decided to change the subject. "So, what does your tattoo mean?"

"It's a reminder to forget something."

"How very *Memento* of you." I ran my gaze over the Chinese symbols, thinking: *What can't you forget, Kor?*

three

Forgetting wasn't my problem. Remembering was. Somewhere deep inside the recesses of my brain, I knew images of my father existed. Like a primordial tattoo that was branded during conception.

But when I try to remember back, the earliest memory that surfaces is of a baby bird lying in the parking lot of our complex. I remember wanting to help it. Save it. I went to scoop up the baby so I could somehow put him back in his nest, and my mother grabbed my wrist. She told me if I touched it, I would contaminate it and the parents wouldn't help it; they'd leave it to die. Horrified, I started crying. But Mom assured me the baby bird's parents would get it back up in the nest.

I stayed with it, keeping out of sight. Eventually two birds did fly down. I remember the sound of their wings slapping against the air, their beaks hinging wide, the squawking angry screams. They flew, one at a time, up to the nest and then back down. But eventually they gave up. And it was quiet.

As if they knew the baby's parents would not be coming back, Mrs. Patterson's cats began stalking the helpless creature. I kept chasing them away, but it was getting dark and Mom was calling me inside. I couldn't bear to leave the baby bird unprotected, so I scooped it up. Its naked little body, so fragile, struggled for life in my hand.

I made a soft nest in my bathroom sink, where I gave it drops of water. I dug up worms for it to eat. Two days later it was dead.

And I was left to wonder what might have happened if I hadn't touched it. Would those squawking birds have returned, would they have ever gotten their baby back in the nest?

Mostly I wondered what had touched me that kept my father from even trying.

I sat down on the curb in front of the Mini Mart, put a cigarette between my lips, and began searching for a light. My fingertips fished blindly along the bottom of my bag, bumping into sharp obstacles, but no lighter. As always, we stopped so Kori could check out *Source*. She never buys magazines, just reads them there in the store like guys do. Which leaves me to wait outside like her bitch.

I repositioned my bag on my lap and pried apart the opening as far it would go, pulling things out to be able to see inside. A PSP, three Altoids citrus tins (two that held games, one that held sours), one Altoids mints tin, iPod, wallet (heavy on change), cell phone, crushed thingy of Oreos. I dug around, finding everything but my lighter.

"Shit, where'd it go?" I growled. It must have flown out during the Josh debacle.

A man coming out of the Mini Mart was suddenly standing right next to me, so close I would've had to bend backward to get a good look at him. "This what you're looking for?" he asked.

I glanced at a Colorado Cares postcard flyer he held out. Did I look that pathetic? Sitting in front of the Mini Mart digging for the number to some cheesy crisis line—wait, don't answer that!

I took it, wadded it up, and tossed it across the parking lot as far away from me as possible.

I'm embarrassed to admit this, but the crisis line postcard probably did belong to me.

Colorado Cares is the teen help line run through Peak County Medical. My amateur psychologist mother volunteers there after her regular nursing shift and makes me distribute the postcards at school. I'm tempted to write on them: "Do NOT call between 3:30 and 7:30 if you want real help."

"Wasn't what you were looking for, huh?" the man asked. He probably thought I needed much more than a telephone number.

"Thanks, but no," I said as I continued to search my bag. The unlit cigarette bounced between my lips, but I stated the obvious anyway: "I'm looking for a light." I rummaged until I felt heat lick off the flame he held out to me. "Oh, thanks, man." My eyes flicked up to him as I cupped my hands around his larger one. Just quick enough to catch his shadowed outline, before settling on the red glow of my cigarette.

I don't look too many people in the eye. It almost always leads to something more. I don't know why that is. I guess for me it is such an invitation, an acceptance of risk, a big door opened wide—who wouldn't be curious enough to walk through? So I'm very careful not to invite too many in.

He flipped his wrist, snapping the lighter shut. Perhaps he meant the punctuating noise to cause me to look up at him. I didn't. Most guys don't even realize I'm not looking at their face when I talk to them, but that's because they usually aren't looking at mine either. Whatever the case, I was having a hard time staying focused on the horizon. And I could tell this guy wasn't just staring at my skirt or my boobs—I could feel his eyes moving over me, trying to place me perhaps.

"You can have it, if you want. I've got another," he said.

As he handed the lighter to me, my fist just opened. "You're sure?" I asked, my fingers already closing over it.

"Yeah. Sure. Keep it." He trailed the pads of his fingers across the heel of my palm, not so subtly.

"Thanks, that's real cool of you," I mumbled, flipping the lighter over and over in my fingers.

I couldn't help but be impressed feeling the weight of it. A Zippo. Chrome with the *Dukes of Hazzard* flag on it. I wondered how to scratch the logo off and wondered what he looked like. I mean, judging from the logo, he probably had a mullet and a beer belly. And still I was drawn to him. Next to the now barren fish tank, it was probably the nicest thing any man had ever given me. If my father was in my life, I wouldn't have been able to say that. Knowing so depressed me. It also made the gesture so much more touching than it was.

I smiled, flicked my eyes up to him, just enough to seem appreciative but not enough to encourage further conversation. Kori would be out soon.

I took a long drag off my cigarette and stared at the damp cement surrounding me. Just a year ago, I might have thought of this moment as fate. I would've analyzed how my mother's note made me late, and in running to school I knocked down Poor Josh, and in the ruckus lost my lighter. I might have drawn it out to include Cole's mother and Kori's magazine habit. But the bottom line was—I would've fantasized that those muddy work boots pointing at my hip belonged to my father.

That fate had finally brought him to me.

I would've reached out with both hands and grasped hope. Now I knew hope slid through fingers, and I didn't believe in fate. It had let me down far too often.

And still, I wanted to look.

I mean, my father probably wasn't the guy standing next to me, and if I looked at him, I'd know that. But I wanted to pretend he was something he wasn't. Even if it was only for two-point-five freaking seconds.

Then I had to do it. He'd been standing there so long, waiting for me. The average person wouldn't do that. And there was this strange sticky air hanging heavy between us. So I had to look up at him.

I had to.

Like the fingers of God, the sun poked my eyes with blinding white punishment. All I could see were shadows and light.

My heart thumped hard.

I shielded my eyes with my hand. As his features came into view, my heart flattened. He was too young to be my father. It had happened too many times for my heart to deflate in disappointment like that. But it always did.

I allowed myself just one shared smile before dropping my hand and returning my gaze leg level. I'd seen all I needed to.

But . . .

I had also seen dimples, good teeth, a very flat belly, and no mullet. He was probably out of college. I figured he'd come from the truck pulling the trailer filled with lawn-mowing equipment, since it was the only one left at the pumps, so I was pretty confident he at least had a job.

"So, what? Are you just hanging out?" he asked.

I tilted my head, looked at his legs. His shins were covered with little grass clippings, making it look like his leg hair was green. Ah, a fellow alien. No wonder I was so drawn to him. I reached out and dusted some off with the pads of my fingers; he didn't flinch or move away or stammer.

"Yep, just hanging out," I agreed belatedly. Then amended, "Well, walking home."

He squatted down, all his weight on his toes, bending creases into the worn leather of his boots. "You wanna ride?"

His eyes—green flecked with amber—were no longer hidden by glare.

Did I want a ride?

I wondered if, now that he was down on my level, he could smell the wet trash clinging to the pavement the way I could. Would he take my hand and lift me away from it, tell me I shouldn't be sitting here? Maybe he would say something like, *"Let's get you out of here."*

My teeth worked against the insides of my bottom lip as I dropped my hand down to the curb, my cigarette sticking out like a broken sixth finger as it grew ash. I glanced at his eyes. His dimples flashed, prompting me to answer yes.

Yes. Yes. Yes. My lips tweaked in a smile.

He didn't say anything, probably because I hadn't answered him yet. Kori was still in the store, and I wasn't sure if she'd want a ride. She was funny about things like this. So I just asked, "Is that your truck?"

He rocked back on his heels, his exhaled breath drifting warm under my nose like when a waiter at Chili's whisks a platter of sizzling fajitas past your table and you wish you had ordered those. Only then did I realize how close we'd just been. If I hadn't said anything, he might've kissed me. How bizarre would that have been?

"Yeah, for my business."

After taking a drag, I asked, "Mowing lawns?" Not very brilliant; in fact, bordering on ditzy, but guys liked dumb. And I liked this guy.

He smiled, his white teeth teasing behind the curve of his lips. Oh, yeah. Definite Fajita Sizzle.

"Yeah, mowing lawns. And landscaping. I've got two employees."

"Really?" They must be illegals. Wow.

"Yeah, just a couple of high school kids in the summer. Right now it's just me, though."

Oh. Not quite as exciting as illegals, but the way he'd said high school kids made him seem far older than he was and like he thought I was older too. Most guys did. I wondered if he had his own place. I was sure he did. I imagined it was a one-room apartment with brick walls and a mattress on the floor with a sheet he rarely washed. I probably shouldn't have thought that was exotic, but I did.

I could see myself washing the sheet and fixing dinner. He probably smelled like fresh-cut grass every day. A girl could get used to that. "Just you, huh?"

His lip kicked up on one side, his eyes flickering and as green as the grass he cut. "You got a lawn that needs mowing or something?"

"She lives in a town house," Kori interrupted from behind him. "They have people for that." She lifted me by my messenger bag's strap.

Let's get you out of here.

"And she's jail bait."

four

Lawn-mower guy watched her drag me away and I waved. He didn't wave back. He wanted his lighter and the last ten minutes of his life back. I wanted him back.

He never even got to ask me how a girl with black hair could have such pale blue eyes. Ever since I'd dyed my hair, it was the pickup line of choice. If the answer weren't Clairol, it might have worked better.

"That was rude, Kor." I shrugged her off.

"I can't leave you alone for a second." She sounded tired, exasperated. Like my mother. "You've got to stop flirting with older guys."

She's one to talk. She's done a lot more than flirt with older guys. In fact—she's done a lot with a lot of guys. "And I don't flirt with older guys."

"Oh, please. I've seen you around Cole's father, Miss American Beauty. And let's not forget Coach Rick." In eighth grade she accused me of being a cock tease to our soccer coach. I was so repulsed when I felt him erect a tent during a post-scoring hug with me that I quit the team. I was his best player. He told me so. I've never played a sport since.

"Mr. Blakely is a nice man, I can't believe you'd even suggest that, and Coach Rick was an asshole."

"So was that guy."

"Oh, come on, he just wanted to give us a ride."

"Don't be so naive, Ser. A guy like that would love a little piece like you. A girl who will hang on his every word, treating him like fucking royalty just because he pats her head once a month between beatings."

"Fuck you," I said without emotion. This was just Kori being Kori.

"A ride is a ride. A fuck is a fuck. It is what it is."

"So why couldn't he give us a ride?"

"Because he wanted a whipping bitch."

"You just blew holes in your is-what-it-is speech. Besides, how do you know he didn't just want a fuck?"

"Because he was trying to impress you with his truck and business and saving your poor little messed-up life with his stupid lighter, and you were eating it all up with your shining puppy-dog eyes, because he had that *I'll take care of you* vibe that you lick up. Yeah, he'd take care of you all right, with his fist. And anyway, if all he wanted was a fuck, he would have approached me."

"Ouch. Tough love."

"Just love. Period."

"He wasn't *that* old," I muttered. Then: "If I wanted to date a high school guy, I would."

She rolled her eyes and pulled out her cell phone, putting it to her cheek. With a sharp inhale, she mimicked Josh's facial expressions with frightening accuracy. "Um, hello. Um, S-S-Serena? Y-y-yes? H-hello, I um . . . I um . . . I . . . Um. I—oh, never mind." I attempted (poorly) to restrain my laughter and to get away. She jogged after me, grabbing at my thermal sleeve. "N-no, wa-wa-wait! I want to ask you out! Yes! S-S-Serena! And . . . I-I-I lalalalove you! Wait! No! Oh God, I mean yes. Wait! Oh, na-never mind."

"You're such a shit, you know that?" But, unfortunately it was the truth. The only high school guy to show real interest in me was Poor Josh.

The truth about the key is that I wear it so everyone will know I'm a latchkey kid. I don't know if people still use that term, but I guess they used to, because that's what my neighbor Mrs. Patterson calls me, and she's older than fossilized dinosaur dung.

Anyway, people should know that my mom leaves me alone, every day, all day long. The authorities should be contacted. The record should state that Destiny Moore is not the perfect mother everyone thinks she is!

Unfortunately, she has everyone snowed, including my friends. They seem to think my having the house to myself all the time sounds like a pretty freaking sweet setup. They have this whole fantasy concocted that I spend my afternoons smoking pot, drinking Colt 45s, watching porn, and hooking up with cute boys. But the truth is much more pathetic than that.

That's right—Destiny's child is all alone. Boo-hoo. Where is my violin music? Where are my harps?!

My mom's name is Destiny, even though she goes by Desi these days. I don't really remember my grandparents, so I couldn't say, but I guess when you live in a town called Kismet and *boom!* you end up pregnant after your supposed menopause, you might think to name your child Destiny.

Mom says it was destiny that I was born too. She got pregnant with me when she was still in high school, which pretty much means I was a total mistake. When I ask her if she's had any regrets, she always says, "Having my beautiful baby girl was fated in the stars."

Fated in the stars? Please. I puke a tiny Disney-colored rainbow in my mouth every time I think about it. Besides, somehow I doubt that little claim would work if I turned up pregnant. "Oops, Mom." Big sarcastic shrug. "I guess it was just fate." Yeah, I'm pretty confident she would pitch a major hiss.

That's Destiny Moore, hypocrite, for you, and I'm Serena. At least that's the name on my birth certificate and the one I'm going with. Truth is my mother was too drugged up to speak or write legibly. She intended to name me Serenity, which, in addition to being representative of an emotion I don't possess, is the name brand of choice for adult diapers. All I can say is thank God for human error and Demerol.

"You're late!"

Okay. Honesty time here. I'm not really home *alone*. I kind of have a self-appointed babysitter.

Two seconds after I was safely inside our town house, our elderly neighbor Mrs. Patterson waddled through the door using her own key. She smelled like cat piss. I'd never counted how many cats she has, but they seem to be everywhere. I saw an episode of *Animal Precinct* where some guy had over a hundred. Cat collectors. That's what they call people like her.

"You're late!" she squawked again. She repeats things.

Her voice is all scratchy, and even though she sounds bitchy and angry, she isn't. She's just deaf—her throat is always sore because she has to shout to hear herself speak. And some really nasty things can happen with her and phlegm, but I hide my horror.

"Yeah, my ride never showed." I neglected to mention I had other offers.

"You want spaghetti?"

"Not hungry yet."

She's always eager to get dinner started as soon as she walks through the door. It's a constant battle to push it off until six thirty. Every five minutes she throws out another dish idea until I bite. Macaroni? Fried chicken? Some nice chicken noodle soup? She usually starts that around six—adding adjectives like *nice* and *warm* and *refreshing* and *hearty* and *good old-fashioned*.

It was hard to smoke pot, drink Colt 45s, and watch porn with Mrs. Patterson asking me if I wanted good old-fashioned smothered steak and taters. Not that I really wanted to do any of those things, but it would be nice to shut myself in my bedroom and go online, and no, not to chat up child molesters, thank you very much. I was itching to get online and work on the latest game I was programming. But I didn't want to be rude and shut out Mrs. Patterson, seeing as how she shuffled her walker all the way across the driveway just to be with me.

I'm sure in the *Lifetime Supply of Tampax* movie of my life they would change her character and make her more of a quirky but lovable old lady who manages to impart wise life lessons every time I end up in a pathetic predicament. But in real life she is nuttier than squirrel poop. Only Quentin Tarantino could do her justice, and he'd probably give her about a hundred more cats and a really dope ride, like a '67 convertible 'Vette with a vanity plate that read PUSYLDY.

"Serena! Board's up!"

Yep, instead of creating a computer game with an onyx fortress that needs defending against evil human hybrids, I'm playing Trivial Pursuit with a ninety-five-year-old lady who is probably wearing a Serenity pad as we speak.

If only my friends could see me now. I bet they wouldn't be so jealous.

Mom rolled in at 9:03 P.M. and immediately began stripping off the facade of perfection. First to come off were the shoes, immediately followed by a loud sigh of relief. Then the hair was let down. The sweats came on and the makeup came off. By 9:07 P.M. the conversion was complete.

I'd watched her transform from the perfect, put-together woman to comfortably flawed mom almost every day of my life. When I was little I thought it was fun—like living with a superhero, except it was the mild-mannered version that was so much cooler. Now I just rolled my eyes and walked toward the bathroom to get ready for bed.

"Serena, can you come back in here for a minute?" I cringed hearing the stilted, false voice she uses when she parents. Apparently she hadn't reverted completely to Cool Mom.

"Yeah?"

"There's something I need to talk with you about."

I'd completely forgotten about the Post-it note by then, but it didn't matter. The big "Let's talk" confrontation was a major waste of worry. I should've guessed, seeing as how she didn't punctuate "Let's talk" with an exclamation point.

The crimes: using her tampons, using the last of her tampons, not throwing away the empty tampon box, not telling her she was out of tampons, not adding tampons to the grocery list. Gee, guess someone was on the rag. I gave her a halfhearted "Sorry," since she was so sensitive and all.

When I first got my period, she told me virgins couldn't use tampons. In retrospect, I don't think she actually believed this, but probably thought it was a clever way of keeping track of my hymen. So I'd expected her next question to be: "When did you start using tampons, anyway?" To which I would've replied: "Wouldn't you like to know?" But she didn't say another word about it.

She probably thought our sharing feminine hygiene products signified some sort of bonding experience. She has delusions that I'm the Rori to her Lorelai, but the Gilmore Girls we ain't.

five

On the first day of class, without saying a word, my social psychology teacher, Dr. Ramsey, commanded my attention with the quote inked on the wall above his desk like a tattoo:

> *To punish me for my contempt for authority,*
> *fate made me an authority myself.*
> —Albert Einstein

A teacher with contempt for authority always had my interest. And my fascination with Doc hasn't lessened since.

Under a head of thick brown hair, Doc's face was a little longer than most. But he didn't look horsey or anything. More than anything, he reminded me of a puppy—a little too excited, a little too expressive. In fact, the only thing that actually made him look doctorish or scholarly were the clear round glasses he was never without.

"Today, students, we are going to be tempting fate." Doc smiled devilishly as he spoke. "We are going to tempt fate into giving us anything we want. How does that sound? Uh-oh, I see skepticism on some faces." His voice was filled with humor as he strolled among us pointing his finger at the doubters like me.

It wasn't really that I doubted Doc; it was that I didn't believe in fate—tempted or otherwise.

"Have you ever heard of a self-fulfilling prophecy? Can anyone give me an example?"

Participation is huge in Doc's classes. But I never raise my hand. In his class, it just wasn't the same as regurgitating a date in history or the answer to an equation. When you answered a question in Doc's class, you almost always ended up revealing something about yourself you normally wouldn't. So even though you're seated in your little desk chair, it feels like you are up in front of the class giving an unprepared speech. Naked. It's awful. Not recommended for the faint of heart.

"No one wants to start? Everyone's ready to nap? Ah, the perils of the after-lunch period. Okay, let's think about this. The basic premise is assumption, right? If you think you're ugly, you will become ugly, right?"

In Doc's class you have to pay attention. One minute the lecture may seem all touchy-feely, but then somehow he's able to break things down and dissect fact from fiction until things start making logical sense. He makes you believe the unbelievable.

Like this theory he has about how our subconscious was superpowerful and how our internal drives could be set like a GPS toward any goal we had in mind. It was a bit out there, but the way he explained it made it seem more rational than my mom's self-help affirmations and chakra cleansings. *If you think it, you can be it*" and crap like that.

Now, as much as I adore Doc and hang on his every word, I have to admit I'm still a complete skeptic. So when he told us to list five things that we never would dream could happen to us this term, I was my typical cynical self.

1. Be on the front page of the *Kismet Courier*. *Heh.*
2. Sing in front of an audience. *Without puking.*
3. Become BFFs with a cheerleader. *Again—without puking.*
4. Fall for a high school guy. *Um . . . yeah, don't think so.*
5. Find my father. *A girl can dream, can't she?*

Just as I was tucking my paper into my notebook, he added, "And I want a copy."

I sucked in a breath, realizing just how sarcastic my list was. I started to wad it up, but then he winked.

"Here are some envelopes. Write your name on the outside and seal them up. Trust me—I don't even want to know what you guys have planned for yourselves."

I slid my list into the envelope, and as I sealed it, I couldn't help but imagine I was indeed sealing my fate.

The corners of my mouth rose slightly at the thought. Maybe I *would* finally find my father.

I used to fantasize the traditional secret agent scenario, and it made a lot of sense because my grandparents were dead. So I sort of rationalized that my father's enemies discovered his true identity and they came and killed his family to teach him a lesson. The only way he could protect his wife and child was to leave them. I would've been very young, since my grandparents have been dead for as long as I can remember. "Old age," Mom claims. That is all well and good, except I think I can remember the shoot-out. Anyway, since the bad guys would always be watching, he's had to be very careful. I'm sure he wants to contact me, though.

I used to imagine him hiding in the drapes, behind pillars, in closets so he could always stay close and watch over me. Now I'm not so sure. I mean—hiding behind a pillar isn't exactly stellar spy work. The standards on that have definitely been raised by *Alias*. But he has to be pretty good, considering I've found out more about where bin Laden is hiding than where my own father is.

The more logical choice, given my mother's tender age when she conceived and all, leads me to believe that it wasn't some CIA man but someone here in town who did the honors and donated his sperm to the Serena Moore Project. Someone who had no idea that he was even my father. Someone like my social psych teacher, Doc Ramsey.

I know it's a little mental, but my mom's so secretive about who my father is that I have to come up with crazy alternative realities.

I told Kori about my Doc Ramsey Paternity Theory, because, well, if Kori and I really were twins separated at conception, he would be her real father too, and so she should know. She wasn't appreciative or surprised.

"It was only a matter of time before you thought that. You need to get over this father fetish shit. What's so great about them? Just look at mine."

"Come on, it's possible, right?"

"Doc doesn't even look like us."

She was too sweet to point out that I only looked like "us" because I dyed my hair black and got a straightening iron for Christmas. With my icy blue eyes and widow's peak, I also bear a striking resemblance to a Siberian husky.

With a daughterly smile, I handed Doc the envelope as I headed out of his classroom. I probably should have been paying more attention, because right as I stepped out of his doorway some spazzy, chicken-chested kid barreled into me, knocking my mondo history book out of my hands. Corner over cover it sailed until one of the corners went right into the back of some guy with long choppy chunks of hair that were as dark as Dr Pepper.

"Sorry!" I called pushing through the now crowded hall toward my latest victim.

"S'all right," he said, bending to pick up my book. I dropped my eyes as he handed it back to me. "Here."

Our thumbs brushed together, and a chill zapped through my skin, straight up an artery, sliding into my heart like a baseball player taking home.

I gulped.

Nothing like that has ever happened to me with a high school guy before. A less cynical person might have thought she'd just achieved number 4 on her list. But this was me, so naturally I was coming up with a logical, non-fate-related answer. Like how it was just some weird molecular thing with the commercial-grade carpeting in the hallway and the Mexican silver of his ring.

I didn't dare look at him in case I'd just "had that special feeling" for some meathead baller with bad breath. Or worse, maybe I'd just totally assaulted a really hot senior whose grandfather owns a chain of hotels and a hobby winery.

Crap. Why didn't I put that down on my wish list instead being so vague? Oh right, because I didn't believe in it.

While I was kicking myself for not being more specific in my sarcasm, I gave him an embarrassed chuckle—my yeah-yeah-I'm-a-big-klutz chuckle. I find a little self-deprecation goes a long way when you've just assaulted someone. Especially if he might be like the total hottie of your dreams.

"You know, I think this is going to bruise," the guy said rather proudly. "Whadda you think? How does it look?"

He hiked up his T-shirt to reveal his summer-tanned back. With his other hand he tugged down the studded belt on his jeans.

In a chiseled plane above his hipbone, the golden brown was turning pink. Below the pink, more golden brown, and farther down a clashing swath of white, and not the cotton Hanes kind.

"Well?"

I swallowed hard. "Looks great," I murmured, admiring his butt.

"Funny, it felt like it hit higher up than that," he said, amused. *Busted.*

I looked quickly up to his face. Strands of nearly black hair fell across his eyes as he checked again for bruising. Then with a swift shake of his head that knocked his hair out of the way, he looked up and his eyes locked on mine.

A blaze of heat seared my cheeks as I realized who I was talking to—correction—staring at. Anthony Beck. Junior. Used to be skinny-and-pale-wears-sweaters guy. But now . . . not so much.

Now he was tan-and-hunky-goes-commando guy.

And I couldn't stop staring at the dark tips of his bangs tangling with his gorgeous, spiky boy-lashes.

I tried to stay composed and aloof and sexy all at the same time. It was hard. I could feel my lips getting freakishly moist à la Poor Josh, and prayed he wouldn't stick around long enough for the drool to start. But he was leaning against the wall with his weight on his hip, like he better get all comfortable because we'd be chatting for a while or something. "So, do you hit guys often?"

"Actually," I mumbled, thinking about Poor Josh, "there have been others."

Anthony chuckled, his eyes unsnapping a little too easily from mine.

I looked quickly away too, and spotted Kori as she battled her way through the hall, rushing to make it to her last class, which was at the other end of the T-shaped hallway.

"Kind of aggressive, doncha think?" he asked. "You know, most girls just tap a guy's shoulder to get their attention."

"I . . . I wasn't trying to . . . I was sort of a victim myself."

"Yeah, saw that. Hit-and-run freshman style."

I cocked my shoulder and started to say something like: "Yeah, I know. *Freshmen.*" But then Kori came around the corner and yelled, "Stop drooling over Becks and get to class, Ser!"

I lifted my hand to flip her off, but dropped it quickly as I spotted Principal Teasley's bald head bobbing along a good foot or so above the crowd as he patrolled for people using cell phones or guys showing off their tan lines. Thankfully (and perhaps wisely), Teasley turned in the same direction as Kori.

"Sorry I hit you," I said, looking back at Anthony.

He pushed off from the lockers and his mouth cocked up on one side. "Don't worry about it. I like aggressive girls."

I would have happily concluded the day with my run-in with Becks, but in my world, there's no such thing as ending on a positive note. I have Mr. Click—that's Dick Click if you're not in his history class, but if you are, then I'm sorry, it's Mr. Click to you—last period, which sort of puts the kibosh on my happy endings. In the movie of my life, I have him cast as a Bob Newhart type that has been attacked by a pack of rabid chipmunks.

As I dragged myself into his classroom, he was scratching the chalk against the board in that harsh way he has, like he's punishing the chalk. Sometimes the chalk screams in pain and we all get punished. I glanced at the board. (Cue the *Jaws* theme music.) Just when I thought it was safe to go to school and *not* hear about my mother. Mr. Click wrote the words *Manifest Destiny* on the board.

I can't wait for the jokes to start up again. *"Look, it's Destiny's Child!"* Ha-ha. Not.

Mom was late last night—this time a double shift at work—again. Which begs the question: why did Destiny even bother having a child? These days I've spent more time with a breath strip in my mouth than with her.

I can't honestly say I want to spend more time with her, though. I mean, yeah, that would be a start, but it doesn't really help if I can't have a decent conversation with her that doesn't involve: (a) ridiculous rules I've broken, (b) hypocritical bullshit, or (c) the words *Oprah says* . . .

After banging out some drivel for my paper on Manifest Destiny, I pulled up a game development site I've been using and navigated to the programming area, bringing up my game.

The beauty of game development is that whatever you don't like, you can change. You build the world. You make the rules.

Like a runner with her precious high, I let my fingers take over in a way that moves my brain so fast it actually becomes calm. The endorphins fill me, and my mind turns into pure melody, screaming guitar riffs, and pulsing crescendos. All because of a keyboard and some lines of code. This is precisely why I have to keep my obsession a secret. I mean, really, how geeky can one girl get?

Within seconds I'm lost to the keystrokes. And then, without warning, my concentration is shattered by an IM.

shaym: Kori?

I paused, saving my game. You learn the hard way to do that as often as possible. I thought about how I wanted to respond to shaym—as myself or as Kori.

I remembered her comment about the fake ID, the doubt in her voice that I could, even in name and address only, pretend to be her. And here I had the perfect opportunity. It was tempting. Very tempting.

With fingers trembling above the keyboard, I took a deep breath.

My heart rate sped with temptation. I willed my fingers to stop shaking.

Kori was always pretending to be me online, saying really embarrassing things. Sexually explicit, I might add. This was no different. I'd tell her about it and she'd laugh. She'd even be impressed if I could pull it off. That's how she is. But me? I'm a different story. Pretending to be Kori, just the thought, was enough to make my nerves feel like bacon on a hot skillet.

shaym: Kori? ru there?

My fingertips hovered, grazing the tops of the keys. And then, as if they had their own minds, my fingers began typing.

dynamitehackr: im here
shaym: remember me?
dynamitehackr: how could I 4get?
shaym: i can't believe i found you

I forced myself to take a deep breath. To stay calm. Find out as much as I could about this person without him getting suspicious.

dynamitehackr: how did u?
shaym: saw ur pic

You couldn't tell if the photo on my site was of Kori or me, which was exactly why I chose it. In the black-and-white photo, with my eyes shielded by a shadow, you couldn't tell their color—the only physical feature that separates us now that I've grown my hair out and dyed it black.

shaym: u look good. been a while.
dynamitehackr: how long?

I waited, but shaym had gone silent on me. He was still online, though, making me miss the days of mouth-breathing junior high phone stalkers. At least you knew there was someone on the other end. For all I knew, shaym was taking a piss break or worse. Then I worried I'd tipped him off. So I tried a more familiar approach.

dynamitehackr: seems like 4ever
shaym: sorry bad dial-up
shaym: about 2 years? seems longer

Two years? I counted back to the summer before eighth grade. Before Kori and I became friends. The summer she changed. Two years? It did seem longer. Like the Kori I knew had been that dark angel forever.

shaym: how ru? ok?
shaym: i
shaym has logged off

How ominous. The Internet can be such a dangerous place, especially when you're alone and have dial-up. Heh. Like me.

My mom rapped her knuckles on my door. "Serena, computer."

If there's any light or typing noise seeping out from under my door at eleven o'clock, my mom will knock. I think she read in one of her books that enforcing a curfew is the key to having a safe and respectable teenager. So I shut down the computer, turned off my lights, and yelled, " 'Night." Then I stuffed my pillows under my comforter and climbed out the window.

six

The walk to the reservoir was an easy one—all lighted side-walks and no creepy treks through the woods. Even from a distance, I spotted Kori doing cartwheels on the crumbling rock of the retaining wall. She was there every night. These days I was sneaking out to meet Kori more often than not.

As soon as I was in earshot, Kori called to me. "Hey, kitten!"

The force of her shout caused her to bobble, and my heart made a white-knuckle grab of my rib cage. But she just laughed. She was fine. She's always fine.

"You're going to kill yourself!"

"Only if I bomb the dismount." She winked. Then she did a perfect pirouette. The balance beam was her favorite appara-tus from her gymnast-wannabe days. They came before her cheerleader-wannabe days, which came before me.

"Just get down, please. Please!"

"Oh, relax," she said, and then did a handspring off of the wall. "Come on, get up and try it. Just stand. It's at least three times as wide as a beam. Easy."

"Yeah, no thanks."

"Wuss. So, how was the porn, latchkey girl?" Kori asked.

"Great. The child molester said to say hello. He's grooming me; do I look well groomed?" I struck a sarcastic pose.

"I just love what he's done with your hair."

"He wants me to run away, cross state lines to meet him. He seems like such a winner. I think he's the one. I really do."

"Yeah, the only person in the world who totally gets you." She pumped her fist over her crotch like guys do.

"You totally get me," I reminded her.

"Then let's run away, cross state lines."

"Hmm . . . where should we go? Nebraska? Kansas? New Mexico? What other states border us?"

"I don't know, I flunked Colorado history, remember?"

She reached into her backpack and tossed me a beer. Her older brother Kieren buys them with his fake ID. He's not very good about hiding them or keeping count. He's also easily distracted when I strike up stupid conversations with him while he's trying to brush his teeth before bed. I don't think it's my wit and charm so much as the boxies and snug-fitting tank top with no bra. Kori claims my flirting with her brother is revolting and since we're like sisters, it's also kind of incestuous. I think it's harmless, and besides, who can argue with the results?

Kori started rolling a joint.

"Can I get a hit?" I asked when she exhaled.

"No. You talk too funny."

It took me a minute to realize she was talking about the first and only time I'd tried it. Kori let me, as a test, she said. Since then she hasn't let me try it again. I guess I failed.

"My voice sounded weird?"

"No," she said. "You used big words like *cathartic* and *amalgamation*. Complained about tribes of dieters."

Diatribes? My first reaction was to say that those weren't big words. That, thanks to *Dawson's Creek* reruns, all teenagers talked like that. But I didn't want to admit to ever having been obsessed with the show in case she remembered the monster crush I had on Pacey's older brother, the cop who turned out to be gay, which was so typical of my luck with guys.

My second reaction was to deny everything. I mean, I didn't even inhale.

"No, I don't," I said way too indignantly for someone who didn't have a clue what she was talking about.

"Yes. You. Do. Don't you remember you said *tabula rasa*, but Kieren thought you said *tabula rasta* and asked what it meant? And we decided it was the blanking effect really good Jamaican weed has on the brain? Remember? We even played a drinking game—whenever you used a word no one else knew the meaning of, we took a drink. We ran out of booze."

I didn't remember any of this. It was all an enigma (drink). But I didn't tell her that.

She placated (drink) me by telling me that drugs are for the boring people, not for geniuses like me.

"Historically speaking, the true creative geniuses were all addicts," I told her.

"No, kitten, they wouldn't do this if they were true geniuses."

I ached to tell her that she was a true genius; that she understood all of the intangibles (drink) of life, the beauty and the poetry of existence that someone like me couldn't even fathom (drink). But I knew all she could see were her Fs next to my As.

I pulled my legs in, rocked onto my feet, and stood on the retaining wall. Just another slip down the slope to hell. A slope that had gotten progressively slicker since Kori had talked me into getting my tongue pierced. Speaking of slick slopes, I looked down from my new footing. It wasn't but two feet off the ground from the land side, but the lake side dropped down to . . . Oh God . . . I couldn't look. My ankles wobbled, but . . . okay . . . as long as I wasn't looking down, right?

In addition to the fear of abandonment, self-torture is one of my "issues." Or "subscriptions," as my mom calls them. I get twelve a year for the low, low price of $12.95.

Mom thinks that because she is a nurse and reads all these self-help books and works at the crisis line that she's some kind of expert on helping people. But it's all a joke. The only person I could count on to have my back, to really be there for me, was Kori.

As I was standing on the edge I was thinking that if I weren't so terrified of pain, I'd probably be one of those depressed chicks who cuts. But for now just standing on a retaining wall was plenty psycho for me. I made myself turn around and look out at the lake. It wasn't so scary if I kept my eyes on the horizon. But dip too high or too low . . .

"Do you feel it?" Kori whispered, her voice hovering in the air like one of her smoky exhales.

I swallowed as I leaned just enough to look down the slick planes of rock. I did feel something. Something I couldn't turn away from. A grip in my gut and the sudden need for air.

"It isn't fear, is it? It's anticipation. Like the last rush of heartbeats before a hot guy moves in for a kiss. Addictive, isn't it?"

Slowly I ran my gaze down the length of one blade-sharp edge. In the moonlight it looked silver and crazy ragged, like a hunting knife. I imagined the blood it would draw, and shuddered. But just as I stepped backward, I heard Kori scream.

"Don't fall!" exploded in my ear as she pitched me forward with her shove.

Her arms caught me around my hips, yanking me off the ledge and against her as she started singing Shakira and making me dance crazy.

"What the hell did you do that for?!" I jerked away from her, doubled over in case I might puke.

"Relax, kitten, what are you afraid of?"

"Easy for you to say!" I gasped, pulling in air. Several breaths later, I was able to bring her into focus. My fingernails had dug so deep into her forearms that blood dripped from the crescent indentations. She scarcely noticed.

"Living won't kill you." She smirked at my doubtful expression. "What? You aren't going to die tonight. So for one night only, you can do anything you want to."

I was still so scared, so mad, I was spitting my words. "How do you know."

It wasn't really a question, but she had an answer. "It's too soon." She said it simply, as if that was all there was to life and death.

I drilled her with my eyes.

"What? Are you honestly telling me you've done everything you want? I sure as hell haven't. I don't want to leave anything undone."

"It doesn't work like that," I said through my teeth. "You could have killed me!"

"I would never let anything bad happen to you, kitten. I was in complete control. Reflexes like a cat," she retorted. "But what if the worst happened? Are you ready, Serena? Are you?"

A sick feeling slithered into my stomach, snapping my emotions from anger to unease. "Don't say things like that. Don't put that out there."

She looked around. "Out where?"

How could I explain? What would I even say? That I didn't want her voicing things, whispering in God's ear, reminding him I was here and going about my life just fine without his pesky influences? Sounded too much like my mother's cosmic kookery, and I didn't believe that shit anyway. Not even when it was packaged all pretty in one of Doc's lesson plans.

I shrugged her off, my heart still pumping too hard to concentrate. "Just never mind."

"Oh, out *there*." She grinned wickedly. "You're afraid if I say it out loud, it just might come true?"

She cupped her mouth to yell.

"Don't, Kori."

But she did. She always does.

"Serena thinks she will die tonight!" It echoed across the water, making my stomach turn. "Hey, God, Serena wants to die tonight!"

"Stop it, Kor!"

She just laughed. "Stop pretending you believe that crap. I bet you didn't even put anything serious down for Doc's assignment. Let me guess. You put stupid shit, didn't you? You're afraid to even put something meaningful. It's no wonder you can't do a cartwheel on the dam. You can't even risk writing some words on a piece of paper."

"I'm not scared of a piece of paper." Was I too scared to tempt fate? Or did I even believe in it anymore?

"You're scared to do. You're scared to be. You're scared to live. You're always scared, so you must like it, and you love the cozy, safe feeling of escaping reality even more."

"And doing a cartwheel on the dam will prove what?"

"It will prove you trust."

I sighed. "You said that about the belly ring and I did it. You said it about the tongue piercing and I did that. You know I trust you."

"I didn't say me."

I shook my head, stepping back up on the ledge. I was irritated enough at her prodding to just do it.

"Don't you even want to know what you're playing for?" she announced like a game show host.

I cut my eyes at her, not amused.

"When it's your time, it's your time. And it's so *not* your time." She grabbed my wrist and pulled me down to the ground.

"What the hell is that supposed to mean?"

"It means I'm ready for another joint," she said. Then, as she gave my nearly full beer can a shake: "And you've got a wounded soldier on the field."

I took a long drink of warm beer, wincing as I swallowed. I was still angry with her, and more than a little bit tired of playing her games. Even the ones she didn't know were being played. So I asked her who shaym was.

Her face contorted even more than usual as she took a deep drag. "Shame?"

"S-H-A-Y-M."

Kori was in the process of straddling the wall, sitting down, so I couldn't see her expression. "How do you know that name?" Accusation filled her tone, giving me chills.

"He found you. Well, found me. Saw my pic. Thought I was you." I knew I was babbling, but I couldn't stop myself. "He IM'd me while I was online. I let him think I was you."

She snorted. "Did you now?"

"Yeah, it was kind of fun being you."

"I bet. So what'd you talk about?"

"Nothing really. He got disconnected. Dial-up. So who is he?"

"No one you would know. Just another guy who couldn't resist my charms."

I laughed. "Since when do you withhold your charms?"

Kori faked a hurt expression. Something dark surfaced in her eyes—sadness? worry?—that made me almost believe it, but hurt was one thing Kori Kitzler didn't feel much of. Not physically or emotionally.

"What do you want me to tell him if he comes back?"

She laughed as she leaned back onto the wall. Her shrunken T-shirt scooted up to reveal a one-carat diamond. Its twin dangled on my belly button, courtesy of her fifteenth birthday gift from her mother, who would freak if she knew the ones in Kori's ears were zircs. "Tell him . . ." She spoke around the joint held tightly in her lips. "Tell him you want to meet him. Run away. Cross state lines."

I finished my beer and stretched out on the rock ledge with her. We both stared up at the star-splattered sky. Our heads were touching, but our bodies were pointing in different directions.

Her hand floated into my sky of vision, coming high and from behind, reminding me of the sun slowly arching against the heavens. Her fingers wriggled, beckoning mine. My arm craned back, awkward and painful, but I knew she needed me to link our fingers together and tether her to me. When she's high, she thinks her body is going to dissolve, or something equally crazy, if she's not holding on to someone else. I wondered if it would terrify her to know I felt like that all the time.

Most people get all slothlike when they're high. Not Kori. After about thirty minutes she abruptly sat up. "So let's do something."

"What?"

"Like with Doc's assignment. Except I get to tell you what to do and vice versa."

"You mean dares?"

"Yeah, whatever."

I rolled my eyes.

She shrugged. "You can even go first."

She'd been daring me to do stuff for weeks now. I wasn't sure how this was any different, but anything had to be better than putting more holes in my body.

"Okay, fine." I narrowed my eyes as I thought about what to dare her. I wanted to be sure and put a stop to her crazy dares once and for all. The only way to do that, though, would be to dare her to do something she wouldn't do. As I looked out at the lake, I grinned. "I want you to go skinny-dipping in the reservoir."

Without even waiting a beat, she said, "I want you to do the same."

"What? No. You can't do that."

She jumped up and started walking. "You had so much fun pretending to be me. Now's your chance."

"That's not what I meant," I called after her. I had to jog to catch up. "Look, I'm sorry I pretended to be you. It was just onli— Shit. Kori, wait up!"

Kori led us toward the beach. And by *beach,* I mean a flat section of land covered with chunks of rock. I watched as she pulled her shirt off.

"What are you doing?" I asked while glancing across the water to where the lights of the town radiated.

"You mean"—Kori turned toward me, but continued walking backward as she unbuttoned her jeans—"what are *we* doing?"

I stepped over a puddle that was Kori's shirt. Her Converses.

Her Habituals. The smell of the lake was strong. Water, algae, and rock. But so was her cherry almond perfume.

"It's freezing in there," I said even as I pulled my hoodie off, then my boots. The wet rocks felt like giant ice cubes under my feet. "I'm not going. It's stupid." And yet, I seesawed my jeans down my legs.

Kori ran in. The thunderous splash of her body hitting the ice-cold water shocked me.

My stomach turned. A part of me felt like I was just thrown in front of a truck with no brakes. Another part of me thought Kori was the truck with no brakes and maybe I could stop her if I only jumped in front of her.

But instead I just stood there in my underwear.

Her repeated screams echoed over the water. So loud it was painful. I understood her screaming kept the cold from cutting her too deep. But the noise held me in its grip, paralyzing me. Her voice seized; her last noise was just a hoarse croaking sound. Then she raced for the shore, water catching the moonlight in the air around her. It may have just been the sobering effect of the icy water bath, but she looked so much more alive than when she'd gone in.

And I felt the opposite.

The feeling only lasted a moment. Enough for me to know it had happened. Then I heard branches snapping and gravel under running boots coming from our left.

"What the hell?" a deep, masculine voice yelled.

Just as my eyes connected with Anthony Beck's, I realized I was still half-naked. *Shit.* I dropped down to scoop my clothes up, covering myself.

"Dude, what is it?" Another male voice came from the dark mouth of forest. Quarterback hero, Adrian17. "Bears?"

Anthony flashed a wicked grin. "Well, yeah, sort of. They are bare." His eyes stayed on me until Kori shook the wet tips of her hair out on him. "Hey! Shit, that's cold."

I used the distraction to tug on my clothes.

Kori pulled up her jeans and asked, "Got any beer left?"

"Not as much as we had an hour ago. Where've you been?"

I shot her a look. *She'd known they were there?* But before I could accuse her of orchestrating this whole embarrassing encounter, I remembered it was my own bright idea.

"Skinny-dipping. Obviously." She shoved her feet into her shoes, cramming the heels down. She had on only her jeans and a black lace bra.

"Jesus, we thought someone was getting pulled apart by a mountain lion," Anthony said as he pulled a still shirtless Kori against him, briskly rubbing her damp body with his palms.

I swallowed, feeling a sudden dull weight in my stomach. More than ever, I wished I'd been the one to go running into the water. Instead, I averted my eyes from Anthony's hands on Kori's body as I zipped my jeans.

"You're freaking insane," Adrian said with admiration. "Not even on the hottest day in August would I go in there."

"Afraid of the shrinkage?" Kori asked with a wink.

"Honey, you would wish for a little shrinkage," he said, grabbing his crotch. "Freaking Loch Ness Monster, baby."

My eyes cut from Anthony's lingering hand on Kori's bare back to the ground as I picked my path through the rocky beach.

We followed Adrian to their campfire. About a half-dozen other people were there. Juniors, all of them. A blond girl eyed Kori and her bra. She didn't look happy to see either. But, as with most people, she would spend her evening watching Kori as opposed to ignoring her.

After Kori slipped her shirt on, finally, she fished a beer from inside a cooler and handed it to me.

I looked over to where Anthony was picking up a guitar. He strummed on it a few halfhearted times. His fingers moving slowly and deftly across the strings caught my eye and I couldn't look away. I found myself slipping into the sound long before it progressed into the intro to "Chasing Cars" by Snow Patrol.

Kori's head popped up. "Ooh, I was telling Serena what a rock star you are! Sing for us!"

I couldn't help but notice the way Anthony's eyes got all twinkly when Kori spoke to him. He shook his head, and I noticed his cheeks were flushed. He gave a modest cock of his lip. "You first."

She stood as he handed the guitar to her. As she took it, she curled against him like a cat, and I heard her whisper, "Best two words a boy could say to me."

Anthony gave a low laugh and traded places with her. As he sat down next to me on the log, his elbow bumped my side and my heart jumped. I wasn't usually nervous around guys I liked. Older guys were different, easier. I had something they wanted but they knew they shouldn't have. It gave me power. Confidence. But with Anthony sitting right next to me, my nerves were snapping like the split wood in the fire.

I kept my eyes on Kori. She slipped into the guitar strap as if it were a shirt. As she started strumming, I let my eyes wander, finding faces that were on the one hand familiar and on the other complete strangers. They were people Kori felt comfortable with, even the ones who clearly wished she weren't there. But that was Kori. She could transcend the whole stupid high school hierarchy.

She started singing. Her voice, even more throaty and dark

from all the screaming before, filled the empty places inside of me. I shivered.

"Cold?" Anthony asked.

Our eyes met and mine fled quickly. Cold was the last thing I felt sitting next to him. In fact, I felt as hot as the fire dancing in front of us. I wanted to say something, anything . . . but my mouth felt like it was filled with drying glue, and all I could do was lamely shake my head.

Wait until it is night before saying that it has been a fine day.
—French proverb

seven

Only those who couldn't drive or get a ride off campus for lunch had to endure the state-mandated "crap-trition." So the cafeteria was a JV jungle complete with a survival-of-the-fittest social hierarchy.

There were five round tables, set up just like dots on a die— one in the center and four surrounding. And boxing those were several rectangular tables set along the walls. Naturally the BBs and PPs (*officially* Blond and Beautifuls and Perfect and Populars, in case you were curious) have claimed the round tables, like they're freaking knights and ladies. There is the one for the JV cheerleaders, the one for the JV jocks, the one for the JV jock supporters (and I mean that literally and figuratively), the one for the JV Hauties, aka social fashionistas, and ours. That's right, ours. The four defectors: Lexi from the brainiacs, Cole from the fashionistas, Kori from the cheerleaders, and me from the computer geeks, at the big eight-person, primo, round-real-estate table.

It was Kori's idea, just to have a laugh. She thought it would be hysterical if we showed up early and took one of the round tables. We picked the lowest upper rung of the social ladder, the JV drill team. They only had the title because the school's administration didn't feel rejection benefited perky blondes, so they created a whole new group to accommodate all the leftovers from cheerleader tryouts. It wasn't like they had a lot of clout. Not that we had any either, but we did have the table.

The drill team girls were, understandably, horrified. They stared at us, unable to comprehend. Some looked to the JV cheerleaders, but they found only laughter. A couple of drill team girls stomped their Kaepas and huffed, but they eventually had to sashay on over to the rectangle tables and wedge in between the debate-the-obvious geeks and the free-the-granola-trees freaks.

Unlike Chelsea Westad—who continues to eat at the round tables because no one at Pizza Hut gives a shit who she is—we can't wait to give up our table. As soon as Cole—the first of us to turn sixteen—gets her license, we will gladly abandon the table, and peace will be restored to the land. But not a minute sooner. After all, you don't go back and hunt slimes after you've hit level fifteen. *Cough*Cough* I mean, once you've sat at the round tables, you could never go back to the rectangles.

As Chelsea Westad and her black-and-blue entourage swung past our table, she made a grand production of checking her ringing cell phone's LCD and . . . wait for it . . . here it comes . . . "Hey, Destiny's calling, must be for you, Serena!" Snicker, snicker, barf, barf. The friggin' BBs think they are sooo original, starting up with their shit again now that Mr. Dick Click has so kindly reminded them of my mother's bizarro name with his Manifest Destiny assignment.

Once Chelsea was long gone, I muttered, "God, she's such a bitch."

Kori's lip quirked up sympathetically. Then she scribbled something on a napkin and shoved it toward me. Apparently, after last night's skinny-dipping screamfest, she'd damaged her vocal cords or something. The choir teacher, Mizz Stella, told her she wasn't allowed to speak if she wanted her most valued instrument to heal.

Tell her off.

I rolled my eyes at her. I probably should've stood up to Chelsea, but what would the point be, really? It would only make it worse.

I shot Kori a mocking smile. "Too late. The moment's passed."

This time Kori was the one to roll her eyes.

She snatched the paper back, scribbled frantically, then with her middle finger pushed it back to me.

I dare you.

When I didn't respond, she said, "You owe me."

The hairs on the back of my neck sprung up hearing the ragged edge of Kori's words. Her poor throat sounded as shredded as the back of Mrs. "Cat Collector" Patterson's couch. What was left of her voice sounded like pure evil, and it was way too early for Kori's particular brand of evil.

She again scribbled on the napkin, then shoved it back at me.

Don't be such a wuss.

"What are you guys talking about?" Lexi asked before popping a french fry into her mouth.

"Nothing," I muttered. I didn't really want to get into the whole dares business with Lexi. Like Mom, Lexi had "concerns" about Kori's "influence" over me. But Lexi'd probably agree if Mom told her the sun was purple. Changing the subject, I asked, "Weren't they wearing their cheerleading uniforms yesterday?"

"Spirit week," Cole said as she pulled Kori's note over to read it. "You're being a wuss?"

"She wants me to tell Chelsea off," I explained, crumpling up the napkin. Luckily with Kori silenced, they didn't need to know about the dares or the heinously embarrassing nakedness that was last night. "I don't know why parents insist on naming their children stupid things."

My friends were kind enough not to mention the fact that no one was actually making fun of *my* name—it was Mom's name they were making fun of, which of course I realized. But that so wasn't the point.

"Oh, fuck it," Kori's hoarse voice croaked. "I don't know what you're crying about. *Kitzler* means 'clitoris' in German." She actually looked proud of this, but of course, none of us believed her. "I'm serious. Google it."

"I'm not *Googling* German clitoris!" Lexi said with a huff.

Kori, Cole, and I burst out laughing, and Lexi's egg-shaped face flared as red as Kori's Coke can when she realized that what she'd said sounded perverted. "*That's* not what I meant! That didn't come out right! Stop laughing at me! You guys are *so* juvenile! Gah!"

When the table returned to order, mainly because we had to breathe, Lexi started again. "It's not your mom's fault, and besides, doesn't everyone call her Desi now anyway?"

"Clearly Chelsea Westad didn't get that memo."

The whole nickname thing came up when Kori, Cole, Lexi, and I had our first sleepover at my house. At thirteen you do stupid stuff like that, make up new names. So there we were—Alexandria, Nicole, and I—and we decided that we would all have four-letter names like Kori. We thought that was cool—you know, because it was like having a four-letter word for a name—real taboo and all. We were thirteen. Give me a break.

So anyway, we became Lexi, Cole, and Rena. It was really great there for a fraction of a second, and then I walked into my kitchen, where the new and improved Lexi, formally known as Alexandria Devlin, was licking the cookie dough from one of my mom's beaters. Mom always does that sort of thing—makes cookies, popcorn, brownies. That's why Lexi doesn't believe me about how annoying she can be. The double chocolate chips disorient her.

I heard Lexi telling Mom all about our new cool names and everything. Mom hadn't even asked her; Lexi just spilled it out. Lexi's like that. You can't tell her anything. She even told Mom she could change her name too. Mom thought that was cool (she is always *trying* to do cool things in front of my friends) and her name could be Tiny, but that would be dumb. For once I wholeheartedly agreed with her.

"No, no," Lexi said, all smiles as she licked the second beater clean, completely ignorant of my death-glare. "You could be Desi. The letters don't have to all be in a row." It was true; we had made that rule just for Lexi, because she pouted about being Lexa or Alex or Dria or Xand, which I personally adored. And so, as the legend goes, that is how Destiny Moore became hip, cool Desi Moore.

"Kinda like Demi Moore, huh?" Lexi had chirped.

I just muttered something like "Yeah, whatever." And from that moment on, I never called myself Rena. Everyone else, Mom included, kept her four-letter nickname.

Funny, because I was the only one who really wanted to change. Go figure.

Destiny. I hate to admit it, but I much prefer Desi. I'll never call her that, or Destiny, for that matter. I think it's dumb the way Cole calls her mother Regina. Well, most of the time she pronounces it differently. You know, like that place in Canada, rhymes with *vagina*. But even so, it's dumb. And Cole Blakely doesn't have to do things like that to be cool. She exudes it without even trying. It emits from her like the glow from gold.

She doesn't know it, though. That's why she hangs out with us.

Or maybe it is just to piss off her old friends the PPs.

That's what I like most about Cole, the way she loves to piss people off. Usually she's subversive about it, but when she's not, it's a riot. Like this one time in art she took craft shears to her Juicy Couture sweats. Some of the Hauties cried out in horror when they saw it. The others pretended not to notice, but they did. Oh, they did. And within a month her cropped couture was en vogue. Everyone was doing it.

After lunch, we reconvened in the art room for smokes. There's no sixth-period class there, so it's always abandoned. Various half-completed art projects and splattered drop cloths gave it a more refined atmosphere than our other option—the south parking lot Dumpsters.

"So what's with the sack of flour?" Cole asked. We'd all been eyeing it in Kori's arms. Not asking her about it, since she wasn't supposed to speak. We should've known it would be too hard for her to stay silent all day.

"Thought you'd never ask," she returned with a grin. She hoisted it onto the high craft table. "This is my baby."

Several other students had also been carrying similar packages, so we knew she wasn't crazy. But still.

I eyed the sack of flour. It was one of those basic five-pound jobs, but she'd decorated it to look like Charmmy Kitty, which touched my heart. For our fourteenth birthday, she gave me a plush version, because "Charmmy has a key around her neck too." I gave her a Badtz-Maru. It was one of those weird twin moments, aided by the popularity of Hello Kitty.

"Baby, huh?" Cole raised her professionally arched eyebrows knowingly at me.

"Yep. Doc Ramsey knocked me up."

"Cute." Cole smirked. "Does the school board know?"

"Don't look so smug, he's gonna knock both of you up next period."

Cole and I exchanged fearful looks; we both had him right after lunch.

"It's not fair," Lexi wailed, since she was the only one of us who hadn't gotten into one of Doc Ramsey's social psych classes.

Kori dropped an arm over Lexi's skinny shoulders and said, "I bet he'll knock you up too, honey, all you have to do is ask."

"Yeah, Lexi, just ask him to slip you his seed." Cole laughed, but I didn't think it was very funny.

Kori caught my discomfort before I could disguise it. "Okay, guys, enough, we're upsetting Serena."

I snubbed out my cigarette in an impromptu ashtray I'd made of leftover clay. "Aren't you supposed to be shutting up, Kor?"

"Oh, don't be so touchy."

"Serena's hormonal, you know—being pregnant and all," Cole said with a wink.

"Ha-ha. Anyone got any, like, Visine?" I asked, pulling out my Altoids mints. Cole tossed me a bottle, while Kori mocked me for scrambling to appear chaste for my favorite teacher.

Cole and I giggled through the entire flour-baby-making class. I'd decorated mine as a Baby Badtz-Maru, and Cole's was a candy-colored Louis Vuitton print. You could take the girl out of the fashionistas, but you couldn't take the fashionista out of the girl.

"I feel bad," Cole said when she finished.

"Lexi?" I asked, thinking about how sad she looked every time we talked about Doc's projects. Now we'd be carrying around flour sacks, and she'd be left out. "Think we should make her one?"

Lexi and I go the farthest back; we both lived in the same row of town homes for a couple of years until about three years ago, when Mrs. Devlin started trading up with a new husband and a new house each year. For a few short months in seventh grade, Lexi lived next door to the Blakelys, and that's when she became friends with Cole. The marriage didn't last, but Cole and Lexi's friendship did.

I used to be jealous of the way Cole took care of Lexi, until Kori and I became friends. I still remembered what it was like to be left out, though.

"I'll go see if Doc's got an extra," I said before heading to his desk.

I returned with it as the bell rang. "I'll decorate it in supervised study," Cole said, scooping it up. "Have fun in history."

I squished up my nose. "See ya."

When I stepped through the doorway, I spotted Anthony Beck's T-shirted back. All I could think about was how he saw me half-naked, and I bolted toward Dick Click's classroom, but seeing Dick and his greasy comb-over, I kept moving.

Dick's classroom was once the last frontier of the school. Then they built the new auditorium connected by an extra-wide hallway, which, in addition to showcasing various students' artwork, included a new bathroom that was only supposed to be used during events. So I darted to it and ducked in the last stall for a quick smoke before having to deal with Dick's class. I propped my new Baby Badtz-Maru on the back of the toilet tank, then leaned against the wall and tapped out a cigarette. Just as I got it lit, I heard someone coming and had to quickly snuff it out. I waved my hand to disperse the smell, then crouched on the toilet, hiding my boots.

Two girls came in and camped themselves out in front of the

mirror. Through the crack I could see Chelsea Westad's white-blond hair. Another girl shoved her way into the stall next to me and was . . . oh joy . . . throwing up. Fun.

Cheerleaders are so disturbed.

Below the partition I could see the soles of two shoes facing upwards. "*Go Adrian #17*" was written in heavy blue marker on the white rubber soles of both.

I sought out better reading on the stall door. Being a new bathroom and all, there wasn't much. Of course, there was the requisite Kori Kitzler bash; every bathroom stall in Kismet probably had one—this one was: *Kori Kitzler invites you to her Rainbow Party!* Beneath it was a couple of words that looked like the poor person didn't even know how to spell. The first attempt—apparently *Who is you*—was smeared. What remained looked to be the question:

Who are you?

What a stupid thing to write on a bathroom wall. The bubble gum font made it clear it was one of the BBs. I pulled out a marker and wrote *I'm Chelsea Wetrag* beneath it.

"Jesus, Marci," Chelsea sniped, "how much did you eat anyway?"

Marci groaned and then muttered, "Too much."

I shook my head as I heard her heave again. I really didn't want to be late because some bulimic cheerleader ate two too many french fries.

Flush. "You got any mouthwash?"

"Here, have some gum. You know, throwing up is so bad for you."

"So are uppers and laxatives, but I don't see you stopping," Marci growled.

My ankles burned and my toes were falling asleep, but I didn't try to readjust, for fear I would fall off the toilet seat. And that would just be embarrassing.

"God, Mar, bitchy much? Come on, we're late."

And out they went. Idiots.

The bell rang just as I turned the knob on Mr. Click's door. Karma was returning the favor for my making Poor Josh late. Unfortunately, Dick has a zero-tolerance policy on lateness. One he never expected anyone to actually break, which explained why his beady eyes swelled at the sight of me and confusion flopped like a fish across the deck of his face. Heaven pity the fool who missed the first minute of his lecture. Since he read verbatim from the book, they might never get caught back up with the rest of the class.

"Principal's office," he declared with a dramatic jab of his javelin-esque map pointer. Clearly its impressive length was making up for inadequacies in other areas.

My trip to the principal's included a "we-are-going-to-talk-about-this-when-you-get-home-missy" phone call from my mother.

I spent the remainder of the period "thinking about what I did," whilst being subjected to the torture of extreme air-conditioning and the sight of the office staff—aka hot-flashing, menopausal women in elastic-waistband capri pants—fawn all over Adrian17. He apparently cut last period and was ballsy enough to flaunt it in front of Principal Teasley, who did nothing but clap him on the back and tell him to slaughter the Rolling-wood Ravens this weekend. I swear, as star quarterback he gets his ass kissed more than a new Pomeranian at the dog park.

I shouldered my way through the hall after final bell, think-ing there was no way the impacted corridors met the current fire safety codes. Proving my assumption, I spotted Kori just as the backpack on some guy in front of me slammed into her, knocking her into her locker. She kicked back her leg and tripped him; he stumbled into the crowd, jostling three cheerleaders. They squealed and started whacking him repeatedly with their pompoms. Just another fine example of our high school's version of paying it forward.

"History was evil," I growled.

Kori pried her glaring eyes off backpack guy. "Halls are evil!"

I flashed the principal's note at her. "Yeah, I'd say they're about even, drama. Mom's picking me up."

Then I proudly showed off my new flour baby.

"So did Doc tell you guys how long we're supposed to lug them around for?" Kori asked.

"No. But remember that Web site thing, the Postcard Secret thing we're supposed to check out for a month before doing our own? I bet it's like that."

"A month? Hell no. What are we even supposed to do with these things? Did he tell you guys?" she asked.

I thought about how Doc had unceremoniously plopped one into my arms. I'd laughed, almost dropping it, and with a sheepish grin, said, *"Heavier than it looks."*

"That it is," he'd returned. *"That it is."*

"Not really," I told Kori. "We spent the whole time decorating them. Maybe we're supposed to be keeping a diary or something. Write down when and what we feed them?"

"Forget that," she said. Then: "You should've seen Marci Mancini's face when he assigned it. The horror that it wouldn't match her shoes."

"Yeah, doesn't exactly make the perfect accessory, does it?"

"Hey, did I tell you? I asked Doc if it was too late for me to get an abortion."

"That's sick, Kor."

"Well, he didn't say no."

"Really? That's weird, because Ashley gave him this huge speech about abstinence—"

"Ashley Simsroth? The chick who always saves a seat for Jesus at her lunch table?"

"Yeah, don't let her *Passion of the Christ* panties fool you—total abstinence advocate."

Kori laughed. "Well, that settles it. She's sooo not invited to my rainbow party."

"I saw that! I was a little hurt I had to hear about it that way. Anyway, so Ashley tells Doc that she practices abstinence, so she can't possibly get pregnant. And Doc was all, 'So, I guess the Virgin Mary was a liar, huh?' and she started hyperventilating."

"Yeah, 'cuz Mary is her homegirl."

"Right. So now she has the Immaculate Conception Flour Baby and is treating it like the Second Coming. So what did Doc say to you . . . about the abortion?"

"Nothing really. He just kind of smiled like he thought it was cool." Kori coughed out a little laugh. "So, why were you late to Dick's? Isn't he, like, right next door to Doc's?"

I shifted uncomfortably. "Yeah."

"Oh! You were flirting with Becks again!"

My mouth went dry. "I wasn't flirting with him." Then: "It's obvious he likes you."

She snorted. "He most definitely is *not* into me." I was relieved, even if I wasn't entirely convinced. "So? What were you doing?"

I thought for a moment about telling her the truth about why I was late. How embarrassed I was after seeing Anthony. Or more precisely about him seeing me. Naked. Nearly naked. But that would mean having to cop to crushing on him a little bit.

"I went for a smoke."

When I caught the devious twinkle in her eyes, I realized she already knew I was evading Anthony when I ducked into the bathroom. And worse, she remembered I owed her a dare.

As soon as her lips started to part, I screamed, "No!"

eight

Yes! It's perfect." Kori snickered; she loved watching me squirm. "What? You dared me to go skinny-dipping in the lake and I did it. You wussed out on me, as usual, which means you owe me a dare. Fair is fair."

Hmph.

"What? You don't have to marry Becks, just make out with him. Come on. That's a great dare. I'd love to be dared to suck hottie face."

"That's hardly a dare for you."

"True, I do like sucking hottie face."

"I'm not making out with him. I don't even know him."

"Exactly. Kiss for the sake of kissing. You don't have to know him; you don't even have to like him. In fact, it's better if you don't."

"This is messed up. Even for you."

"No, it's brilliant. It'll make you a better person."

I stopped and stared at her. Well, more at her pupils. They weren't nearly as dilated as I was expecting. "It will make me a better person?"

"What? You're always going after losers," she scoffed. I started to object, but she cut me off. "Any guy over nineteen who dates a high school girl is a loser. Think about it."

"So they're older, so what? Why does a guy liking me have to mean he's a loser?"

"Oh, Ser, just stop, would ya. Don't you ever get annoyed with yourself?"

I rolled my eyes. "You and your flattery."

"I love you too much to pull my punches. So, it's done. Tonight you will be making out with Becks."

"Sorry, can't."

"Yes. You. Can. He'll be at the kegger tonight."

"A kegger? Tonight?" I asked. It wasn't even the weekend.

"Spirit week. We'll all go."

I flashed the note, actually feeling thankful for it. "I'll be grounded, remember?"

"Since when does that stop you?"

"Fine." I closed my locker door and started toward the front exit. I looked over my shoulder at her and confessed, "But I'll just wuss out of it too."

"Over my dead body," she called.

"Stop it with the morbid death and dying stuff, okay? Leave it to the goth kids; they're more convincing anyway."

"I know you don't mean that! I'm just as depressing as they are," she called after me, but I was already rounding the corner making my escape. "And you will be doing the dare." And then with dramatic flourish, she announced more than asked, "If not tonight—when?"

I should've known that I was in serious trouble when my mother showed up at school in a suit and heels. The hairdo she'd sprayed in place looked hard enough to repel a hollow-point bullet or two. She headed straight to Principal Teasley's office, so she could personally apologize for my behavior. The way she strode purposefully down the hall and into his office, you'd have thought she was at the county courthouse and I was on trial. Or maybe that's just because I was humming the theme song from *Law & Order*.

I'm sorry, but I just can't take this version of her seriously. I've been to Oz. I've seen behind the curtain. And the woman behind it wore mismatched socks and giggled when she burped.

"I don't know what she's thinking, that's not how I raised her to behave," I'd heard Mom tell Teasley. Just a little dramatic for being five minutes late to class, but whatever.

"You're grounded, starting tonight," Mom said as she came out of Teasley's office.

"You don't even want to know what happened?" I probably shouldn't have started with that, considering I didn't really have a good excuse.

"This is unacceptable, Ser. Completely." Even as she was saying this, her head ducked down and the blond bangs that usually fell away from her face stayed plastered in place as she scrawled off her signature on the note Teasley's secretary had given me. "I'm serious—no phone, no TV."

If it got me out of *Gilmore Girl*s reruns, it was well worth it.

"Fine," I said, turning my phone off and setting it in her palm. "It wasn't on purpose."

"Oprah says there are no coincidences—everything has a purpose." *Crap*. Not Oprah. I'd already had my cell phone grounded; I didn't need to be tortured too. She waved the principal's note at me. "This is fate's way of giving you a wake-up call. Oprah says you get a whisper first, then you get a little pebble upside the head, next it's a brick, then a brick wall, and then the whole wall falls down on you. This is your whisper, Ser."

Hmmm . . . I was sort of hoping it was a pebble, because then I could chuck it at her.

"Okay, Mom. I'm sorry. Can we go now?" I pried the note from her tightly pinching fingers and handed it to the principal's secretary. *My whisper?* Was she serious?

I shut myself in my room as soon as we got home, turned up the stereo, and went online in stealth mode, disabling my IMs. I didn't want idle little chitchats. I wanted to get that lost feeling, that floating fog.

I signed onto my game and picked up with my coding, trying to get into that hacker haze I needed. I was just free coding. My brain full of delicate state—*juggling priceless eggs in variable gravity*, as my fellow aliens would say. I basked in the white noise vibration of it.

Some hours later, a clinking noise overtook Rob Zombie's "Dragula," jerking me painfully out of my hacker mode bliss. It took me a second to realize it was a pebble hitting my window. After quickly saving my game, I unlocked my window and looked out. Kori's eyes stared up at me, concerned.

I glanced back into the house, thinking Mom would be knocking soon, and even if I wasn't grounded, she wouldn't be pleased about seeing Kori there.

"I'll be quiet!" Kori shouted up. Loudly.

With a groan, I waved her up and waited while she climbed the handyman's ladder.

"Seriously, be quiet. I'm in enough trouble," I said as I helped her crawl through my window while trying to carry her flour baby. As she stood, I stared. The skinny wench was giving me a serious case of pelvic bone envy. She was wearing a pair of black leather pants that were cut so low she had to shave her special place just to wear them.

She hooked a thumb in her front pocket, which inched them down even farther, if that was possible. "What? Don't tell me you forgot."

I looked back at her face.

"The party? The dare?" She went straight for my computer monitor. "I tried to catch you online."

"Stealth, sorry."

She turned back to me. "Your cell went straight to voice."

"Mom grounded it."

"Well? Is she shipping you off to Brat Camp?" In addition to being heavily involved in Colorado Cares, Mom is also lead advocate for Wilderness Wonders.

"We 'talked,'" I said, making air quotes.

"So why didn't you call or come out to the lake?"

"Shit, what time is it?"

"Eleven forty-five."

"Shit, sorry, I got carried away," I said, but I was more concerned about why my mom hadn't come to bang on the door. It wasn't like her. "Hang on."

I looked down the hallway toward her room. The strip of air beneath her door seeped black. My stereo had blared way too loudly to go unnoticed all this time. Inching along the hallway, past the photos of Mom and me, my blood pressure spiked. I glanced back and saw Kori hugging my door, rocking it on its hinges as she watched me.

I drilled her with me eyes and mouthed, *"You're not supposed to be here."*

Kori mouthed back, *"I'm not worried."*

"Just go!"

I waited until Kori disappeared into my room, my hand

poised on the knob. Then I pressed my ear to the door. No sound. My tongue swelled against the back of my throat, beating hard with my heart as I slipped into the darkness of Mom's room. If Kori were shameless enough to steal up behind me and grab me like she had on the dam, I would have screamed like I had never screamed before. She would have had to peel me from the ceiling—that is how terrified I was in my mother's dark room realizing she was gone.

I fumbled for the lamp switch just to be sure. The sudden brightness revealed nothing but her tidy furnishings.

Where was she? Why hadn't she told me she was leaving?

The sound of water running in her bathroom swirled in my ears and I moved confidently toward its source. She only had a tub, no shower. There was no way she would be running a bath at that hour, and if I had a private bathroom, I'd probably have tried the same trick. That's why I opened the door without hesitation and the water running straight down the bathtub drain didn't surprise me at all. Instead, I felt like I'd been punched in the gut. How often had she abandoned me without so much as a word?

All these years, I had been one of only a few people to have seen the real person behind the carefully hung curtain my mom displayed to everyone else. And while I didn't always understand her need for the deception, I'd been okay with it. I knew the real person. I'd seen the wizard. And that was the person I'd loved. But as I stood in her bathroom staring at the water as it ran down the drain, I realized that all this time there'd been another curtain, one I'd never known existed.

The vulnerability of the empty house pulsed behind me until I reached my room. I was never more thankful to see Kori. The only person I could truly count on anymore.

"So, what did Mommy Dearest say?" Kori asked as she whipped her straight hair into a funky knot.

"She's not even here." My head couldn't wrap around that.

"What do you mean she's not here?"

"I don't know, I think she might be . . ." I could barely form the words that came to mind. "On a date?"

"A *what*?"

"I don't know! She's not here and she didn't tell me she was leaving."

"Okay, okay, calm down."

Kori was used to her parents' disappearing acts, so I didn't want to make a big deal about it in front of her. But it definitely was a big deal, a very big deal. "I'm fine. Let's just go to the party, okay?"

I could tell by the way Kori looked at me that she didn't believe that I was fine, but she also wasn't about to make me talk either. "Well, you're not going dressed like that. Go get changed."

I hurried, grabbing up my shortest skirt as I headed to the bathroom to do my hair and makeup. All I could think about was Mom. She'd never been a big dater or anything. Let's just say *Dr. Phil's Relationship Rescue* was more of a vicarious read for her. But maybe now she was making up for lost time. I wasn't sure how I felt about that. But I sure as hell didn't like her keeping it from me. Abandoning me without so much as a sticky note.

All those nights I thought I was so clever sneaking out to the dam, making my movements stealthy and covering my tracks, I wasn't fooling anyone. There wasn't anyone to fool except myself.

I returned to my mom's room and retrieved my cell phone from the drawer of her bedside table.

I walked back into my room and saw Kori at my computer. "What are you doing?" I asked.

"Just waiting for you, kitten," she said coyly as she pushed the power button on my monitor.

"That's the monitor," I said. Before I could stop her, she'd jabbed the PC's power button. "Kor, you're supposed to actually shut it down."

"Whatever." She looked at the "Let's talk" Post-it note collection that was growing like mold over my desk as if it were the first time she'd ever seen it. She flicked one of them with her finger. "Why do you keep all of these? If that isn't a cry for help, I don't know what is."

She turned back and looked at me. I just shrugged.

"So you're grounded, huh?" Kori said as we left the town house. She put her arm over my shoulder and hugged me against her as we walked toward the park. "What else did she say?"

"She's disappointed in me." The feeling was mutual. "And this is my whisper."

Eagle's Nest Park felt more like a nightclub than the outdoors. Everyone from Kismet High jostled against one another, bumping up close even though the secluded park had acres to spare.

I hopped onto a cement picnic table, flinching at the cold sting biting the backs of my thighs. I had Baby Maru hidden away in my messenger bag behind me on the table. Lexi sat on the bench below me, crossing her legs, and put hers in her lap. It was decorated in pink poodle swirls. Cole's flour baby was not attending the kegger. She'd paid her younger cousin, who was only six, to babysit. And when I'd last seen Baby Charms, she was in the crook of Kori's arm as Kori was slipping into a van better known as "The Easy-Bake Oven" for a smoke with Parker Walsh.

I wondered what hope any of us had for Flour Baby Mother of the Year.

Cole stood in front of me with a devious look on her face. Her chin tucked like a cat focused on its prey as she watched Chelsea, Marci, and Brittney fawning over Adrian17. Another gaggle of groupies huddled just to his right, too shy to actually approach him.

"You know," Cole started, a sly grin forming. "I've always wondered what it'd be like to date the star quarterback."

Lexi's legs unfolded quickly, like she was springing into action, and her eyes went round in that cute anime way. All lashes. "You wouldn't!"

I smirked. It had been a while since she'd been up to her old tricks of pissing off the BBs and PPs.

"I'm just thinking that . . . well, he and I might have some things in common. You know, like we both have great hair, and I'd bet money we both lost our virginity to Nickelback."

I grunted. "Yeah, you and every other BB and PP."

"You have a boyfriend," Lexi reminded her. Not that Cole was all that serious about him. It was more of a friend of the family kind of thing. And he did live in Denver, which was almost an hour away.

"I wouldn't consider this cheating. No. This is more of a social experiment per se."

I turned my attention to Cole's new mark to find Brittney DaSalvo presenting her cleavage to Adrian at advantageous angles. (After going to a one-day modeling seminar, she is all about knowing her angles.) Chelsea played it a little cooler since she had a boyfriend-point-five. She kept making these weird little jerking motions with her chin, like *"Come on, boy, you and me, let's go into the bushes!"* Marci took a step back, but kept that desperate-to-catch-his-eye look, alternating it with awkward laughs that seemed to be out of step with whatever they were talking about. Hey, third in the queue for the QB ain't bad. Besides, I'd heard rumors she'd already had her turn on the Adrian17 Express over the summer.

"He's got twenty girls in line for him already," Lexi said, unintentionally throwing down a challenge.

If any girl at Kismet High could get cut-zees, Cole could. Her self-imposed lower social standing made her all the more mysterious and intriguing than the always accessible BBs and PPs. Add in her unbelievable coolness and it was a devastating combination.

"Cole." Lexi's tone flattened in warning, but Cole was already shaking out her Aniston-esque hair and heading straight toward Adrian. He became caught in her spell from the moment she hit her stride. And in that very same instant, Chelsea and Brittney folded their arms over their chests, feeling the chill of already being in her shadow.

"Did you see that?" Lexi asked.

I assumed she was referring to Cole's breezy execution of the Adrian17 fan club. But just to clarify, I asked, "See what?"

Lexi swiped her hand through the air, gesturing incredulously at Adrian and Cole.

"What about them?" I asked, sensing she was somehow hurt by all of this, but not really understanding why.

"This is just a joke for her. She doesn't even like him."

"Do you?"

"No! I'm just saying . . . she makes it look so easy. She likes a guy, she walks up and gets him. Why's it so easy for her?"

"Lexi, don't even sweat it. The guys Cole and Kori go for are just toys for them. That's why it's easy." And then I thought about Kori's dare and Anthony Beck, and I didn't want to be like

Lexi worrying and being scared. I wanted to be like Kori and live for the moment.

"Do you ever wonder why Kori became friends with you?"

I swung my gaze around. Looked at Lexi for a moment and then lied. "No, I don't." Then a few beats later: "What the fuck kind of question is that?"

"No, I just mean . . . she and Cole are so different from us."

"You and I aren't that alike, Lexi," I said, because I wanted it to be true. I knew it sounded harsh, but I blamed her a little bit for making me open up a wound, reminding me of my insecurities and not being the slightest bit aware of it.

But the truth was, Lexi and I were more alike than I wanted to admit.

Cole and Kori were the brave ones. Lexi and I were timid. I hid my vulnerability, making quite the job of it. But not Lexi. Lexi kept hers proudly on display, and sometimes looking at her made me feel like I was standing in front of a mirror naked. All the raw spots glaringly obvious. And sometimes when Lexi's all buddy-buddy with my mother, I also ask, *"Why's it so easy for her?"*

Just thinking about my MIA mother made a familiar, antsy energy start up inside of me. I felt it every time I thought about my father leaving me. I usually channeled my anxiety by programming games on my computer, but out here in the park that was impossible. My fingers twitched like a dreaming dog's legs, finding imaginary keys, reaching for letters to string together. Muscle memory, it's called. My fingers could run code lines even if I were in a coma. I could hear the gentle tapping of my fingers on my plastic beer cup like a Morse code repeating an SOS.

Save Me. Help Me. Hear Me.

But Lexi, oblivious to my unease, continued to babble.

I finished off my beer in a long chug, as eager to get a little drunk as I was to have a reason to get away from Lexi and her reminders. As if right on cue, up came Poor Josh. I was so not in the mood to patiently wait while he P-P-P-Porky P-Pigged his way through a conversation with me.

I couldn't handle sitting still. My bones twitched with desperation to move and get away. "Hey Josh, Lexi was just asking me about the Gorillaz. They're like your favorite group, right?" I said, stabbing out what was left of my cigarette. Then, because I knew neither of them drank: "Does anyone need another beer? I'm going."

And I was out of there, shouldering my way through the musky heat of too many people—sweaty boys, perfumed girls, grungy stoners who never washed their flannel shirts. Marijuana seemed to waft off them all. If it weren't for the mandatory Colorado history class, I would have sworn *Cannabis sativa* was the state plant. They don't call it the High Country for nothing.

After filling up my cup, I went to look for Kori. Walking through the thickest part of the crowd, I felt a little wad of panic—part claustrophobia and part fear that I wouldn't be able to find her—churning inside me. But people moved aside and made space for cool currents of air, scented with pine and bonfire wood.

I searched for Kori, managing to catch only glimpses—her black hair being whipped over her shoulder, her hand thrust high in the air to keep from burning someone with the glowing tip of her cigarette.

The mass of people around her was thick. I circled around it, finding a less crowded path. Just as I was about to elbow my way in, I heard a voice say, "What's your damage, Heather?"

I turned to see Parker Walsh sitting with his back against a tree, flashing me a puckish smirk. His hair looked mangled and his eyes were thin little slits, as if he were looking up into the sun instead of the pitch-black night.

"Are you talking to me?" I asked, annoyed by the delay as well as the delayer.

"Yeah. What's the matter?"

"Nothing."

"Sure there is. Kori's all in a freak too. What is it with you girls?"

"She was fine earlier."

"Whatever. She's all worried about something." I thought I heard sincerity in his otherwise mocking voice.

I glanced toward Kori; she was smiling and laughing. "Kori's fine."

"Is she?"

"Yes, Parker, she's fine."

"Are you?" he asked, the agitating sarcasm back in place. Why did I even bother trying to talk to him? No doubt his brain was in some alternate universe where my messenger bag was a killer unicorn or something. I drank my beer, nearly finishing off the full cup.

"Yeah, she's fine and I'm fine, okay?" I said, finishing off my beer as I started walking toward Kori. I just wanted to go home. And the sooner I could get to Kori, the better.

About halfway in, the crowd seemed to close around me. Tighter. An awful trapped feeling came over me. Too many people, too much heat. And then the weight of an arm dropped over my shoulders. My eyes slanted to find a hand with a silver thumb ring dangling over my right boob. It was attached to none other than one very fine Anthony Beck.

"There's my dangerous girl."

My heart danced.

"If not tonight—when?"

With three plastic cups worth of keg-pumped liquid courage already in me, I was a lot less shy about the whole "bare sighting" as it were. I smiled and held up my hands. "I'm completely unarmed. Look, no books."

He eyed my messenger bag. "I think, just to be safe, I'm going to have to keep you next to me all night long," he said, tucking me closer against him.

I laughed. "You're afraid of my empty cup?"

"Empty cup? We'd better get you a refill, keg's getting low," is what he said. What I heard was: *"Let's get you out of here."*

nine

Anthony led me away from the party, instinctively knowing I needed to get away from the crush of bodies.

He tugged me a little closer to him. Whispered, "I wanted you to be here."

"Yeah?"

As we neared a park bench, he took his arm away. "Yeah, I wanted to talk to you."

After he sat with his legs spread the way guys always do, and his elbows propped up on the back on the bench, there was no room left for me. I had no choice but to stand in front of him. I fiddled with my plastic cup, unease swirling in the pit of my stomach. I just knew he wanted to talk to me about Kori. Find out what her favorite song was or where she liked to eat. I tried not to let my voice waver as I asked, "So, what's up?"

"I don't know. I just, I keep seeing you around."

My heart quickened. "Me?"

"Yeah." He gave a short laugh. "I wanted to talk to you last night, but I got the feeling you didn't want to talk to me." Heat flared over my cheeks. And he tilted his head, amused. "Wait. You weren't embarrassed about being caught skinny-dipping, were you?"

"No," I said quickly. "I thought, I don't know. I thought you were into Kori."

"Kori?"

"Yeah. I mean, you were kind of all over her after she got out of the lake. Just seemed like, you know, you were into her. And I didn't even go in . . ." I stopped myself before I babbled too much. Although, judging from the look on his face—a mixture of confusion and curiosity—I'd crossed that line already.

"Why didn't you go in the lake?"

"I just didn't." I looked at my boots. This wasn't my idea of fun. In fact, I seriously was ready to start telling him Kori's favorite TV shows. "I didn't think she would do it, okay?"

"That bothers you?"

"Yes. I mean, no. It doesn't bother me that she did it. It's just, I was there, I was ready. I didn't have a good reason not to follow her in. I just . . . I got scared."

Behind us the party was a drone of noise, a bundle of tangled energy. Around us settled a still and patient silence. In the cold air, I could see Anthony exhale. He sat forward and started taking off his watch. When he held out his hand for mine, I thought he was going to suggest we go skinny-dipping together.

His fingers wrapped over mine. Reluctantly, I let him pull me closer. "This isn't waterproof," he said as set his watch across my wrist. The wide leather band still held his warmth. Then, as he buckled it in place: "Now you've got a reason."

Anthony passed me the stub he'd been given as we made our way back to the party. I hesitated about bringing it to my lips as I watched him work the keg. That was always Kori's call. In addition to not wanting me to talk funny, she doesn't want me to end up like her. She tells me I can only smoke when she gives it to me. That's our rule.

I desperately wanted to take a couple drags to settle the racing rat in the wheel that was my brain. I'd just spent the past hour snuggled in Anthony Beck's lap talking about everything and nothing at all. You know, the kinds of things that keep you up at night smiling as you remember them? And now I'd worked myself into a panic because he hadn't kissed me and I so wanted to kiss him. I'd held my breath savoring each second, but then he'd brought me back to the party and the moment had passed, and I just needed to calm down.

I couldn't spot Kori anywhere. Instead my search halted on Marci Mancini. She'd wandered off from her friends and was making a funny face as she stared down into her plastic cup of beer. After flicking a glance at the flour baby nestled in the crook of her tanned arm, she lowered her nose to the cup and sniffed. With a violent shake of her head, she tossed the full cup of beer out onto a nearby shrub. I rolled my eyes. She probably *only* drank Zima.

First she cradled her flour baby. Then she held it out in front of her with both hands, as someone might lift an actual child to look him in the eye. Even from the distance I could see her forehead all wrinkled in the same way it'd been when she contemplated drinking her beer.

The BBs are so bizarre sometimes. I knew it was just a sack of flour and all, but I couldn't even watch if she was going to toss it into the shrub with the beer. And when my gaze swung around, it collided with the dazzle of Anthony's emerald greens. Oh hell, it was just one drag.

I pressed my lips around the joint and inhaled deeply.

Anthony was laughing and saying something, but I couldn't

quite hear. He took the joint back, sucked on it before passing it off to someone else. Realizing I hadn't heard him, he bent in closer to my ear, his breath licking currents of warm air across the surface of my skin as he whispered, "I'm scared too."

The words *"Of what?"* tripped over my lips.

The hard tip of his nose brushed against the edge of my ear as he spoke. And then I felt it, the buzzing of fear—no not fear, anticipation—rising up hard inside of me. And it felt alive. Addictive.

A shiver made a hard escape down my spine when the soft edge of his tongue traced along the outer shell of my ear, before finding tender places to tease. He switched ears, and as he did, he reached down to take my beer and set it aside.

"Of this," he whispered as he brought my palm to his chest.

His heart bumped a hard, fast beat. Just like mine.

Like water left boiling too long—a wave of heat blasted past hidden levees inside me, cascading down my ribs, down my belly, down, down, down.

He looked briefly into my eyes, his fingers taking gentle command of my jaw while he kissed me. It was one of those movie-worthy kisses, slow-motion and—cover your eyes, Baby Maru!—full-on. It lasted way longer than it needed to, but (Oh thank God!) it didn't show any signs of letting up.

I let my hands rove over him, upward until my fingers were pushing into his hair. I wound chunks of it around them and pulled his mouth harder against mine. My world turned in a slow swirl.

"Serena!" Kori shouted in my ear. I snapped to attention, nearly biting off Anthony's glorious tongue. "Geez, slutty much?" she said, smiling like a proud—yet clearly dysfunctional—parent.

With one strong hand, Anthony kept hold of my face. His

eyes shared secret things with mine as the pad of his thumb made a focused swipe of my lower lip, drying it off with a satisfied grin.

Before I could smile back at him, his hand began to travel down my side, stopping just below the frayed denim hem of my skirt. I held my breath, feeling his fingers curl around the back of my thigh, as if they were merely wrapped around my arm or something equally benign and friendly.

Kori coughed, gaining back my attention. She lifted a pierced eyebrow and the guilt flooded me. I confessed to everything. "I had some bud."

She smirked one of her burgundy-lip smirks. "That's okay, just don't talk."

Kori gave the key around my neck a tug as she told Anthony to make sure her kitten got home okay.

I got lost in Anthony's eyes again, and by the time I turned back to her, she'd walked off. "Hey, where are you go . . . ?" I called to her, but stopped, seeing her and Baby Charms disappear into Parker Walsh's blue Mazda. Before I could even worry about it, Anthony pulled me into another drenching kiss. The force of him coming toward me sent us back, back, back. The cold steel of a parked car stopped me as Anthony kept coming, filling every gap of air between us.

Sliding my palms inside the back of his shirt, I pulled him even closer, because there was no close enough . . . no fast enough . . . no enough enough.

Like a roller coaster ride slamming to an end, Anthony dropped his forehead against mine. "I'm, sorry," he said while trying to catch his breath. "I'm . . . uh . . . I didn't mean to just attack you like that."

I swallowed. "That's okay. I like aggressive guys."

His eyes locked with mine, and he took my hand, lacing our fingers together. "Let's get out of here."

Under my breath, I whispered, "Best five words a guy can say to me."

When I awoke in my bedroom, I smelled of Anthony—Axe, male sweat, and something else . . . oh yes, golf course grass. Embarrassing memories exploded around me, but I soldiered on past the oh-shit-what-happened stage of post-public-macking stress syndrome. No, we didn't have sex. I don't want to talk about that.

I was too depressed, seeing as how I'd just done the whole drunken-slut-girl routine with a guy I really liked. And I was sure whatever magic had possessed me at last night's kegger was lost and Anthony was probably already regretting it and planning to avoid me until he graduates.

His watch was still wrapped around my wrist. And I wanted so much to keep it. So much so, I left it on while I showered, holding it carefully out of water. But while I showered, it wasn't Anthony I was thinking about. It was Mom.

Steam had coated the bathroom before I even crawled under the hot spray. Guess that faux midnight bath hadn't gotten her clean.

I was torn with feeling excited by the notion that she might've been secretly meeting my father and upset knowing it was more than likely just some loser guy.

I did a double brush on the teeth, rinsed and repeated, and almost passed out before I made it back to my bedroom. I opened my window to its fullest to clear the stench of drunk-girl. A jackhammer-like noise pounded my brain and I turned to see my cell phone buzzing across my end table. I grabbed it up and through my blurry eyes read the message:

Meet b4 school? ;-) A.

My heart revved a little. *Did Anthony Beck just text me?* I mean, sure he had his tongue down my throat, but to text me the next day? That was definitely not avoiding me. In fact, that was dangerously close to relationship territory. I looked at the clock. Shit. If I hurried, I could meet him.

CU soon. S.
:-) :-) :-) A.

I snapped my phone shut with a smile and busted ass to get ready. I was happy, officially happy, and then I saw Mom in the kitchen peddling her breakfast-wares like a cheating man with roses. Toast? Eggs? Bacon? Cereal? Bagel? (Which she dropped when she got a close look at me.)

"Serena!" she screeched. "Your eyes!"

Crap. I looked like shit. Not exactly the look one went for when meeting up with a hottie junior. I fished out an ice cube from the freezer and rubbed it against my eyelids one at a time.

"Have you been . . . ?" Her hand tried to soothe the words out of her chest with odd little circles.

God only knew what she thought—probably not that her little girl was playing tonsil hockey on the eighteenth green, but the last thing I needed was an unscheduled parental lecture when Anthony Beck was waiting for me.

I held the ice cube away from my eye so I could glare, and pain tore up my optic nerve, spearing my brain. "What?"

I slammed my eyelids shut and dabbed them again with the cold ice. Sucking in a deep breath, I braced for the drugs question to rear up sans sticky note warning, but nothing came. "Have I been what, Mom?"

I dared her to say it. I don't know why I prodded her. Knowing I was clean certainly didn't hurt. Last night I didn't even inhale, not really. Not that I gave a damn what she had to say, but I really didn't have the patience to wait for her to spit it out either.

"Serena?" She tried to make eye contact. "Have you been crying? All night?"

Crying? Why would I have been crying?

"You know, I remember getting sent to the principal's office when I was in eighth grade. I cried so hard my father couldn't even bring himself to punish me."

God, how lame. Especially for a girl who got knocked up at seventeen.

"If I'd known you were this upset about it . . ." She got this faraway look on her face, no doubt remembering that she hadn't even been at home last night.

Briefly I debated taking the excuse she was handing me. I could've shamed her, asked if she'd heard me, told her I was so upset that I'd come to find her and couldn't. But truth was, after learning that she'd been gone all night without so much as a word to me, I really didn't even want her guilt anymore.

"Computer," I said, dropping the ice into the sink. "I was up late working on my history project. I wanted to get it done early, you know, to make amends for my being late to Mr. Click's class." I had the paper on my computer if she chose to call me on it. "I guess I just lost track of time. Hope my music didn't disturb you."

"Your music?" She didn't just take the bait, she snatched it. "No, I must've slept right through it."

My breath escaped, everything in my heart bled out. She actually did it. She lied to me. Stone-face lied.

At that very moment—for only the thinnest slice of a second—I no longer thought of her as my mother, she was just a woman standing in the same room as me. It scared the shit out of me.

I dried my face with a kitchen towel before I met her eyes for one quick moment of truth. I expected to see guilt, shame, but found nothing.

"You really should be more careful with your eyes. Maybe we should get one of those screen diffuser things."

Yeah, that and a sticky note will solve everything. "Whatever."

I hurried to school, completely pushing everything with Mom to the back of my brain. I took a deep breath of the cool morning air and filled myself with its freshness. Anthony Beck was waiting for me. He'd text'd smiley faces, for crissakes. Three of them! I didn't even feel hungover anymore.

But as I got closer to school, I could tell something was wrong. Anthony wasn't hanging by the front stairs. Nobody was.

The school stood in front of me. Post and beams, river rock walls, a little landscaping to give it that Colorado lodge look. But this morning it looked lifeless, like it was a weekend or spring break or something.

And then I could make out a faint bleating noise. A car alarm? And as I got closer, I started to hear a muffled mass of voices. Other students were here somewhere. I just couldn't see them. The new performing arts auditorium blocked my view.

Then I heard the siren.

The faster I moved, the closer I got to the noise, and the louder and more indistinct it became, until it grew into a massive hive of sound.

Then Principal Teasley's voice shouting loud and clear over everything, "I need everyone to get inside! Now!" It came from the back parking lot, and as I got closer, I started seeing people, lots of people moving toward me, returning to the school. On their faces—confusion, fear, sadness. And as they headed back toward the school, I pushed my way through them.

"Serena!"

I turned and spotted Cole and Lexi maneuvering through the crowd toward me. Tears streaked Lexi's swollen cheeks. Cole took hold of my elbow and turned me around, told me we had to get to class.

"What happened?" I asked.

"There was a car wreck. It's bad. Don't look. Teasley wants everyone inside. Let's go."

The ambulance sirens were louder; coming up the long straight road everyone called "The Strip." As I turned toward the noise, I saw the wreck. Spiderwebbed glass bleeding red. Smoke steaming from folded metal hoods.

"Is that . . . ?" My words caught as Cole tugged me toward the school. I jerked free and turned back.

Parker Walsh stumbled out of his crunched blue Mazda; wet blood blackened his pant leg.

I started moving toward him, to get a closer look, but a pair of arms came around me. It was Anthony. "We need to go inside," he said. But I held my ground. From the distance the scene before me didn't make sense.

Parker struggled through the smoke, disoriented, his hands trying to push it aside like he was tangled in a large white bedsheet.

He kept disappearing and reappearing with the breeze. I watched, trapped by Anthony's arms, as Parker bent over, leaned inside the window of the mangled red Mustang like he was trying to talk to whoever was inside.

I closed my eyes, remembering Kori getting into Parker's car the night before.

Anthony was speaking, but I couldn't hear anything except the bass beat of my own blood—pounding like angry fists on my eardrums. I'm sure the car alarms were still bleating. The ambulances had their sirens on. But I couldn't hear any of it.

Anthony's grip tightened as I struggled against his arms. "No," I whispered. Then I started screaming, "Let me go!"

"Teasley said we had to go inside," he said softly, not releasing me.

"But, Kori's in . . ."

Anthony softened with shock. His hold became more of an embrace than a restraint, and I broke free from it.

There is no shame in not knowing; the shame
lies in not finding out.
—Russian proverb

ten

I felt a hand on my shoulder but I didn't look up or open my eyes. "Serena, it's time to go." My mother. The nurse at the desk had called her when I'd come into the emergency room. I remembered hearing her. Then I remembered the accident.

"Serena, we need to leave." Her voice caught. I heard her swallow before she spoke again, this time with authority, urgency. "The family is coming and they'll want some privacy."

She choked out air. I could hear her tears and I opened my eyes. Her voice had seemed so faraway, yet she was standing right next to me wearing a pair of navy sweatpants with her hair still in curlers. It was just a dream. I was still in our town house. In my bed. There was no way this was real. My mother wouldn't be caught dead looking like that in public.

"It was just a dream, Mom."

The clarity and force of my voice shocked her. Her head moved side to side as she pulled me into her. Her voice soft and gentle. "I'm so sorry, honey."

"Just a dream," I repeated.

"No," she whispered. "Kori died. So did the two other boys, Curt and Brian. Parker is in ICU."

My head shook in disbelief but my mother's hold only got tighter.

"Kori died instantly," she said as she stroked my hair off my face and tried to look into my eyes. One hand rubbed my back. She was desperate to soothe me. "She didn't suffer," she said over and over. But Mom didn't know. Not really.

I didn't go back to school. I went home, put Pearl Jam's "Black" on repeat, and stayed in bed until the funeral.

Between cycles of deep sleep and restlessness, I thought about all the ways I could get to wherever Kori was. Most involved too much pain to think about for too long.

So instead, I thought about a story Mrs. Patterson had told me when I was younger. It was about a man and a woman who had been childhood sweethearts. They'd gotten married, had beautiful children, and were as in love with each other on their fiftieth anniversary as the day they'd married. On the way home from dinner one night, the woman had an aneurism and died. That very night, the man went to sleep and never woke up. Died of a broken heart, they said.

I closed my eyes and waited. But every time I woke up, reality stood over me. I was still here. Kori wasn't.

I don't know how many times I tried, how much time had passed, but it wasn't enough. My heart wouldn't give out, but it wouldn't come back to life either.

Everything inside of my skin hurt, everything on its surface was numb.

And then came the sudden blinding sting of sun as my mom snapped the drapes open. Then the impatient jab of her finger as she rammed all the buttons on my iPod until she silenced the singular voice that had rolled over in my head for what I supposed had been somewhere between three and five days. I felt the loss of it instantly. I needed to crawl back into the darkness, wrap myself in Eddie Vedder's cries of why.

Mom said I had to get up. I had to go to the funeral. I felt her watching me, waiting for a response. "Cole and Lexi have come for you." The way she said it made it sound like they were taking me off to the funny farm.

They're coming to take me away. Hoo-hoo, haa-haa, hee-hee.

I started laughing maniacally but then quit when I caught my mom choking back tears. I clamped my lips shut and tucked a stray hair behind my ear. "What?"

"I don't understand why you're laughing."

"I'm laughing because this is ridiculous. Kori can't be dead. She just can't."

"But she is."

"But I don't feel it!" I screamed. "Don't you think my heart would have broken by now?"

Maybe I *was* dreaming. Maybe this whole thing was just one bad nightmare. The only way to find out for sure was to go to the damn funeral and see for my damn self.

Cole and Lexi came in as Mom left. They'd come by at least three times; called every hour, it seemed from all the ringing. So far I had yet to talk to them. I couldn't face them. I know that's awful. They needed me as much as I needed them, but until then, I just couldn't. I didn't want to acknowledge the reality of what had happened. I couldn't say the words.

Lexi made my bed with clean sheets; Cole shoved me into the shower before heading straight for my closet. She pulled things out but found nothing appropriate despite my wardrobe being heavy on black. It had been years since I'd been to church, and I'd never been to a funeral, not one that I could remember, anyway.

When I was younger we went to church a lot. Correction—we went to a lot of churches. Mom's explanation was simply that there was more than one way of thinking, and she'd certainly explored them all. In her *Where's Waldo?* approach to finding Jesus, we attended just about every church imaginable. But I don't think I'd ever been inside Our Lady of the Rockies.

Inside, it was like an overturned ark. The riblike boning of the roof formed the massive hull. Giant oars pitched out on each side. The stained glass revealed a watery underworld complete with mermaidlike angels—not flying, but floating—outside of the windows. It made me feel a little bit claustrophobic. A little like I was drowning.

I recognized a few other students and teachers, but essentially strangers crowded the foyer, filling it with their gentle voices. I felt so far removed from it. Like this whole other world existed that Kori belonged to, but I had never even breathed its air.

"Let's just get seated," Cole suggested, and Lexi and I followed her.

I had to keep hiking up the dress Cole had picked out for me. My eighth-grade prom gown. The dress was simple—not shiny, not taffeta. But it was strapless, and now that I actually had them, my breasts bulged obscenely from it. Cole had paired it with the black shrug she'd brought to wear with her perfect and stylish sheath dress.

I looked fine, but I felt stupid. It didn't help that I was carrying my flour baby. No one else was. I guess it was one of those universally understood things. Note to self: you don't have to do social psych homework during a funeral.

As we moved inside, I caught sight of Chelsea Westad and her family huddled close to "The Surviving Kitzlers." What exactly did that mean, anyway? That they survived the tragedy of losing their daughter? And wasn't it a little soon to be declaring that victory? Or was the term *surviving* used more broadly? As in they had succeeded in living on this earth longer than she had? Judging from the smile on Mrs. K.'s face, it was a toss-up.

I glimpsed Mom's blond hair and black suit as she snuck in late; she had dropped us off at the main entrance of the church before heading off to find a parking spot in the overflow lot. She took a seat in the back row even though we had saved a place for her.

Next to me Lexi sniffed back tears. Cole stayed strong and fed her tissues.

The funeral was numbing. Prayers, sermons, psalms, prayers, psalms, sermons. It was a total out-of-body experience. Inside, sea waves of sickness rocked through me while erratic clips of music kept repeating in my head—chafing hands, broken glass, and all the love gone bad.

I needed to get back to that black world. This bright one was moving way too fast. Spinning out of control. My brain snagged, over and over, repeating audio clips of Kori like a CD with a scratched surface, unable to skip past a lyric. Just spinning and skipping, skipping and spinning. The sides of my stomach jerked and clamped, ripping flames of acidic bile up the back of my throat with every convulsion. I needed to throw up. That's what happens when you've been jerked upright and thrust out into the sunlight after spending four days in the horizontal position in a perfectly good dark room. I felt blind, slimy, like a larva forced out of its dark, safe cocoon too soon. Born to a new world that I had zero chance of surviving.

I needed to prove to myself that Kori was really and truly dead. In all honesty, that was the only reason I was even at the funeral. And I'm not entirely convinced I got proof of that.

The person in the coffin was dressed and coiffed in a way I'd never seen her. Laid out was the girl that her parents had always dreamed she would be. She was not anyone I'd ever met. Not the true Kori.

Two carats of cubic zirconia winked from her ears. No doubt they'd removed the real diamond from her belly, thinking it was a fake. I slid my palm over my stomach, feeling the hard bump of the real diamond's lonely partner. I feared that if they knew, they might come and rip it from my flesh and replace the fake ones in her ears before it was too late. Before she was deep in the earth and they couldn't fuck with her anymore.

I looked back down at her. They fucked with her plenty already.

The black fingernails that had once raked through my hair were the color of ballet slippers. Not even a hint of black remained, not even the little crescents along the cuticles that polish remover never seemed to get. Her eyebrow ring—gone. They'd plugged the hole with some sort of fleshy paste and spackled over it with makeup. The ink tattoo never happened. This girl would've never even thought of it, much less have the creativity to pull it off.

Of course, this girl didn't look like she'd been in a car crash either. Which only served to strengthen my doubts.

"You look like shit," I said through burgeoning tears as I kneeled at the casket, setting Baby Maru next to me. I pulled the tears in with pure spite. I wasn't about to cry over this girl. I didn't even know this girl. "I bet you hate them for doing this to you.

"I had a feeling they would, though," I whispered before making a paranoid glance around to make sure her parents weren't watching me. When I was certain their attention was elsewhere, occupied with other people giving condolences and stock tips, I leaned over and secured a garnet necklace of mine she'd always borrowed around her neck. I tucked it beneath the crisp white Peter Pan collar of her dress, ignoring the starched feeling that both the fabric and her skin shared. "Now you're beautiful, bitch."

I picked up Baby Maru, cradled him against my chest like a pillow as I stood up. "You weren't supposed to leave me. I still love you, though. I always will, my dark angel."

When I looked down at her, I heard the words she spoke at the dam, so certain and so sure. *"It's too soon."*

Earlier, while cradling the porcelain in the tiny bathroom of the east buttress of the church, I'd heard through the thin plywood door all about the major land deal Kori's brother Kyle had scored. Now, in the receiving line, he looked appropriately somber in his suit, but I couldn't shake the feeling that he was going to slip me his business card as he shook my hand. I resisted the urge to lean toward him and whisper in his ear: "Did you know that *Kitzler* means 'clitoris' in German?" and instead simply nodded and moved to the next person in line.

A glaze completely covered Kieren. Kori'd always said she didn't think she could have survived without Kieren. And I instinctively knew it went both ways. His hand gave mine a limp squeeze. *He will never be okay*, I thought. Not that I would either. But at least I didn't have to go home with the rest of the Kitzlers.

I scarcely knew her parents, probably because they scarcely knew their daughter, but I greeted them anyway, because they were next in line and the movement of the line was the only thing that kept me going.

I clasped Mr. Kitzler's large hands.

"Kori?" His whispered voice snagged. "Kori?"

He turned to his wife and started again with the panicked whispers. "Is that? Kori?"

I wasn't sure what kinds of antidepressants he was on, but it didn't help that he'd never seen me with black hair; never known how much I looked like his daughter. I started to move along, unsure of his emotional state and not liking the way he sounded so panicked, but his grip didn't release. It was like he had one more chance to look at Kori and wasn't ready to let go.

"Honey, you know Serena. Serena Moore."

Embarrassed, Mr. K. dropped my hand quickly. And I took the opportunity to move away from him.

"Oh, look! You have one too!" Mrs. K. reached for Baby Maru as I tried to pass by her. I stepped back, holding Maru protectively to my chest. "What is it supposed to be?"

"A baby. A class project," I said numbly.

"Oh! *That's* what it was. Korianne had one with her. We had no idea what it meant. We questioned it for hours—you should have heard some of the ideas we came up with!"

She started laughing. It poured like gasoline on the burning anger inside of me as I imagined their worry over a mysterious sack of flour instead of their own daughter.

I swallowed back anger and accusations. "Do you still have it?" My breath burned in my lungs as I waited. When she eventually nodded, the heat beneath my eyelids receded and the fist my heart had made loosened. "Can I have it?"

Her black hair was pulled back in her signature tight twist. Gold earrings dropped from her lobes. Her forehead wrinkled up as she peered at me as if I were a curious oddity. The calm, untroubled look she'd worn all day could no longer be explained away by Botox. She studied me. Probably thought I was high. Probably wondered why I was wearing a prom dress and a man's watch to a funeral.

"Please, she would want me to take care of it."

I could tell Mrs. K. didn't want to deal with it, with me. She didn't want me stopping by, and she wasn't about to come to my house. I wasn't Chelsea Westad. And I wasn't the twin sister of the girl in the box. She wrestled with the fact that it was just a sack of flour; what value could it possibly have? Her daughter's academic career was over, not that it'd been going anywhere before. But then she let out a charitable sigh. "I'll bring it by the school. I'm going to bring her books by the office tomorrow."

I tripped over the words to thank her as my mind digested the fact that they'd already addressed the issue of what to do with the dead girl's textbooks.

Immediately, I thought of Kori's room, of all the things we'd traded over the past two years. Photos. Trinkets. How many of Kori's secrets lay vulnerable in the Aspen Grove house? In a panicked moment, I spat out, uncensored, "If there is anything of hers, you know . . . that you're ever going to throw out, I'd really appreciate it if you'd . . . let me have it. Anything."

Her mother's skinny lips twitched like two little red worms on a fishing hook. Behind me, I could feel the warm smile of the lady waiting next in line. I could feel her listening to me. "You were very close, yes?" the woman asked, stroking my back. "I'm so sorry for your loss, dear."

I didn't nod; I didn't want to risk losing contact with Mrs. K. Her lips inched, spreading into a stretched smile, like she would never have agreed if the woman touching me couldn't hear. "Of course, dear," she forced out.

"Thank you."

I stepped out of the way and straight into Doc Ramsey's embrace. My nostrils slammed shut at the smell of Doc's suit jacket; he'd hugged a lot of women with very bad taste in perfume. I added the Ralph Lauren Romance Cole had spritzed me with to the mix as I clung to his size and strength. "Just so shocking," was all he said as he took my elbow. I nodded and let him lead me out of the church.

"Let's get you out of here . . ."

eleven

K ori wasn't dead.
    You couldn't just slap a Laura Ingalls-Ashley dress on her,
put her body in a box, cover it with dirt, have the choir sing a
sappy Nickelback song that half our class had lost their virginity
to, and tell me she was gone. She wasn't gone. Her fingerprints
were still on Baby Maru. Her scent still lingered on the throw pillows in my room. The silky cascade of her voice still smoothed
out wrinkled lyrics in my ears.

So to say she was dead wasn't really the truth. And I desperately needed to know the truth.

I had walked to the dam alone at night many times, but this
was the first time I didn't know for certain if there would be anyone there to greet me. This time the night pricked at my skin.
This time noises needled my heart, jolting me with every rustle
and snap. I needed to do this, though. I needed to know.

When the cracking wall of the dam came into view, I realized
there was no tobacco or hemp lacing the fresh air, no smoky voice
turning ordinary songs sexy, no plop of rocks tossed absently into
the water. No cartwheels. No Kori.

I could've turned back. I'd gotten what I'd come for—proof
that she was in fact gone. Instead, I crawled onto the ledge and

leaned back, tucking an arm behind my neck to cushion it. The stars winked at me and I stared at them, wondering where within them Kori was and how I could possibly get there when I was so tiny, so helpless.

I imagined what she would say if I could get up there.

"You didn't even bring beers. Man, are you useless or what?"

And as if she were here with me, I breathed in the sweet scent of cherries and almonds. My lips stretched into a contented smile. I knew it was wrong to enjoy the illusion. I didn't care. I wanted so badly for her to be with me. To have her telling me everything would be fine as she stroked her black nails through my hair.

A tingle zipped across my scalp. I didn't imagine that. I jerked upright, scrubbing down my arms as I whipped around. Trees, road, water, darkness.

The wind hadn't kicked up. Lightning hadn't licked the sky or struck me down. Sudden waves weren't crashing against the dam. It was the same exact level of noise, the same chirps of night insects, the same rustling breeze as when I'd first arrived.

I swallowed down a lump of tears.

What will I do without you? How often did people say those words? So casually. So confident that they will never really have to figure out how.

The first time I'd lost Kori was about six months into our friendship. She'd had a major falling-out with her father, so instead of going with her family to the Caribbean, she spent spring break at our house.

I could tell Mom was not pleased. She didn't approve of Kori or Kori's so-called influence over me. And it didn't help that Kori enjoyed provoking her.

"Hey, Destiny, do you think my dad didn't want me to go to the Virgin Islands because I'm not a virgin?

"Hey, Destiny, do you think if your boyfriend has sex with another girl, you should take him back? Do you think it's more his fault or the skanky ho's?

"Hey, Destiny, do you use birth control? I'm trying to decide which one is best."

It went on and on, and at first I was envious, because I used to be able to ask Mom anything. But by age eleven or so, that had changed. Unexpectedly my questions took on a whole new life. Instead of answering questions directly, she'd say *"Why are you* (By *you* she really meant *my* daughter) *asking about that?"* or *"Where did* you *hear that word?"* or *"That's not something* you *need to worry about."*

Ask the wrong question and suddenly you were watched more closely than one of Professor McDugan's petri dish experiments.

So naturally I thought Kori's relentless questioning was brilliant and Mom's growing unease, hysterical. But as the week wore on, the questions got more graphic and personal, and Mom's patience got thinner and thinner. And when the week was up and Kori'd gone home to her family, Mom told me I wasn't allowed to be friends with her anymore.

From that moment on, Kori wasn't allowed in our house, and I wasn't allowed to go to hers. It was by far the biggest fight Mom and I have ever had, and in truth it was still going strong. After only one week without Kori, I panicked. But Kori just laughed it off. *"Don't worry, kitten, they can't keep us apart."* And she was right. With Mom's crazy work schedule and the Kitzlers unaware of the arrangement, policing us was nearly impossible. Even so, it didn't matter what lengths it took, I refused to give Kori up.

And now she was dead and I still couldn't let her go. I didn't know how.

When I awoke the next morning, I forced myself through the motions of getting up, showering, brushing my teeth. Amazing as it seemed to me that I was able to accomplish these things, I was too numb to congratulate myself. But I could tell Mom was both impressed and relieved to see me awake, moving, heading for the shower willingly and without assistance.

She'd taken off from work, so she'd been around for the past couple of days. I appreciated the effort; I just didn't want to talk to her. Not now. Not like this.

Not with Kori out of my life. Not with Mom having gotten her wish.

If it weren't for picking up Baby Charmmy, I probably wouldn't have ever gone back to school. But now that I was up, I just wanted to go through the motions. It was all I could handle.

Walking through the school halls was surreal. It was as if I awoke to find the sun had dropped away, leaving the Earth to revolve in a different direction. I didn't quite know where to put my feet as I tried to walk along its surface. It took my complete attention to simply not trip on myself.

Since I'd stayed home the past couple of days, I'd missed a lot of the crying and emotion. Cole told me it'd been brutal, but she was holding up. She had to, for Lexi. She didn't say that, but I knew. It was how she was. Lexi's tears had stopped, though. Now all she talked about was the future.

Her chest should have been so heavy with ache she couldn't even pull in enough air to speak. But all she did was talk, talk, talk.

Her sudden passion for learning French and going to Paris and getting a boyfriend and trying out for the next school play and maybe learning to snowmobile grated on my nerves.

I didn't understand it. I couldn't even see a future. The world in front of my eyes was as hollow and dark as it was behind them.

The only future I could think about was the one with Kori. *"I'm just waiting for you, kitten."* I heard her voice replaying in my head for the thousandth time. And every time I heard it, I thought, *They can't keep us apart. Whatever lengths it takes.*

And I meant it, even knowing there was only one way to accomplish it and that I didn't have the guts to do it.

An image of Kori trapped in a coffin flashed behind my eyelids, when I saw Charmmy secured in a Ziploc bag on the counter in the school's office.

The delusional idea that Baby Charms was suffocating tore my senses apart. Yellow and blue make green, keeps Mrs. K.'s life safe and clean. I yanked the seam open and pulled Charms free from the plastic.

Two deep slits formed a gaping cross at the top of the flour sack. Clearly the K.s had investigated the substance inside, unable to trust that it was just ordinary enriched white flour like the label promised. Did they rip it open? Lick an index finger and swab the substance? Rub it over their gums? Perhaps the odd artwork—a kitty with a key around its neck—made them suspicious. Because everyone knows that's the new secret code for cocaine.

I pulled a length of Scotch tape from the roll on the counter and sealed the gaping flaps.

Five pounds of fake baby to lug around was tough; nearly ten pounds was sure to be exhausting. *"You're just trying to impress Doc Ramsey,"* Kori's voice chided loudly in my head.

"I'm too tired to even argue with you."

I must have said it aloud, because the principal's secretary looked up from her Sudoku puzzle. She just smiled one of those sympathetic smiles that never makes anyone feel better, and told me, "Mrs. Kitzler said you could clean out Kori's locker, if you'd like. Tomorrow one of the custodians will break the lock and let you in."

"That's okay. I know her combination."

"Okay, honey. Bring us her books when you're done?"

I nodded and headed out, meeting up with Cole and Lexi to go to lunch. When we walked toward our round table, my filled tray bobbled. The vulnerability of sitting there without Kori hit from all directions. I could see the drill team licking their chemically whitened teeth and extending their acrylic claws as they edged to make their move.

Cole's hand was firm on my back. "She'd hate us if we gave it up." Cole was good at reassurance; she'd had a lot of practice watching out for Lexi. But it was Kori's job to watch out for me.

Who was going to do it now?

The thought plagued me through the Very Special Assembly we were required to attend after lunch. It came complete with three rehabbed teens, two Mothers Against Drunk Driving, and a state trooper *in a pear tree.*

I barely listened to Principal Teasley as he reiterated what everyone else had been mumbling about—drinking and drugs are bad. *Bad! Bad! Bad!* Don't do them. You'll end up dead or in prison, where surely Parker would be soon. It was almost as if he was happy to have proof that everything he'd told us was true.

His speech fell just shy of him jumping up and down, shooting finger-pistols at us and yelling, "I told you so! Huu-ahh!"

Yeah, his bald head's a regular crystal ball.

He concluded with an informative declaration that the Friday night football game would be played as scheduled, and the Kismet High Cougars would kick ass in Brian and Curt's honor.

Before I could even contemplate Dick Click's version of history, I had to have a cigarette. I ducked into the bathroom and before I could even get my lighter out, two girls came in. What was it with this place? Didn't they know students weren't supposed to be in here?

I assumed the toilet-bowl squat position as quietly as possible.

"Do you have that new Anna Sui lipstick?"

Brittney DaSalvo.

"Which one?"

Chelsea Westad.

Crap. Nothing was worse than getting trapped in the bathroom with the Blond Bitches.

"Did you see Marci scarfing the caf food? My gawd!"

"I know!" Chelsea cackled. "She's totally freaking out over Adrian and Cole."

"Whatever, like she has a chance anymore. Have you seen her stomach? Hello? No. You have to do something."

"What? Why me?"

"Because! You're the captain of the squad. We can't have a cheerleader with a muffin top oozing over her skirt. It's too gross. We just can't! This is a crisis."

I just shook my head, imagining her calling in to Colorado Cares: *"Um, hello? Yes, this is Brittney DaSalvo. Well, see, here's the thing . . . I have this friend who has gained five-point-five pounds. No, really, it is a friend. No, it's not me! Ugh! Hello? Yes, just five-point-five pounds. Well, what do you mean not to worry? This is a crisis!"*

Brittney clicked her lipstick cap back on. "She must be stopped."

Chelsea extracted something from her purse. Through the crack I could see her blotting her nose with powder. Blah, blah, blah, I tried to follow the logic of their discussion on lipstick names. It was unreal to hear people talking and behaving normally—well, normal for demented cheerleaders. Normal for me was long gone.

"So, Marci said you went to Kori's funeral. You're so random anymore."

I pressed my lips together, my heart hammering at just the sound of Kori's name.

"Our families go way back. You know that."

"That's right. Didn't she, like, hook up with your brother in seventh grade?"

"Who didn't she hook up with?" The edge to Chelsea's voice was undeniable. She smacked her lips. "How's this color on me? Cute?"

"Oh, *beyond*."

I wondered if I could puke and not make any noise.

"I heard Parker Walsh is paralyzed. Can you believe that? His family's going to sue the school for putting in that speed bump and not putting up any signs."

"Just because they sue the school doesn't mean they'll get any money." Chelsea smacked her newly polished lips. "Everyone knows it was all Parker's fault."

My lighter slipped in my sweating hand, and I had to press it into my thigh to keep it from falling as I waited on each word. All

I wanted was an answer, and I didn't want the answer for why Kori was gone to be: because of Parker Walsh.

If Parker was the reason Kori was dead, then I was to blame too. I should have stopped her from getting in his car.

Brittney gave a playful laugh. "Oh, I don't know about that. I've heard other theories."

"Yeah?" Chelsea grunted. "What other theories have you heard, Britt?"

"I heard Kori was pregnant and went to meet her baby's daddy. Hey, I bet that's who killed her! He tried to make it look like an accident, and messed with Parker's brakes or . . . maybe he hired a sniper to take out a tire!"

"That's stupid, Britt. She was with Parker. What do you think happened? They had a total coke binge and were still tanked when they drove to school."

"See, I told you—an overdose. He tampered with their drugs."

"Britt."

"What? I heard she was going to meet someone . . . some guy who got her pregnant. Parker took her to meet him at a motel to get abortion money and drugs. Like he couldn't have given them bad drugs?"

I could almost hear Chelsea's eyes roll. Or maybe those were mine. These were not exactly theories I could use.

Chelsea smacked her lips together again, fluffed her fingers through her hair.

"I'm so sick of these stupid rumors. People need to quit talking about her." Chelsea clasped her purse shut. They were leaving. The bell would be ringing soon.

"You're just jealous because they aren't talking about you anymore."

"Could you shut up already?"

"Wow, bitchy much, Chels?"

Chelsea's cheerleading shoes squeaked across the tile. The door whooshed open. "Just don't believe everything you . . ." The door whooshed shut.

I was about to drop my feet to the floor when I heard another set start squeaking. I didn't have time to deal with this. As soon as I heard the door open, I started out, catching the distinctive sable-colored ponytail of one Marci Mancini as she squeezed through the door. Her Coach purse caught in the opening and as she jerked it free, a postcard tumbled down to the floor.

I expected it to be one of the Colorado Cares cards promising 24/7 shrink-wrapped psychology that the teachers had passed out during the assembly. It wasn't. It was a sonogram picture.

The bell rang. *Crap.* Dick Click was not going to be happy to see me. As Oprah would say, this was my pebble.

After school, I stood at Kori's opened locker. Lexi and Cole were long gone, as were most of the students. I'd wanted to do this alone. Not to reminisce or mourn. As I stood there, staring at her locker, her things, there was really only one thing I wanted: to know how to start.

"Serena?"

I turned to find Anthony Beck standing behind me. When I'd thought about Anthony, I remembered his face in fragments. Clipped shots of his cheek, one side of his nose. His face all close—morphed like through the peephole in our front door—as he kissed me. I couldn't quite remember what he really looked like. Now I knew—he was absolutely gorgeous.

And I was the slutty, no-self-esteem girl who had been too busy sucking hottie face to save her best friend.

We made clumsy eye contact, but my mouth refused to speak.

That's the downside of the drunken hookup. You think you've blasted past all the awkward stages, only to find them waiting—torn and dented—for you on the other side. And ultimately it's ruined anyway, because chances are you didn't really appreciate—or in some cases, even remember—all the firsts. First touch, first time smelling his T-shirt, first kiss.

Now he was standing in front of me and I wondered if we had ever touched, kissed. That night was so long ago, across a rift in my world so big I could scarcely remember what had been on the other side.

"Hey, it's okay," Anthony said softly, almost under his breath, as he moved toward me. He stopped when he got close, not close enough to touch, but close enough to feel like there was no barrier between us. I wasn't used to someone just moving into my space like that, but at the same time it felt too comforting to step away.

He reached out and stroked his hand down the back of my head. The way one might do to a small child. And I leaned into it. Then he gave me a small lopsided smile. "I've been thinking about you."

As I stood there next to him time seemed to race forward, speeding up, and my heart started beating faster, too fast, and I pulled away.

"Do you need a ride home?" he asked, not seeming all that surprised or offended by my change of heart.

"My mom's coming to pick me up. I had to go see Teasley."

"Everything okay?"

"Yeah," I said, turning back to the task at hand. "No biggie. Just late to Dick Click's class."

I was pretty sure my mom would go easy on me, all things considered.

"This is Kori's locker?" Anthony asked.

"Yeah. I'm just cleaning it out." I heard the stiff edge in my voice, but didn't know how to soften it without opening myself to more pain.

"You want help?"

His eyes tried to make contact with mine, but I avoided them by staring into the locker at Kori's books and papers. I feared if I looked into his eyes, a part of me might cross over into a place that no longer felt safe.

"No, I'm good. Catch you later, okay?" Again the words came out too rigid. But I'd already started pulling things out of Kori's locker and if I stopped, even to apologize, I might never get started again.

"Okay, then." He stood there for a minute, watching me turn old tests and worksheets into wadded balls, before walking away.

I threw myself into the process, not slowing down even after he was long gone. All the adrenaline-filled garbage can stuffing came to a screeching halt when I got to her notebooks, though. And once again my heart filled with an unbearable weight.

Almost every notebook had more doodles than notes, and a cold part of me wanted to throw them all away. An angry part. The part that blamed her for riding with Parker, for leaving me to clean out her locker like her bitch.

But I couldn't bring myself to trash them. And I knew I shouldn't keep them. Not all of them. Just one. I looked through them, my search stopping on the one with *Doc Rocks!* scrawled on the cover. Her social psych notebook. It slipped through my fingers, fluttering to the floor and landing on its spine. I bent to pick it up, but stopped short when I saw the page it was open to. Amidst all the various doodles was Kori's Tempting Fate list.

I dropped to my knees to get a closer look.

Her words kept coming back to me. *"I don't want to leave anything undone."* But now it was as if she was talking directly to me. Daring me.

twelve

When we first became friends, Kori was obsessed with playing truth or dare. It was all we did. Kori, without fail, chose dare. There was nothing she wouldn't do. Lexi would hem and haw and eventually decide on the lesser of the two evils. I always chose truths. And Cole usually did the dare and then would confess the truth anyway. I don't think she really grasped the concept of the game.

I, on the other hand, learned very quickly how the game really works. How revealing truths can be more problematic in the long run. An unscrupulous player, say one who always takes dares and never truths, might . . . oh, I don't know . . . use your truths to get you to do dares later. The ol' *"So you have a monster crush on Matt Wood? I'll tell him, if you don't cut in front of Chelsea in the lunch line"* while all you've got to come back with is, *"Oh, yeah? I'll tell everyone you ate mayonnaise-covered ice cream."*

Um, yeah. No.

But even knowing this, I still had a hard time doing her dares. Eventually the consequences of telling the truth became too risky and I had to start doing them, and slip by slip, it became easier. Or more precisely, harder and harder to stop. But Kori never changed. She never had to. And now, two years later, staring at her notebook in the privacy of my bedroom, I finally had access to all those truths Kori had kept tucked so safely inside.

I reread her Tempting Fate list, remembering how there was nothing Kori wouldn't do, nothing she put off, nothing she was afraid of or had to think about. Nothing she wanted to leave undone.

And now in my hands, I held a whole list of things.

1. Sing with Bleeder Valve.
2. Get a tattoo.
3. Work things out with Shay.
4. Confront D.
5. Tell Serena.

And she was daring me to do them for her. Things I didn't even understand.

What did she want to tell me? Who was D.? And why did she need to confront him or her?

Things I couldn't possibly do—sing with Bleeder Valve? Get a tattoo?

But there was one thing—work things out with Shay.

Maybe there was something I could do about that one. I mean, I wasn't so sure about dealing with some guy I'd never met, but I did know how to get in touch with him.

I hadn't turned my PC on since the night of the party, and watching it flicker to life felt both weird and good. When I saw the message that the computer hadn't been shut down properly, I remembered Kori using it, turning it off as soon as I came in the room. At the time, something about it struck me as odd, like she didn't want me to know something. Now I was certain it had something to do with Shay, or more precisely: shaym. Obviously he meant more to her than she let on, but why all the secrecy?

I pulled up the chat history log, my heart racing at the sight of the last exchange.

dynamitehackr: i need 2 meet u
dynamitehackr: 2nite
shaym: ru sure?
dynamitehackr: please
dynamitehackr: Golden, The Sleep Inn, 2:00 am
shaym: idk
shaym: Kori. ru still there?

The Sleep Inn? In Golden? Brittney DaSalvo's words replayed in my head, *"I heard she was going to meet someone . . . some guy who got her pregnant. I heard she went to meet him at a motel to get abortion money . . ."*

Kori had gone to meet someone. It was at a motel. No matter how misguided Brittney's theories were, she did seem to have an awful lot of facts. Of course, she was the police chief's daughter.

While Parker might've been the last person Kori saw, Shay was the last person she went to see.

I racked my brain. Golden was thirty minutes away. When Kori had jumped in Parker's car, it'd been about one thirty, leaving her enough time to meet Shay. It was the last place she went. The last thing she did. As with any mystery, it was best to work your way backward. It was how I always designed the mazes in my games.

But who was Shay? And why did Kori really go there to meet him?

There was only one person who would know. The man himself.

I jumped hearing the knock on my door.

"Coming!" I called, getting up from my desk.

"Serena, Cole and Lexi are here to see you," Mom said.

Of course Cole and Lexi had to come over; I hadn't left them any other choice. I'd been avoiding the regular calls and text messages.

I watched as Cole and Lexi came in and made themselves at home in my room as they'd always done before. But now it felt like an invasion.

I knew I was being shitty. I recognized the red around Lexi's eyes, the sullen weariness that hung over Cole's coolness, but it was silently understood that any and all pain associated with losing Kori was mine to hoard and feast on alone. If I didn't want sympathy, then no one was getting any.

"So what are you doing?" Cole asked, totally disregarding my privacy and reading the chat log on the screen. "Meeting strangers at motels?"

"No!" I said emphatically as I punched the monitor power button. No, *that* didn't look guilty at all.

Out of the corner of my eye, I caught Lexi gnawing away at the crook of her thumb. She looked like a beaver with a sapling fruit tree. Her chestnut eyes, round and wide, stared back at me. She didn't like what she saw. It worried her.

"Look, I didn't meet anyone at a motel, okay. It was Kori." I turned the computer monitor back on and explained about shaym and how he'd thought I was Kori and how she'd been on my computer arranging to meet him the night she died.

"So what are you doing still talking to him?" Cole asked.

"I'm not. I mean, I might. I'm thinking about it. He might not know what happened to Kori. Maybe he'll meet me. Maybe he knows something."

"Knows something?" Lexi shifted nervously. "About what?"

"I don't know. That's why I want to meet him. I mean, why did Kori go see him?"

"Ser, Kori knew a lot of guys, dangerous guys. I don't think there's much mystery here," Cole said, and Lexi nodded. They were certain shaym was a drug dealer. "Let it go."

But it was too late; shaym had come online and I'd already started typing.

dynamitehackr: i need 2 see u

shaym: Kori?

dynamitehackr: Kismet Mini Mart on Pine and Lakeshore

shaym: now?

dynamitehackr: can u?

shaym: ok

shaym: im sorry about the other night

dynamitehackr: cu there

thirteen

When Kori and I would hang out at my house, we'd go through Mom's self-help books. At Cole's house we would read *Vogue* and do the quizzes out of *Cosmo*. Lexi always put Audrey Hepburn movies on. And at Kori's, we gave each other *Rolling Stone* interviews.

Liza Wicked was Kori's rock star name. Cole's was Siouxie Chainsaw, I was Aimee Killz, and Lexi was Luz Noir. But I don't think you could really call Luz a rock star, since the only instrument she played was the Norwegian flute.

AIMEE: Your voice has been compared to that of an angel in a blender. Liza, your thoughts?

LIZA: I owe my unique voice to my parents. Mother was a sword swallower and Father was a hypochondriac who gargled Dove soap to cure his [makes finger quotes] cancer.

AIMEE: The combination certainly works for you. Some are saying your hit "Girl Fight" is a loosely veiled comment on your much speculated feud with Fergie. What do you have to say about it?

LIZA: Fergie and I are great friends. Nothing but respect. "Girl Fight" is more of a comment on the feminist guilty pleasure of mud wrestling.

AIMEE: Is it true you wrote it while staying at a nudist colony?

LIZA: It's true I stayed at a nudist colony. [laughs demurely] But I don't think I got very much work done while I was there. I found inner peace by looking outside of myself. The scenery there was unlike any other. So many peaks, so many valleys. Our flutist, Luz Noir, talked me into going.

AIMEE: A nudist-flutist. Fascinating. What can you tell us about the controversial *Maxim* photo shoot? Was the black light your idea?

LIZA: I wish I could take credit for it, but it was the brain-child of the amazingly brilliant Zeke Lagerfeld. [gives peace sign]

AIMEE: Are the rumors about you and Zeke true? Everyone's talking.

LIZA: [winks] Don't believe everything you've heard about me, darling.

The Liza Wicked persona was not so far off from the real Kori. Rumors seemed to abound around both, and in the end you never knew what was real, what to believe.

Sitting in the Mini Mart parking lot watching a black Yukon Denali pull up, I had a feeling I was finally going to get to the truth.

Through the tinted glass, I could barely make out the driver.

I studied it for any signs that it might be Shay. I'd done the same with every car that had pulled up in the past hour.

"I don't think he's coming," Lexi said. Her expression was a mixture of relief and joy, which annoyed the hell out of me.

"This might be him."

Lexi and Cole had insisted on coming with me, so we all sat on the curb watching the SUV. As the door opened, I held my breath.

"Or her," Cole said with a smirk as a platinum blond woman stepped out.

I grunted. "She wasn't having a lesbian affair with some Aspen Grove golfer's wife."

"You never know." She laughed. "Who's to say Shay's even a *him*?"

I shot her a look.

"I'm just sayin'. It's one of those names."

"He's not coming," Lexi repeated for the tenth time. "It's been over an hour."

"He might be coming from Golden or Boulder." Golden was the halfway point between Kismet and Boulder. I'd calculated all the options, the distances. And that one made the most sense. They'd met in the middle. Not something a drug dealer would've done.

Cole dusted off her butt as she stood. "Well, I'm going inside. Anyone want a Slushee?"

I shook my head.

As she went inside, the sleigh bells hanging on the door clanged. I scanned the street and watched as a black Acura with deeply tinted windows pulled up to the pumps. My skin tingled. "It's him."

Lexi stood up quickly. "How do you know?"

"I just do." I hoisted my pack onto my shoulder as I stood up. "Wait here."

A man's leg stepped out of the driver's side. Lexi stammered something as I started walking toward the pumps. I couldn't really hear her over the sudden pounding of my pulse. I was scared, like I was with all of Kori's dares, but I also felt something else, something that kept me walking. And it wasn't anticipation. It was determination.

The man who stepped out of the Acura was dressed well, a suit. Dark car, dark hair, dark suit. He was good-looking, slick. Twentysomething. More city than was typically found in Kismet. A downtown guy, loft district. Not exactly what I'd expected, but truth be told, most of the time I didn't know what to expect with Kori.

The closer I got to him, the shorter my steps became. But he wasn't watching my approach, he was getting gas. I hovered on the opposite side of his car, thinking maybe he wasn't Shay after all. But as soon as he got the pump going, he scanned the storefront like he was looking for someone. I cleared my throat. "Hi," I blurted. When he turned I caught my reflection in his mirrored sunglasses. I'd done my eye makeup thick, let my hair hang loose and free, and replaced my usual layered shirts with a tight-fitting one. I looked so much like Kori, I wasn't even sure it was me. At least on the outside.

His grin was slow, easy. "Hi."

"So, it's . . . um . . . good to see you."

The man nodded. He looked apprehensive, but then he grinned and asked, "Can I help you with something?"

My thoughts raced. I steadied myself and started speaking. "I wanted to . . . um . . ." I stalled. Whatever Kori's business was with this man, I had to get him to believe I was in on it too. I dropped my chin and gave him a knowing look. ". . . meet with you?"

He looked me over, taking in the Kori-style sex-kitten-rock-star clothes on my body. Maybe he was a music producer. He looked like he could be. "You want to meet with me?"

"Yeah," I said, smiling, giving him another knowing look. "Meet with you. Work things out."

He swallowed, nodded, then bent down to my ear, grabbing my wrist and squeezing it tight as he whispered, "If this is a setup, you'll regret it, little girl."

I pulled back just a hair, my eyes round and innocent as I lifted my chin. "It's not a setup."

He waited a beat, letting his grip stay tight on my wrist a few more seconds of warning, before it loosened. His fingertips grazed my skin, caressing. The sudden softness unnerved me even more. "So how much?"

"Um . . ." I stalled again. I'd never bought drugs. I had no idea what to say, how to word my order, or even what sizes they came in. "What?"

"Charge? How much do you charge? For the hour?"

Okay, so maybe he wasn't a music producer.

God, had Kori really turned tricks? It did explain the motel, though. "No. I'm not offering . . . No!" I snatched my hand back and took off.

I didn't see Cole or Lexi, so I hurried toward the safety of the store. I couldn't get there fast enough. I just wanted to be inside sharing Cole's Slushee and pretending I'd never had this stupid idea. What did it matter anyway? Kori was gone. Who cared who she'd met or what she'd done in the past?

Just as I had the door in my sight, someone grabbed my arm. A guy's voice came from behind me. "Kori?"

I was so wired from what had just happened with "the john" that I wheeled on him, swinging my book bag and hitting him right in the crotch.

Then something really random happened. And unlike my generation, I don't use that word very often. But considering everything, I think this qualified as effing random.

Because before the guy even dropped to his knees, Kismet's finest were hopping the curb in their car with sirens blaring. I looked at the person doubled over at my feet. He had slicked back white-blond hair and was wearing a wife beater that showed off the tattoos covering his arms. I'd seen him a few minutes earlier watching us from across the street. But I'd dismissed him quickly as a poser, which was so not Kori's type.

Obviously, I was wrong.

"Shay?"

But all I heard was a gurgling noise coming from him.

While I waited for my mom to pick me up at the police station, I thought about this time during the summer before freshman year. Cole and I were with her father, driving fast in his Porsche along the mountain road from Boulder up to Estes Park. We were going to stay at this famous haunted place—the Stanley Hotel. It was in this really supercreepy Stephen King movie that Cole totally forced me against my will to watch like thirteen times so we'd be completely freaked out. We almost didn't go, not because we were scared, which we were, but because Mr. Blakely tried to back out. He hadn't wanted to take us in the first place and had too much going on with work, but Regina Blakely put her Jimmy Choo down. He was going to spend time with his daughter.

We'd stopped at a convenience store near Lyons; Mr. Blakely was taking a call. He'd been taking a lot of calls. He was irritated. With the caller and with us. Cole and I were fourteen. We didn't understand about those kinds of things. Didn't understand that our giggles and gossip and obsessive quoting of *The Shining*—"*All work and no play makes Jack a dull boy*" was particularly entertaining for us—were making it hard for him to talk on the phone. And even if we did, we didn't care. He'd been jerky about the whole thing, why should we be nice?

Before he burst a vein in his forehead, he'd whipped his beloved 911 into a parking lot. With a slammed door, he was out of the car.

For some reason, Cole and I thought this was hysterical.

Maybe we thought we had won the battle that had been raging inside those sleek metal walls. I don't know. But we weren't satisfied. We wanted more.

Cole slid her long tan legs over the center console and sat behind the wheel of her father's "baby." In the rearview mirror, I could see her eyes were filled with tears. I can't say for certain if they were from our laughter or from something I didn't even realize was taking place. All I remember was her throwing the car into reverse. Everything was spinning like an amusement park ride, gravel splattering in a hailstorm around us, the blaring of a horn coming from somewhere I couldn't quite place. Before I could even register that the blur of color whipping past my window was the source of the long wailing honk, there was a sudden smack of a stop that seemed to yank the entire planet to a halt.

The quiet gave way to pain. And then came Cole's whispered, "He's going to kill me."

Through the windshield I watched Mr. Blakely run to the car, his cell phone deserted in the gravel behind him. "Are you all right?" As if there were cotton in my ears, his shouting was muffled. "Are you both all right?"

We were too terrified to answer yes, because we knew he'd unleash on us. But we both nodded, our chins quivering from the fear of what had happened and of what was about to.

"Get out of the car. Both of you, get out. Let me see you." We slowly extracted ourselves from the steaming metal, knowing the car was much more compact than it had been before. And that we might share its fate.

But Mr. Blakely didn't pop a vein.

"You girls scared me to death," he whispered. He looked us both over, like he needed to see for himself that we were okay. "That car came so close to hitting you, I thought I'd lost you both." Then he pulled us to him, his arms so tight and solid that our chins stopped quivering and our hearts stopped racing and all we felt was safe.

That is what love is—the ability to push aside all the stupid stuff, no matter who brought it on or why, and to embrace what's important.

When the police called my mom and told her about the "Mini Mart Mugging," I knew she'd be mad. After all, *her daughter* would never need to be picked up from the police station.

But I also kind of hoped when she'd heard about it, or at least the policemen's version of it—since they really made it out like Shay was some kind of badass—she'd be so relieved and grateful I wasn't hurt, she'd forgive me.

But when Mom came out of the chief's office, she didn't hug me. She could barely even look at me.

I knew Mom didn't believe "the attack" was a random act of

violence against me. I just wasn't completely aware of what she was thinking, or I might not have left my room. Unfortunately after sitting in the holding tank at the police station (Hello? Who was the victim?), I desperately needed to shower. When I came out, I found her standing over the shattered remains of what used to be my computer.

At first, all I could do was stare. "What have you done?"

"It was an accident," she said, looking winded and ruddy, and oddly triumphant.

"An accident?"

"No, no, it fell."

I really didn't care how it happened or why; I just wanted it fixed. I wanted it put back together. I wanted everything in my shattered world put back together. The tears threatened to start up again, but I rolled my eyes skyward to stop them.

"What were you doing moving my computer to the living room anyway? Don't you trust me? Do you think I'm online with perverts having Internet orgies or something?"

"It's not just me; your friends are concerned about this too."

I nodded. It was all clear now. "Lexi. Lexi's the concerned one and now suddenly I'm in some sort of Dr. Phil intervention, is that it?"

"She's just as concerned as I am about how you spend your time online. This just isn't something I can ignore anymore. You spend hours upon hours playing your games."

I gnashed my teeth together to keep from screaming. "I don't play them, I program them."

"It doesn't matter, Ser," she said, standing her ground.

"There's a big difference."

"Not to me."

No, I don't suppose there was.

"Lexi tells me how you can't concentrate, you're dragging ass, and your eyes are all bloodshot. You've been having trouble in school. What am I supposed to think?"

"I haven't been having trouble at school. I'm making all As. The only trouble I have is with Dick—Mr. Click, and that's just because he hates me."

I searched Mom's expression, never having seen her quite so determined or urgent. I was too tired to fight it, so I just sighed. It was one of those ridiculously long parental sighs of thorough disgust and disappointment. It was odd not to be on the receiving end of it.

"I don't suppose having just lost my best friend justifies any of this?"

"We both know this has been going on a lot longer than that. Maybe it's a good thing that you don't have a computer to hide behind anymore," she said.

I bit my tongue before I called her out on her own secret life. The last thing I needed was some paranoid parental crusade over something so stupid. Judging from the evidence at my feet, I wasn't dealing with a rational person. And here I thought I was the one who wasn't handling it well. Thanks, Mom, way to trump me on Sudden-Kori-Death-Syndrome.

It was ludicrous. Some sort of bizarre self-help book intervention: pretend you are crazier than the crazy person to knock her straight! Frightening, but it was working. I felt sane again, too damn sane to continue with this.

"Just so you know, it wasn't what you're thinking."

"No? Don't lie to me, Serena. That guy—the one at the Mini Mart. You met him online, didn't you?"

"Seriously?"

"Yes, seriously. I know all about these Web sites and chat

141

rooms, all of it. You know which ones I mean. The ones like My Spacebook."

I choked, stifling a laugh with my hand. *My Spacebook?* I couldn't make that shit up.

"I've heard some things that, quite frankly, disturb me. A guy like that might know everything about you, what you look like, where you hang out. You may not have invited him—"

"Just stop. Okay. I told you—I don't hang out in chat rooms. It's not even what I'm into. Where'd you even get an idea like that? *Oprah? Dateline?"*

"The police." Mom paused to make sure I was listening. "That guy could've been . . . You have no idea the danger you put yourself in. I can't believe you would do that. What were you thinking, Serena?" She looked at me like I was the stupidest person on the planet.

I still held on to hope, though, because I did understand a few things. Like with Cole and her father, sometimes people who love each other don't always show it. Sometimes love sits inside of our hearts like a bear in hibernation. After her reaction to my "attack," I also knew spring would have to be hard coming, and I didn't have a Porsche that could bring it any faster.

"Yes. Okay. I did ask him to meet me. Happy?"

Through tight lips, she asked, "Why, Serena?"

"He was a friend of Kori's."

"Kori's, huh?" She heaved a sigh of pure exasperation. "Now do you understand why I didn't want you to be friends with her?"

After hearing her callous words, I almost didn't care if it was winter forever.

fourteen

This is a mistake, my inner voice warned, but did I listen? Of course not.

I shifted my weight and rang the bell of a royals-worthy mansion. In this country a structure that size is usually reserved for country clubs or the Osbournes. But in Kismet, it belongs to the Krivvys.

The door opened and a formally appointed—seriously, black dress and white apron—maid queried me. "I'm here to see Josh," I said.

"Josh?" The maid repeated.

I nodded.

"Who shall I say is calling on him?"

Calling on Poor Josh? Gah. Why did she have to put it like that?

"Tell him Serena . . . is calling on him." *God . . . I'm such a crush enabler.*

Her confused smile turned beaming. "Serena! Certainly. Please, come in. I'll just announce your arrival."

I followed her inside the mansion, my boot heels squeaking against the marble floor. While the maid lifted a phone from the foyer wall and spoke quietly into it, I started to worry again about the sanity of my plan. But after Mom's little outburst, I was more determined than ever to find Shay and meet with him. All I needed was a computer and someone who wasn't going to rat me out.

The maid turned back to me with another bright smile. "Right this way."

The house smelled of flowers, and not flower-scented Lysol either.

On the outside it may have been a mansion, but on the inside it could only have been described as a museum. I openly gawked at the lavish furnishings. The paintings looked suspiciously like ones we'd studied during the art history week of my freshman art class.

I knew, of course, that Poor Josh wasn't exactly poor. I'd just never pictured him living in a home that needed less than five minutes' notice to be photographed for *Architectural Digest*. But then again, I had trouble believing the Osbournes really lived in their mansion too.

"This is Josh's wing," the maid informed me as we walked toward a pair of heavy wood doors stained nearly black. As she opened the doors, the sound of gunshots and bombs erupted as if from all sides. Knowing it was synthetic didn't make it any more comforting. "Go right on inside; you'll have no trouble finding him."

As the maid closed the double doors behind me, I turned to see the heavy wood was further thickened by some sort of spiky black foam substance that prevented the sound from disturbing the rest of the residence.

I strode onward, hoping to get this over with as quickly as possible.

Life-sized commandos were taking over a bunker on the largest flat-screen television I've ever seen. It was a wall, and not a small one. A green army helmet swung around; under it, Josh. He fumbled to hit a button that paused the noise and action. Jerking to his feet, he stared at me with crazy round eyes, completely confounded by my presence in his room. Kind of odd, considering the maid had clearly announced my arrival just moments before. I wondered if the maid staff had pulled so many cruel jokes on him over the years that he no longer trusted their announcements.

"S-S-Serena?!"

"Hi, Josh. I, um, need a favor."

He quickly removed his helmet and held it respectfully in front of him, as if reporting to the general. "Y-y-you d-do?"

"Yeah, my computer met an untimely death." *At the hands of my psycho mother.* I coughed and continued, "There's something on the Internet I really need to access. It will only take a minute."

"Oh, oh, okay." Josh maneuvered awkwardly around the black leather couches and suede pillows that had bunkered him. He plodded to a wall of electronics in his combat boots. I couldn't help but be amused that his army pants and black BDU vest perfectly matched the commandos on the screen. "This one's already signed on, but um, um . . ."

I looked at the sweet setup, trying not to be wistful, but my geeky little heart was all atwitter. "Did you build this yourself?"

He nodded, his mop of hat-hair dancing with the motion. He started to wheeze and then glanced uncomfortably at his surroundings, probably looking for any dirty laundry that needed to be kicked under the couch.

"I heard what happened at the . . . um . . . Mini . . .—" He vigorously wiped his hands on his baggy combat pants, then shoved them into his pockets after realizing how psychotic he looked.

"So, this room's amazing, huh? All yours?" I asked, changing the subject.

"Yeah, yeah. I designed it myself." He smiled, surveying the room with fresh eyes. "I've got the, um . . . 360 over there, PS3, DS. But if you like, um . . . old school games, I've got original boxes too. Um, the PCs are all Aliens. The surround sou—"

I gasped, cutting him off as I noticed the unusual larger-than-life painting on the wall behind me. A silver-haired warrior with striking eyes as blue as mine stared back at me. They looked oddly real. Now that was art.

"Sephiroth," Josh and I said in unison.

"Only the most amazing boss of all time," Josh said over my "A complete son of a bitch bastard who deserved everything he got." We both laughed and then I returned to my mission.

Unfortunately, it was more a matter of waiting than anything. To kill time, I busied myself with reprogramming some of Josh's games, and then against my better judgment started hacking into the Peak County Medical network. With a few simple keystrokes, I crossed a line, and instead of looking at my own records, I pulled up Parker Walsh's.

He was the last person to see Kori alive. He knew things no one else did. And, since we weren't exactly friends, I didn't feel comfortable just charging into his hospital room and making accusations and demanding answers.

Besides, I had trouble understanding how the boy I saw stumbling around the crash site could really be paralyzed. Apparently, so did the doctors. His file was filled with medical jargon I didn't understand. I could tell there were a lot of tests being run and rerun—X-rays, CT scans, MRIs, something called electroencephalograms. And even though I had no idea what any of those things meant, I understood that just like I was, the doctors were looking for the answer to something they didn't have an easy explanation for.

At the sound of someone knocking on the door, I quickly backed out of the hospital's system. A woman entered with a tray of snacks. Not the original maid, but one who looked remarkably similar.

Ten paces behind her, a finely appointed woman whisked in as if on a breeze, not at all surprised at having company. Josh's mother. Imagine that.

Her beaming smile zeroed in on me. She clapped her hands before gliding across the room and embracing me.

"Serena, it is so good to finally meet you."

Did she say finally?

Out of the corner of my eye, I caught Josh's grimace. His glowing hot cheeks were melting the camo paint off his face.

"Mom," Josh wailed, clearly in as much pain as I was. "Don't glomp on her like that."

"Um, hi, Mrs. Krivvy. Sorry to show up unannounced like this. I won't be long," I said as I managed to untangle myself from the woman's arms.

"Take all the time you need. Our house is your house." Mrs. Krivvy turned back to Josh with sparkling eyes and I returned to my attempts at contacting shaym.

I checked again to see if he had come online, but he hadn't, probably because he was trying not to drop the soap at the Kismet pokey. I couldn't believe how close I'd been to him and how horribly it all turned out thanks to Lexi and her cell phone.

Mrs. Krivvy patted me on the shoulder. "Well, I'm sure *you two* would like to be *alone.*"

Yeah. *That* would be my cue to leave.

"It's okay, Mrs. Krivvy. I'm actually on my way out." I quickly sent Shay a message apologizing for his wrongful arrest and possible imprisonment. With a sigh of frustration, I logged out; fate had thwarted me once again. "Thanks, Josh. Sorry about all this."

"B-b-bye, Serena."

"Check out San Andreas later. It now serves hot coffee."

Josh's mom turned to me with a questioning look on her face. "What's that, dear? Did you say you wanted some coffee?"

"Oh, no, Mrs. Krivvy, it was nothing. Just an extra feature on an action game." I had a feeling a woman with Louis V wing chairs wouldn't understand about cyberhookers.

"I'm pretty sure after the cops Tasered his nuts that he won't agree to meet me again. So, yeah, thanks, Lex. Now my chance at meeting Shay is completely blown."

I sat my lunch tray down next to Cole's in the cafeteria on Monday and shot a look at Lexi. I could have tossed her by the throat to the rectangle tables. The cops' quick response time had nothing to do with randomness. The second I'd started walking over to the Acura, Lexi had called 911 to tell them there was a mugging in progress at the Mini Mart.

"I'm sorry, Ser, but it was for your own good. Besides," she said, handing over a copy of the *Kismet Courier* that featured the story on its cover, "it says right here that he was in a gang." Trust Lexi to believe that rag. "Front page. Why would they say that if he wasn't?"

"Um, sensationalism maybe?" Cole suggested. Brittney's father had been trying to get a new budget voted in for the police force—which really was just an excuse to buy a fleet of Swiss SUVs like Aspen and Vail have. So anything that even smelled like a crime spree ended up on the front page. *"Gangs in Kismet,"* Cole repeated incredulously.

"I swear—Kismet needs more crime to chill people out," I said. "But the worst of it was my mom totally freaking out on me, like I'd brought this on or something." Which, I guess I had, but I still shot Lexi a look to let her know that I knew she'd played a major role in my mom's hysterics.

As I walked to Doc's class, I saw Anthony Beck's T-shirted back as he pulled a book out of his locker and I stopped cold.

He hadn't been overbearing or clingy or aloof or any of the conditions that commonly plague high school boys. In fact, I hadn't really spoken to him since I'd been snippy with him, but whenever he passed behind me in the evil hallway, he'd stroke his hand down my hair. A subtle reminder that he was there, that he understood something of what I was going through.

I knew if things between us were going to work at all, I needed to make the next move. And everything about Anthony— the way his eyes would go soft, the way his lips would curve, the way his hand would linger on me as he walked past—told me there wasn't any risk. He was a sure thing, a safe place to fall.

And I desperately needed to fall.

He turned and caught me staring. "Hi," I said quickly.

"Hey," he said, flashing me a smile.

"So, yeah." I took a tentative step toward him. "How've you been?"

A metallic bang sounded as he shut his locker. He gave me a quick, apologetic grimace. "I'm sorry, Serena, I have to run, I've got an exam next period. Can't be late." When I nodded, he was already walking away. He turned and pointed at me. "Don't get mugged."

I grimaced. *Don't get mugged?* So much for my soft, safe nest.

At least I had Doc's class to look forward to. Ever since the car wreck, classes consisted of lame group discussions to talk about our fears and feelings. I didn't say a word, even when people who had never so much as said hi to Kori cried about her death. Let's just say the forced group therapy bored the crap out of me. My fingernails have never been so clean. But I'd expected Doc's class to be of help. To make something as illogical as Kori being gone make sense to me. To make that vulnerable feeling that seemed to drip from the school walls go away. To make me feel safe about what might happen next.

Doc Ramsey had that kind of power. An aura of protection surrounded him. It wasn't like he was a wimpy guy or anything, but the sense of protection I got from him didn't come from anything physical. It was more about the way he knew how to explain baffling things, so when you left his class you felt like life was a little less mysterious and confusing than it was before. That the problems in your life had solutions. Having a father should feel that way.

Yes, I'm well aware that Doc's not my father. I keep hearing the dramatic flair of Maury Povich's voice telling me, "It is 99.9 percent certain that Doc Ramsey . . . [Suspenseful Pause] . . . is NOT the father." But that doesn't mean he can't be fatherly to me, right?

I was confident Doc would be able to explain why Kori had died. Why I was still here.

But he didn't have us talk at all. He just popped in a DVD—*Sliding Doors*. He'd started it the Friday before, and ever since we'd had to endure the BBs debating if Gwyneth Paltrow was really English or not and the Hauties' sudden overuse of British curse words. *Bloody 'ell an' bollocks.*

I already knew the ending, because I'd rented it over the weekend. I was so sure there was something significant about it. It just wasn't like Doc to drop the ball by babysitting us with a movie. But after watching it, I was more confused than ever.

I imagine Doc wanted us to determine for ourselves if we really believed in fate and destiny. But I was more interested in what he thought. What he believed. Because I really didn't think he believed the answer to "why" was as simple as which train you had the dumb luck to catch or if your eighth-grade lab partner was a crushy stalker boy who ruined your favorite T-shirt.

But Doc *never* tells you what he thinks. All his lessons are designed to let you determine for yourself what to believe. And that was just it. I wasn't so sure I believed in dumb luck at all.

I wanted a reason, needed a reason, for Kori to be gone.

As I started to leave after the bell rang, Doc called me over to his desk.

"There's something I wanted to talk with you about. I'm going to be meeting with your mother next week."

"Oh . . . um . . . okay." Not having any idea how his grading system worked, I've never been too sure of my standing. Our grades were based on "try factor." *"You'll get out of this class exactly what you put into it,"* he'd said on the first day of class. I figured that just meant I had to contribute to the classroom discussions, but no matter how easy Doc always made it, participating wasn't one of my strong suits. Plus, I never really understand his lessons. I mean sure, I get that they're meant to be thought-provoking, and I certainly had my share of thoughts. More often than not, though, I didn't think my thoughts were the right ones. If I told him that, I expect he would have countered with something like:

"*There are no right or wrong answers.*" So I went with: "I'm not like . . . failing or anything? Am I?"

He laughed, reached out, and gave my shoulder a warm pat. "No, no, not even close. I like to get to know my students' parents. That's all."

"Oh. Okay then."

"Serena, before you go—how've you been doing?" The way his brown eyes radiated warmth and concern, I could tell he was asking about Kori. "Have you been getting along okay?"

"Sure, I mean, yeah, I guess." *Getting along okay?* Who was I kidding? Half my day was spent contemplating suicide. I most certainly wasn't getting along okay. I wanted to go back in time, to start over, to be a child again. To curl into my mother's lap. To feel her fingers in my hair. I just didn't trust she would be there. So I didn't tell him about thoughts of death or even about Kori's list. What I told him was: "I just really miss how things used to be . . . with her."

After a long pause, Doc asked, "With who?"

Leave it to Doc to not let me be ambiguous. Of course he wouldn't assume I was talking about Kori, because I guess I wasn't.

I shrugged his question off as I lugged my book bag onto my shoulder, feeling the weight. "I'm fine, Doc. Really. Perfect."

The charade of perfection swung fully. And this was despite all the rumors and gossip about my "mugging." Each day I'd been to school, I'd slapped on a smile and made a good showing of being "okay" until last bell rang.

My mother would've been so proud.

But being "fine" was exhausting. The smile. The small talk.

By the time I got home, all I wanted to do was close my bedroom door, duck under my covers, and embrace the cold darkness of sleep. As I was tugging the key from my neck to unlock my front door, I stopped. The action pulled at something lodged tight inside of me.

The last time Kori touched me, the last words I heard her speak. *"Take care of her, Becks. Get my kitten home okay."*

I took a deep breath and fought back the urge to assume the fetal position on my front stoop.

I'd started having serious doubts about my own mental health after Mom's computer smashing and crazy spewing. Since we were related, this very well could've been the start of my crazy train's downhill coast into Nutsville Junction, population 2.

I slipped the key in and turned.

All my plans for seclusion and retreat were squelched. "How 'bout some of my famous grilled cheesies?"

Ah, sweet ninety-five-year-old Mrs. Patterson in a T-shirt with a hand drawn on each low-slung breast, above which read: I'M OLD, BUT I FEEL GOOD. FEEL FOR YOURSELF.

Nutsville Junction, population 3.

I couldn't very well crawl under the covers with her there.

"Grilled cheese sounds great. What's up?"

"Well, the devil has his hands full now. Martha Blackwell finally passed on. Lester isn't looking too good either." Ah, to be so blasé about death. Those were the days.

I tried to imagine what it must be like for Mrs. Patterson to have friends passing on with the kind of frequency they did at Whispering Aspens. I couldn't. I couldn't lose the image of the wreck. I saw it with nearly every blink of my eyes, like the zap-zap-zap of an assault rifle.

"Is Lester the one you play Texas hold 'em with?" I asked in an effort to shake the ever-present image of the crash from my mind.

"No, no, that's Leslie. Lester's Martha Blackwell's cat."

Right, a man named Leslie and a cat named Lester. Everything normal at the old folks' home.

"Well, my cat now, I guess. Damn beast doesn't know what to do without that old bat squashing him with her cane."

"So how many cats does that make now?"

"Oh, gosh. Ten, I guess."

That was it? I could've sworn she was up to seventy.

"Are the other cats playing nice? Sharing their kibble?"

"Oh well, you know, there's hollerin' and hissin'. Nothing gettin' the broom out doesn't resolve."

"That's good. Trivial Pursuit before dinner?"

She never had to be asked twice, and was already setting up the board. I went to the kitchen and poured us each a glass of Diet Coke, then returned to the table. For the first time in a long time, I was thankful for her company. She was the only person who'd understand what I was going through without all the pity. She might've even slapped me on the back and said, *"First one's always the hardest."* Or hug me and say, *"You'll never get over it, so stop trying."*

"So, were you and Martha close?"

"Oh, as close as any, I suppose."

"Well, you took her cat in."

"Shoot, kiddo, all my cats are take-ins. The home won't let anyone who lives there add to what they bring with them, so that leaves me."

Mrs. Patterson's family put her into the Whispering Aspens assisted living center over fifteen years ago. Which is crazy, considering they were all set to give up on her, and she's lived just fine on her own for as long as I've been alive. But she'll have the last laugh, letting them pay for her supposed care, while she spent their much-coveted inheritance on a town home in our complex. When she's not hanging out at "The Wal-Marts," she spends most of her time at Whispering Aspens, but it's more of a volunteer thing and a cover for the semi-surprise visits of her family, who all live in Denver. They have absolutely no clue about her town house or her cats or any of it. Especially not their dwindling "early retirement plan."

"Mrs. Patterson, can I ask you something?"

"You've been asking me questions all these years—now you're telling me I had a choice?" She playfully waggled her bushy brows at me.

Oh, a regular riot, she is.

"Does it get easier? Having people leave you all the time?"

"People don't leave you, dear. They just die."

"You know what I mean."

"Yeah, and you're not listening. You think people leave this earth when they die, but they don't. Nothing is finished. Not really." Then she sputtered, "I've never wanted a damn cat. Hate the darn things. But who else is gonna do it?"

She didn't even like cats? Wow. Suddenly the smell of her wasn't so offensive. From now on, when I smell her I will think of friendship and love. And cat piss. Who was I kidding? She reeked like a meth lab.

I expected her to say something profound after that, maybe along the lines of: *"There is just as much beauty in birth as there is in death, and it changes our lives just the same. They both add things to us and take things away. It just so happens death adds cats to mine."*

Instead, she told me, "Sometimes when someone you know

dies, you just have to take the crap that's thrown at you. As long as it's not the cats throwing their own crap, I'm good."

I had no idea how to respond, so I went with: "I got five pounds of flour."

"Well now, flour's a start. By the time people move into the home, the families have already gotten rid of everything so that it's all tidy come trust fund time, but if someone from the church goes, I always stop by the house as soon as I can. I try to nab sugar and laundry detergent, 'cuz I go through a lotta those. Always try to get coffee. I just don't have any need for flour; so I leave it for someone who is big into baking. But next time I'll try to get you some, if you want."

"No, thanks. I think I'm good on the flour."

The big advice on how to handle death from the woman with the most wisdom in my life was basically a grocery list of what to ninja-loot. Considering I'd basically asked Mrs. K. for everything Kori owned, I guess I really couldn't judge.

A turkey never voted for an early Christmas.
        —Irish proverb

-

fifteen

People did leave when they died. Mrs. Patterson was wrong. School continued to be one long, grating reminder of it. There wasn't a hall I could walk down, a place I could sit, or a song on my iPod that wasn't lacking because Kori wasn't there to share it with. When the final bell rang I knew it was time to face the walk home alone. I'd been catching rides with Cole and her mom and I realized I couldn't avoid it forever. But when I got to Aspen Grove, my legs stiffened.

The black iron gates of the subdivision stood open against its river rock walls. Fat blue spruce and scraggly blue atlas landscaping flanked the entry, while fall pansies filled the beds with color and cheer, but I didn't feel welcomed.

Cutting through the neighborhood could shorten my walk home considerably, and Cole lived there too, so it wasn't like I was completely out of my place, yet I couldn't bring myself to walk through the gates. I didn't want to see Kori's house. I didn't want to see her family carrying on, or spot a service truck come to paint her bedroom ballet slipper pink or a decorator with Laura Ashley ruffles cascading over her arms trotting toward a smiling Mrs. K.

Everyone handles death differently, my inner voice chided. Who knew it made some people happier?

I avoided the neighborhood, walking instead on the sidewalk as it rounded the luxury homes. The landscape stretched and flowed alongside the protective nine-foot walls. A friendly reminder not to try to get too close to the people who lived behind them, but for me it was already too late.

I turned down Lake Ridge Road and spotted Mr. Miller's ranch. The horses calmly grazed in the pasture. Behind them Mr. Miller's old timber-framed barn looked like something from another era. The past I could handle. It was the future I was having trouble with.

As I walked the fence line, the horses picked up their heads and curiously watched me. I reached into my bag and pulled out an apple I had left over from lunch. I clucked to them the way Mom and I used to. I'd forgotten about how much I enjoyed riding on the weekends and feeding them with my mom.

The apple I held out was gone before I could blink, so I reached back into my bag for more goodies. One of the horses had pushed against the fence and was mouthing at my sleeve. "Hold on," I muttered, digging for more. This time I made sure the horse took only one grape at a time.

"Hey!"

Shocked by the sudden masculine voice, I whipped my head around to find a guy coming toward me. His faded jeans and a hugging white T-shirt didn't cover him enough to keep me from dropping my jaw a little. He kept his firm and flexed.

"You can't do that."

My heart quickened at the sight of his hard, almost angry eyes. Kori was always the one who did the talking in situations like this. I tried to think of what she would say if she were here, and all I could come up with was: "Just feeding the horses, *sir*." I flicked the last word off of my tongue. Best not to show fear, after all.

His flexed muscles relaxed a little, but not his eyes. Or his tone. "Miller said no treats. Rots their teeth."

I held out the evil, teeth-rotting grapes in my palm, and asked, "Really? Nine out of ten horse dentists would disagree with you."

Without waiting for his reply, because I knew it wouldn't be permission or an apology, I fed them to a black gelding.

The guy moved closer and asked, "So, what are you . . . following me or something?"

I looked back at him, this time really looking. His eyes were almost exactly the same blue as the infamous Mini Mart Mugger's. I snapped my teeth back together and narrowed my gaze. Impossible. This guy didn't have Shay's blond hair, and the only tattoo he had was a Chinese symbol beneath his ear on the right side of his neck.

Maybe he was on the run and undercover. His hair did look freshly dyed.

"So?" His tone bordered on biting. "Are you going to call the cops again?"

Shay—the guy who I'd gotten myself in a shit-storm of trouble to find—stood right in front of me. *And*, I thought looking into those eyes, he was royally pissed off. At me.

Shit.

If it weren't for the fact that this was the last guy Kori had gone to see and I'd been desperate to know why, I'd have assaulted him with my bag and taken off like a track star, but I couldn't shake the feeling that I should stay. That if I understood why Kori had gone to meet him—I'd understand why she was gone.

"I didn't call the cops, my paranoid friend did."

His shoulder twitched, and some of his anger slid away. "Right. Well, just keep your book bag holstered, okay?"

I shrugged it off and set it down as a show of good faith. "Like your hair. Looks better dark. What happened to your gang tatts?"

"I was . . ." He tucked his chin and let out a low masculine laugh. He no longer seemed all that set on intimidating me, so I let myself relax a little. "Okay, this is embarrassing. I was in character, you could say, for my little cousin's birthday. She's obsessed with Eminem. The blond hair was supposed to be temporary. The box lied."

I wanted to smile, because it sounded funny and kind of sweet, and I was picturing him with a turban towel and latex gloves, but still—this was a guy who I'd last seen being hauled into a police car.

"Was it you on the computer?" His eyes hardened again, making me step backward. "The whole time?"

"No. I mean at first, yeah. But I told her about it. She's the one who asked you to meet her in Golden. That wasn't me. Um, did you . . ."

"What she and I did or didn't do is none of your business." He closed the distance between us. I took another step back and he stopped. "So, why did you want to meet me?"

"I . . ." I tried to swallow but my mouth had gone a little dry. "I don't want anything."

He softened, hearing the discomfort in my voice, and said, "Sorry I scared you."

I nodded, not feeling like he was all that sorry.

"I thought you were Kori. You'd been sitting with your friends, and I kept waiting for you to be alone. When you were, I just reached out and grabbed you, not realizing how it would look or seem. Not realizing you didn't know who I was." He flexed his jaw. And when I dared to glance up, I saw that his eyes were vacant and hard. "I didn't know what had happened to Kori. They told me when they brought me in and started asking me all sorts of questions."

"I'm sorry. You shouldn't have had to find out like that."

"So?" he asked, mildly impatient. "Why did you want to meet me?"

"You were the last one to see—" I swallowed, but her name stayed thick and unmoving in my throat.

Shay drew his lips tight, but he gave me a slight nod, like he understood what I couldn't say.

The black horse nudged me, demanding attention, and I turned to him, stroking his face.

Shay shoved his hands into the front pockets of his jeans, appearing only mildly less threatening as he moved closer to me. "You like that one, don't you?" he asked.

"Yeah. He's *friendly*."

Shay's lips quirked at my jab. It might've even been a smile.

I ran my hand down the horse's neck, thankful for the change of subject. While I wasn't as ready to talk about Kori as I'd thought, I still needed to find out more about him, figure out what Kori had needed to work out with him. Was it business? Personal? And why had she never mentioned him to me?

First I wanted to find out what exactly he was doing here and why he was playing sergeant for the Sugar Police. "I didn't get the impression you lived around here."

"Don't." After a few awkward beats: "You shouldn't have let me think you were her online. I might've said something I shouldn't have."

So much for changing the subject.

"Kori and I don't . . . didn't have secrets."

"Right," he said, clearly not believing.

162

I glanced in the direction he'd come from undeterred in my effort to find out more about him. I spotted a half-built pyramid of hay bales by the barn. "So you work here now? I didn't know Mr. Miller was hiring on."

He pinned me with his eyes and stiffly spoke. "Sudden need, I guess."

"Oh." Despite his efforts to end my line of questioning, I asked, "So, do you like working here? With the horses, I mean?"

"They crap a lot."

I laughed. "They're amazing creatures. I could spend all day with them."

His gaze held mine a little too long and he shifted his stance.

I dropped my eyes to his lips and my breath hitched. "But I've got to go," I said quickly.

He didn't stop me. But he did call after me, "Hey, Dynamite Hacker, I didn't catch your real name."

I turned back, looked him up and down in a sarcastic challenge. "Are you going to write it down on some sort of security log? You know, to prove that I've been warned once before you haul me in?"

He held his hands out in surrender. "No, I promise, no citations." He laughed at his previous bad cop routine, probably realizing it was really idiotic and he deserved to be called on it. "Just no sugar cubes."

"Then it's Serena, Serena Moore."

"Serena. I'm Shay, Shay Miller." Miller, of course. Now it made sense.

I repeated the name aloud, enjoying the way the syllables surfed across my tongue. *Shay Miller*. Then: "I didn't know Mr. Miller had a son."

"Long-lost nephew."

"Well, I'll try not to feed them so much that they poop more than they already do, Shay Miller."

We'd only been friends for a few short months when I'd given Kori the plush Badtz-Maru doll for her birthday. But, like dogs, teenage girls had their own calculations of time. Three months could be the equivalent to a whole year. And even as enigmatic and mysterious as Kori was, after three months of being best friends with her, I'd thought I had her pretty well figured out. I knew she'd like the gift, and was even more certain after she gave me the Charmmy Kitty. So I was a little shocked when she took her Swiss Army knife to its back and started pulling out the stuffing.

"Jesus, Kori! You don't have to destroy it!"

She looked up and cocked her lip. "I'm not destroying it, kitten. Here, give me Charmmy."

I reluctantly handed over my new gift, and with an efficient swipe of the knife, she initiated me into the world of secret keeping.

Now all of Kori's secrets were sitting on my doorstep, boxed up courtesy of one of Mrs. Kitzler's employees and handily delivered by Kori's brother Kieren. I knew he was the one who had brought them, because Badtz-Maru was not boxed up. Instead the plush doll was set aside in a grocery sack, which for the Grove Market, where people who lived in neighborhoods like Aspen Grove and Bear Creek shopped, meant heavyweight, sand-colored glossy bags with an embossed logo of an aspen grove and stiff braided rope handles in hunter green. It was more suited for carrying clothes from one of the high-end stores in Denver's posh Cherry Creek neighborhood than food. Kieren was the only other person, besides me, who Kori trusted with the stuffed animal's very special contents. And I was grateful that he'd had the sense to keep those secrets safe from her parents.

After lugging the last of her boxes up to my room, I looked at them again. Judging from their number and weight, her mother had been true to my wishes and sent me everything that was truly Kori's, i.e., anything that wouldn't go with the new guest-room's homage to roses and ruffles.

Looking at them, I felt oddly incomplete. I had since her death. Like half of me had been ripped away. I'd hoped having her things would've helped. But it only made it worse.

I pulled her Badtz-Maru doll from the sack and fished my fingers around inside the hidey-hole she'd made on the day I'd given it to her. I felt a sliver of plastic and pulled it out. Her fake ID.

I turned it over in my hand and thought about her plans to get into that club in Denver. It was her dream, her big chance. Cole's words came back to me: *"She'd hate us if we gave it up."*

If I closed my eyes, I could hear Kori onstage, squeezing out songs with that same fierceness that she lived her life.

"You had so much fun pretending to be me. Now's your chance."

I closed my hand around the plastic ID. My palms started sweating at the thought. It was silly really. I couldn't sing.

"I'm gonna be infamous, Ser."

"Don't you mean famous?"

"Hell, no! I'm much more suited for infamy. Doncha think? Famous people are forgotten. Infamous people live on forever."

"No, they don't," I muttered aloud. I let the fake ID flutter from my fingers to my bed.

I didn't want to cry over lost dreams. I didn't want to push myself past my fears. I just wanted to get high, to float out of my body, up, up and away, and be with her again.

I brushed back the tears with the crook of my arm as if they were merely sweat from a lengthy workout, and resumed searching the hidey-hole. Farther into the stuffed body, my fingers found what I was looking for and pried out Kori's plastic bag, complete with rolling papers and matches. Without further thought, I shoved it into the front pocket of my jeans.

Just as I set Maru on my bed, I glanced back and was shocked to see Mrs. Patterson standing in my doorway. My heart lurched.

She looked pissed.

"Start talking!"

She sounded pissed.

She assumed the you've-got-some-explaining-to-do stance.

"Um . . . I . . . um," I stammered à la Poor Josh. The fake ID stared up at me. My fingers fidgeted at hiding the telltale bag hanging out of my front pocket as I formulated my it-just-fell-there-and-I'm-holding-it-for-a-friend story.

"The jig is up, missy."

"Okay."

"Your mom told me."

I sat on top of the fake ID; Mom knew nothing. Certainly not about Kori's illegal habits. What could the old bat be irate about if it wasn't that? Damn old biddies always snooping around.

I flicked a glance at her, pausing to read today's T-shirt. I MAY HAVE ALZHEIMER'S BUT AT LEAST I DON'T HAVE ALZHEIMER'S. I really hope Tarantino keeps that when he directs the movie of my life, though the way Mrs. Patterson's fingernails dug into the wood handle of her cane, I doubted I would live long enough to see it.

"Mom told you . . ." I lifted the last word, letting it hang in the air, implying my question.

She wagged a bony finger at me. "Yeah, so you can give up your little miss goody-goody act."

Huh? Of course, she probably *did* have Alzheimer's, so maybe this was just the beginning of its manifestation.

I spoke slowly so as not to provoke her. "What did I do?"

"What have you done? What have you done? You've made me watch chicky flickies when we could've been watching *Nip/Tuck!*" She stuck her tongue out at me and made a farting sound, complete with a healthy spray of spit. A five-year-old's or ninety-five-year-old's equivalent to giving me the finger. "Gwyneth Paltrow ring any of your bells?"

"Huh?"

"Oh, you with your romantic comedies and board games, all miss sweet and innocent . . ." Then she busted into a really hysterical imitation of my mother: *"Sliding Doors?* Serena rented this? But she hates romantic comedies . . ." She looked down at me like she'd like to chew me up but I wasn't worth wasting the PoliGrip on.

Admittedly—my mother was correct; I wouldn't normally rent a Gwyneth Paltrow movie. Unless, of course, it was *Seven*.

Holding my hands up in surrender, I attempted to reason with her, because I was all for watching *Nip/Tuck.*

"So . . . let me get this straight. You don't like romantic comedies either?"

"Hell, no!"

Now I was getting a little bit riled too. Here I'd politely endured many an evening of Mrs. Patterson's movies and shows, and even though this was my house, I never complained. I just figured she was older and, well, I didn't want to offend her delicate sensibilities. I should've known there was nothing delicate or sensible about her.

"What about *Jeopardy!?*" I certainly wasn't responsible for her watching that.

"I just watch it to keep your virgin ears clean. The only daily double I care about is the one I get from an extra scoop of Metamucil."

Um . . . cringe. So much for my virgin ears.

I made myself focus. This was a defining moment. Disturbing, but defining.

"So, you're telling me we can watch . . . say, oh I don't know . . . *Sin City?*"

"And *Fight Club.*"

"Yeah?"

As excited as I was at finding a new best friend in my geriatric babysitter, I refrained from asking her if she wanted to chill out and blaze with me. *Although,* at that precise moment, I wouldn't have been surprised at all if she pulled her favorite bong out of her tote bag.

"How does spaghetti sound?" Ah, there she was. There was the Parker Brothers–playing fool I knew and loved. Just like a broken record. Frankly, I didn't have the patience required for the "What's for Dinner" variety hour, even with the new and improved Mrs. Patterson.

"Spaghetti sounds good. If you get the water started, I'll do the sauce. I'm going over to Cole's, though. So no corruptive TV shows tonight. Big history test," I lied. I needed to go to the dam and I didn't think I could wait until dark.

Just in case Mrs. Patterson was having an Angela Lansbury moment, I walked all the way past the turn to Cole's house, passing the Mini Mart, site of the infamous Kismet PD Gang Bust. Only I wasn't quite ready to confront ghosts at the dam, so I ducked inside. The clerk, Samit, waved, remembering me from "The Incident."

"Hey, it's Kill Bill. Have a soda—on me," he gushed, grinning at me as if the mystery perp Shay, aka gangsta badass, had pointed a sawed-off at his chest. I nodded and thanked him before heading back to the fountain. While struggling to get the right balance of ice, I heard the jingle of the sleigh bells that hung on the door.

"You're scaring away our customers, Kill Bill," Samit said, adding the swipe of an air Hanso sword to my new nickname. I could see he was planning to get a lot of mileage out of it. "He saw you and then, *pfft*, took off."

I turned to see a police car rolling up and a guy ducking his head into the hood of his sweatshirt. I recognized the truck he got into as Mr. Miller's. *Hmph.* I put a lid on my drink. *Shay Miller.*

I headed to the cashier, just so the cops didn't think I was stealing the drink, and reached into my pocket for some money. I might as well have stuck my hand into a pit of snakes, because cash wasn't what I touched.

My fingertips jabbed the bag of weed deeper into my pocket, just as the police swung through the door with mustached smiles. There went my oops-it-must-have-just-fallen-there excuse.

As my thoughts spun out of control, Samit waved me off. "No, no, free, I mean it."

"Hey, tough girl," the taller one said, remembering me.

"Hi," I squeaked

"Catch any more bad guys?"

"Me? No." Then I laughed; only it came out as a really stupid and fake-sounding noise. A giggle? Remarkably like Chelsea Westad's. I'm surprised they didn't billy-club me.

I needed fresh air and quick. I needed to get out of there.

The short one clapped me on the arm before reaching behind me for a package of Ho Hos. As his body brushed against mine, I froze in place.

Heat filled the collar of my shirt, flaring up my neck, my cheeks. Could he feel the distinctive bag-bulge of my pocket?

"Thanks for the drink, Sammy," I called, reiterating that I wasn't stealing it, as I slipped through the narrow opening of the door.

"See ya later, Kill Bill."

I didn't look back to see if he added any new kung fu moves to his repertoire. I was too busy evading arrest.

My heart didn't stop racing until I saw the dam. I glanced around. It took thirty minutes before I was convinced the cops hadn't followed me and that I was alone. I pulled the bag out. I worked at rolling the joint—my experience limited to halfheart-edly watching Kori. Satisfied that it looked okay, I lit it and attempted to pull its entire essence into me in one long drag. Time for my soul to leave, I thought before I exhaled. But instead of a nice smooth stream of soul, I started coughing and didn't stop until I'd coughed up what felt like half my lung. How did Kori ever look cool doing this?

"I don't know what I'm doing," I inadvertently said out loud.

The sun's colors began to blur. Orange. Red. Blue.

I thought about Parker. I imagined him lying in his hospital bed, waiting for all those test results to come back, waiting for answers from his doctors. And that was exactly how I felt. Para-lyzed. Waiting. The life I used to have was gone. The future didn't even have a name and I wondered if it was even worth the effort to wait until it did.

And like a gentle breeze, I heard her whisper curling through my thoughts. *"I'm just waiting for you, kitten."*

I figured I was gone enough not to think too hard about what I was doing, and stoned enough not to feel too much pain. I stood up on the dam.

Looking down at the skinny path of the retaining wall, I readied myself. Hand, hand, foot, foot. My stomach quivered, refusing to settle. I swallowed, looked down at the cement, then at the broken boulders. *No*, I told myself, *don't look down. Look at the water.*

But looking at the water made me dizzy. I closed my eyes and instead of seeing the rock screaming closer, this time I saw a car coming toward me. My hands jerked to cover my eyes. Bang! The world shattered into red. Just as I'd imagined Kori must have.

As I opened my eyes, I was staring at my hands. And as I peeled them from my face, I saw Anthony's watch. It may not have been a good reason, but it was a reason. It was hard to remember the way I'd felt when he'd put it on me. So excited for a future with him. For a future, period. I squatted down, feeling for the ledge, hugging it as I lowered my shaking legs to the ground, out of danger.

sixteen

My fingers were twitching. I'd never gone very long without a computer. And even though I didn't have any inclination to do any coding, I did need to feel the keyboard, something. So in supervised study I asked for a pass to go to the media center and work on the Postcard Secret project Doc had assigned earlier in the month. With everything that had happened, I'd forgotten to be checking the Web site as it was updated with new secrets each week. Apparently confessing—even anonymously—your secrets and sins was good for the soul or some such.

And I certainly had my share of secrets. But my real secret was much too big to put down on a postcard. My real secret couldn't be shared. Not even anonymously.

The only person I trusted was dead, and that was exactly what I wanted to be too. I just didn't know if I could make it happen. That was my real secret.

I scanned for images to represent Kori and settled on a pair of beautiful black angel's wings. Then in ransom-note fashion I added the words *"I don't want to live, if living is without you."*

I still had some time, so I pulled up the blog Doc told us

about and looked through the secrets, reading each. One caught my eye. The handwriting looked exactly like Kori's.

I knew and I didn't tell you.

The picture was of a man embracing a woman. The way it was set up, it drew my eyes to the man's hand as it caressed her blond hair, or more precisely, it drew my eyes to his wedding band. She was holding her ring-free left hand up to his face, shielding their identities. A couple having an affair was what the photo looked like. The hair on the woman looked familiar. The red car they were huddled up against triggered a tremor in me and I looked more closely at it. I could barely make it out, but there was something in the car's window.

I held my breath as I clicked to enlarge the photo.

Colorado Cares. Just like the one on the back window of my mom's lovingly used red Jeep Cherokee.

And once again I felt the world as I knew it shatter.

My hand shook as I clicked to close the Internet session. On Kori's list there had been one thing—Tell Serena—that had confounded me more than the others.

I didn't think there was anything on earth Kori couldn't tell me. But if there was one thing, my mom having an affair with a married man would probably be it. Kori had known I'd held out the hope if I couldn't have my *real* father, one day I would have *a* father. And I wanted a good one. One who didn't lie and cheat. One who had a good heart and an easy smile. One who didn't leave his family in the dust.

"I won't kiss you if you eat it," Cole was saying to her new side-kick, Adrian17. I squeezed in behind her in the cafeteria line, pretending all was normal. I slid my tray along the silver rails, grabbing some extra fruit for Mr. Miller's horses.

Adrian pulled her tight against him and kissed her ear. "Yes you will. You can't resist me."

To be perfectly honest, I was shocked her little lark had somehow survived through everything with Kori. It shocked me because I knew the only reason Cole even hooked up with him was to piss off the BBs, and I knew how hard it was for me to even think about boyfriend stuff, and Anthony had definitely not been some stupid practical joke.

The line moved slowly. Ahead of me, Chelsea was taking two cartons of milk off of Marci's tray. As Marci stretched for a slice of pizza, Chelsea dropped the cartons and grabbed Marci's wrist. "You're supposed to be on a diet!"

"It's new. All carbs and dairy," Marci said, nearly pleading. "It's French! You know how skinny French women are. All they eat is cheese and bread."

"Yeah, well, you're an American and it's not working for you." Chelsea tossed back Marci's oatmeal cookie, following it quickly with the blueberry muffin.

Marci's tray was empty except for one yogurt and a bottled water. Embarrassed, she looked down as she passed us on her way to her table. Of course, it might've had something to do with Cole and Adrian playing handsies over the garlic bread.

For two cool people, they were unbelievably annoying as a couple. Luckily he still sat with his jockstrap buddies at lunch, which meant I had a fighting chance of keeping my food down at our table.

Unfortunately the continuation of their ooey-gooey-you're-the-smoochie lovefest picked up right where it was left off. In Doc's class, Adrian took his new favorite seat, sprawling in the chair directly behind Cole. She turned toward him for maximum flirting.

"I'm not telling you what my secret was! No! Tell me yours, then. No. Tell me yours! No. Tell me now. Tell me. Tell me. Tell me."

Kill me. No. Kill me now. Kill me. Kill me. Kill me.

Adrian whispered his secret into Cole's ear and the giggle fits started. I so wanted to vomit, but the pizza wasn't very good the first time.

"You want a ride home?" Cole asked as she turned back toward me. "I'm driving."

"Driving? Wow." Regina had been adamant that Cole wouldn't be learning on her G-class despite Cole having her permit. Considering what had happened when she was behind the wheel of his "old baby," I think it was safe to say Mr. Blakely wasn't letting Cole near his "new baby"—the GT3.

"Thanks, but I think I'm just going to walk." I really wasn't up for Mrs. B.'s high-society chit-chat or *The Regina Monologues,* as was more often the case. Not after learning my mom was a skanky man-stealing ho. I needed a little alone time to digest that.

Besides, I planned on running into Shay again. But I couldn't tell Cole that, or even that I'd found him, because she'd tell Lexi and Lexi would tell Mom. And I don't think I had anything left for Mom to break.

"Okay, if you see me coming, jump out of the way. Lexi says the sidewalk isn't safe anymore." She gave a little laugh, then: "We're going to the football game Friday, if you're interested."

So I can watch you cheer like a BB for your QB boyfriend? "No, thanks."

"Okay. Well, Lexi and I were thinking of going into Denver on Saturday, do some shopping. You should come."

"I said no." My words had sharp enough of an edge for Cole to stare back at me shocked. But I was seriously tired of her efforts to get me to "come out and play" with her and Lexi.

"I was just asking."

"I know; I'm sorry. I just don't want to go shopping. I have plans."

She shot me a doubtful look.

"Well, what about Saturday night? Lexi wants to try sushi, and there's this great restaurant my dad recommended."

"Saturday night's not good either." I didn't have plans, but I had a feeling Mom might, and I wanted proof. Luckily I didn't have to worry about explaining it to Cole, because she just muttered, *"Whatever"* and turned her attention back to Adrian.

"So, let's talk about the Postcard Secrets," Doc said after the second-bell stragglers took their seats. "I assume everyone's had a chance to go to the Web site and become familiar with the various secrets people have sent in. What did you think? Is this a productive way to spend our time? Reliving and recalling our most embarrassing truths? Does this help or hurt us? Is it salacious? Is it a joke? Is it cruel—some people are talking about killing here, right? So is it wrong?"

In suck-up fashion, Chelsea went first. "It's just good to get things off your chest."

"Okay. Good. So are you saying it's cathartic?"

"Cathartic?" Chelsea asked the guy next to her.

Toby Reynolds leaned over and said, "Yeah, like *or-gas-mic.*" Then he bumped fists with Adrian.

Chelsea squished up her pert nose. "Really?"

"He means like liberating," Cole corrected. "Like a release."

"Oh, yeah, yeah, that's what I mean, it's like an incredible release," Chelsea said with a smile.

Toby grunted. "Yeah, that's what an orgasm is, duh."

"*Ladies* and *gentlemen*, let's stay focused. For the purposes of this discussion, catharsis is the act of bringing complex emotions and feelings that burden us into consciousness and affording them with a releasing expression. Sometimes that expression includes artwork and poetry—like we see in the postcards on the Web site. It also involves an element of physical release, a sense of getting the bad stuff out of our bodies, our minds, which is why simply making the postcard is not enough. We have to send it. We have to pass it to someone else, preferably someone who won't also be burdened."

"Which is why an anonymous Web site works."

"Right, Ashley, very good. So let's talk about some of the postcards that stood out to you and why they might be cathartic."

My mind flashed to the picture of the man kissing my mom. A secret picture of two people carrying on a secret life they weren't going to stop. A secret inside of a secret. *I knew and I didn't tell you.*

There was nothing cathartic about it.

As if a stupid little postcard could set people free of their pain, their guilt. Making it all better. So quick. So easy. I wanted to laugh. These cards didn't set people free. The two people in the picture were still carrying on their affair. Kori never had to tell me the truth. And worse, with her little words—*I knew and I didn't tell you*—she came off like such a martyr. No, the post-cards didn't set you free. The postcards made something ugly look beautiful. That's all.

I raised my hand. Doc wanted participation out of me; he was going to get it. He nodded in my direction. "It's not cathartic.

It's mocking. These aren't people telling their secrets to liberate themselves. They covet them."

"Covet. Great word. Interesting. Why do you think they do that?"

"Decorating a card, coming up with poignant prose, sending it to someone? It's like a fetish. If these people wanted to get rid of their secrets, they would. *I cut myself because I feel pain; I don't quit my job because I'm at a job that doesn't test for drugs, but I take drugs because I hate my job; I knew and I didn't tell you.* These are resolvable. Honest? Yes. Sad? Yes, okay, I'll give them that, but cathartic? Come on. If you really wanted to tell, you'd have told."

I was being hypocritical—here I was in so much pain that I wanted to end my life, but I was afraid to end my life because it might be painful. And yet, Doc stood there nodding at me like I'd just said something brilliant.

"Great, Serena."

Maybe he was just happy I'd said anything at all. But all I wanted to do was pull my words back inside.

"So what else?"

Ashley the Advocate raised her hand and at Doc's nod said, "I just wanted to hug these people and tell them it will get better."

Figures.

"Great. Do they all need a hug? Does the janitor who takes the recycling cans and throws them in the regular Dumpster need a hug?"

I had to applaud Doc for pointing out Ashley's biggest pet peeve. She was always getting her chastity panties in a twist over recycling.

"Well, no, not a hug, I guess. But maybe he just needs to be informed of how easy recycling can be."

"Oh, please," I said out of turn. "You'd still judge him if you saw him toss a bag full of aluminum cans away, and so would Jesus." She quickly covered her Immaculate Conception Flour Baby's ears. "And I'm sorry, but that janitor guy knew exactly what he was doing and didn't seem to feel guilty for doing it either."

Ashley attempted to recover from my comment. No doubt she would be praying for me as soon as she did.

"So why did he bother making the card and sending it in?" Doc asked.

"So he could waste the paper, of course." I pivoted to speak to Ashley. "Or maybe you'd prefer to say he recycled it?"

She grimaced at me. "You're so cynical."

"Okay, so Serena is cynical. Serena, did you take the assignment seriously and send in a real secret?"

"Yes," I said, but felt bad lying, so I added a sheepish "Sort of."

"Okay, so maybe not *entirely* cynical. Why send it in at all?"

Doc waited for me with his soft and safe eyes encouraging me, and I wanted to tell him. Not about the secret I'd sent in, but the one I couldn't. I wanted to say that I didn't put my real secret down because I didn't know how to face it, fix it, but the pressure of everyone else being there—knowing and hearing—hardened me. I felt it first as a tightening on my skin, a stillness of my eyes, and then the quickset cementing of my jaw. And the answer I gave wasn't about my own secret, but about Kori's, Mom's. "You send it because you want to keep doing it."

"Okay, spoken like a woman with very good secrets." The pressure lifted as Doc turned back to the class. "So, here we have another view—confession leads to acceptance. Once you've let it out, you can guiltlessly continue your questionable practices. Why is it safe to continue?"

Doc had turned back to me, and now I was so safely entrenched in my hard shell, the words came easy. "Because my beloved little card, all decorated and poetic, now has everybody's prayers and hugs and warm fuzzies. Not only do I do it and do it anonymously, but now you tell me—I understand. I agree. Me too. Don't feel bad. It's normal."

Doc thought about it and nodded. "The dirty little secret is now embraced. It is acceptable behavior."

"Um, I disagree."

"Wonderful, state your opinion, Cole."

"I don't think eating your boogers will ever be acceptable behavior."

"All we can do is hope," Doc said with a smile, and everybody laughed.

Everyone except me.

I stewed about Mom and her married lover through the rest of the class. And as the bell rang and Doc gave me a pat on the shoulder it hit me. He wanted to meet my mother. A big, real smile that didn't even feel stretched or awkward spread over my face. "Hey, Doc? Did you really mean that about wanting to get to know our parents?"

He nodded.

"How would you like to come to dinner on Saturday?"

There was a look in Kori's eyes that day in eighth grade when I came rushing into the bathroom. It was a look I'd later come to know as playful. But playful in the way Mrs. Patterson's cats liked to play with little field mice before eviscerating them for sport.

After everything with Kori and my mom, I felt like one of those little field mice.

Toyed with and tortured.

I'd always thought my unlikely friendship with Kori was fate's way of making amends for all the other crappy things it had dealt me. But after fate had ripped her from me, I realized just how cruel it could be. You couldn't tempt it, you couldn't change it.

But if I believed that, I also had to accept that Mom wasn't responsible for her actions. And I just couldn't do that.

"Miss Moore?" Dick Click asked, standing next to my desk. "Your Manifest Destiny paper? You were supposed to hand it in before class started." *Shit.*

"I don't have it. Well, I mean, I did it. I just don't have it with me."

He put his hands on his hips. "Serena, Serena. Tsk, tsk, tsk." His pleasure in this moment radiated from him, everything from the white surrounding his little eyes to the nana-nana-nana swish of his hips. "And where might it be?"

I didn't really have it anywhere; it had been on the computer Mom dropped. Completed well ahead of the due date, thanks to Mom's constant chiding about priorities. Completed and forgotten and now gone.

"On my destroyed computer."

A thin little smile infected his lips. "Miss Moore, the computer ate my homework is no more an excuse than the dog."

"The computer didn't *eat* my homework. It's an inanimate object. It doesn't *eat* anything." A few of the students laughed at that.

"Then why, pray tell, don't you have the completed assignment?"

Because, pray tell, "My computer was destroyed."

"Destroyed, Miss Moore? Did your house catch fire?"

His sarcasm scrubbed at my raw patience. "No."

"And did gang members bust in and riddle it with bullets as retribution for your having one of their members hauled in?"

I squinted at his *mature* jab at my Mini Mart attack. But this time the stifled giggles weren't for me. How quickly they turn on you, I thought. It wasn't like I'd claimed to have been ganked or anything. The *Kismet Courier* might have, but not me.

"No."

"Then you will get an incomplete."

"I can write another paper." I could feel my voice rising, my throat squeezing with the hysteria of one who was not being heard and needed to shout. "I can have it to you tomorrow."

"Miss Moore, this isn't a paper that can be completed in one day."

Yeah, right, I thought, but I knew pleading would get me further than honesty. "I've already done the research. I wrote it once. I can write it again."

His tweed blazer jumped an inch off his shoulders as he gave an excessively sarcastic shrug. "On what? Your destroyed computer?" He waited a beat, then: "Incomplete. Now, I think you've taken up enough of our class time." He returned to his desk to begin his sacred lecture.

I was all prepared to zone out and behave myself when the screeching chalk pierced through the drone of his voice, shooting me out of my thoughts. A sadistic grin played on his face as he talked about the decimation of the American natives. Did he really think destiny justified their treatment?

Dick detested interruptions. After all, he so kindly left no room at the end of his lectures for questions, because every question would be answered if we only waited until the end. But since I knew my questions would never be answered in any of his lectures, I raised my hand.

Mr. Click's eyes boggled. He sniffed so hard his nose wrinkled, scooting his glasses back in place. "Yes, Miss Moore? Are the gang members back? Do you require a hall pass?"

Dick Click was such a jacktard. But I wasn't going to let him bait me into any more embarrassing arguments. "What about freedom of will?"

"What about it?"

"I'm sorry, but that Manifest Destiny shit is a load of crap. Just an excuse to do whatev—" He started to object. But I objected more. "We're people, Mr. Click. We have free will. We can make choices. Hell, isn't that what makes us so freaking superior?"

"Well, Miss Moore, your free will and foul mouth just earned you a trip to the principal's office."

And for all the Oprah fans out there keeping track—that would be my brick.

seventeen

Considering I was sitting in Mr. Teasley's office for the third time in two weeks, I should've felt more repentant. But after unleashing some of my fury on Dick Click, I felt a glimmer of something good.

I tried to pinpoint it, but before I could nail it down, Mr. Teasley returned to his office and he was not alone.

"Serena Moore, I'd like you to meet Catherine Giles."

I reached out and shook the woman's hand. Everything about her—her shoulder-length blond hair, her long flowered skirt, her yellow cardigan—said: "I'm a counselor." There'd been several like her since the accident. They roamed the halls, offering their time should anyone need to vent or cry or whatever. Sympathy I didn't want filled their eyes.

"Serena? If it's okay with you, I'm going to leave you two alone for a minute to talk about what you're going through."

I nodded because I didn't really think I had much say in the matter, and besides, from the way the woman's eyes went all soft when she looked at me, I could tell Mr. Teasley had already filled her in on all the juicy details.

After Mr. Teasley stepped out, Catherine pulled a chair up next to me.

"I know it must be hard, coming back to school and focusing on things that may seem, well, not as important as they were before." Her comment seemed more like a question, so I nodded. She looked at me for a minute, assessing, and then asked, "Is *that* how you feel, Serena?"

"Not exactly."

"Use your own words. Tell me how you feel."

When I closed my eyes, I imagined Parker, paralyzed in his hospital bed. Not knowing if he would ever walk again. That was how I felt. Paralyzed. Waiting. Needing answers. "I feel stuck."

"Stuck." She nodded like she too felt stuck. "Are you afraid that something bad might happen to you next?"

"Something bad has happened to me. I lost my best friend."

"Yes, of course," she said, nodding in agreement again. I wished she'd stop agreeing with me and give me some straight answers. "Serena, what's holding you back? What's making you feel stuck?"

Just like with Parker's legs, a part of me just didn't have any movement, any feeling. She waited even though I didn't say anything for several minutes. But I wasn't so sure it was acceptable to go around comparing myself to a paralyzed person. "I guess, I don't know, I feel incomplete."

"That's normal. It's natural for you to feel incomplete. A large part of your life has been ripped away."

"I guess."

"Can you tell me how you see yourself filling that void?"

"Filling it?" I asked on the heels of her saying the word.

"Serena, sometimes it's easier to think about loss in terms of physical elements. So tell me, if you were to lose your leg, what would you do? Would you be able to stand?"

"Sure, I'd still have one good leg."

"Absolutely, but what if while you were standing on your one good leg I came up and gave you a shove?"

"I'd probably fall down." *And then kick you with my one good leg.*

"Right. Without both legs, you have no balance. You'd need to use crutches or get a prosthetic leg. Now, with our emotional lives we need to do the same thing. We need to lean on our friends and family. Because until we are able to fill that void, we are in a constant state of unbalance."

When I thought about filling the void, I started to panic. What if Kori were to ever come back and there wasn't a place for her? What if I forget her? "No. I don't want to fill the void," I snapped.

Catherine Giles and her soothing voice never wavered. "I know it's hard to stop hurting. We worry that if we don't feel the pain, don't suffer, then we didn't love. We fear letting go of the pain, because we think we are also letting go of the love. But our loved ones don't wish for us to suffer. They wouldn't be happy to know they are the cause of our pain. If you want to serve your friend's spirit, think about ways that celebrate it. Filling is not replacing, Serena. I want you to think about that. Think about ways you can fill that won't replace."

"Okay," I said, not entirely convinced, but I was ready for her to leave. When she did, I went back to waiting in the office with the extreme air-conditioning torture treatment.

It was nothing compared to the torture waiting for me in Mom's Jeep Cherokee. She shot me a look of disappointment as I opened the door. But all I could think about was the picture of her with that married man. So as I slid into my seat, I shot her one right back.

I waited until we were pulling out of the school before I said, "By the way, on Saturday we are having dinner with Doc Ramsey."

"We're what?" The Jeep jerked onto the narrow shoulder as she whipped her head around.

"Watch the road, Mom, you don't want to have a wreck."

In my room, while being "grounded," I pulled out Kori's boxes. I tugged on a pair of her jeans. Spritzed myself with the scent of cherry blossoms. Slicked on her burgundy lipstick. As I was slipping one of Kori's old-school concert shirts over her lacy black bra, I heard Mom leave to go to Colorado Cares.

"About freakin' time," I muttered.

When I got to Mr. Miller's, Shay was half-naked and turning small piles of manure into larger piles.

It was no wonder Kori spent her last hours with him. He was a hottie of the hottest order. Eyes the color of a well-worn, absolute-most-favorite pair of Levi's. Hair too short to look properly disheveled; instead the dark spikes played in an arrangement of devil horns and little angel wings.

Gotta love a guy with morally perplexed hair.

I could only imagine how much work his conscience got.

As I got closer, I could see he wasn't a fan of the latest Five-No!-*SIX!* blade razors; the stubble on his boxy jaw looked at least a day old, and not that silly high school boy-fuzz, either.

With each lift of the pitchfork, he repeated the affirmation, "I am not shoveling shit."

I started to laugh, and had to gulp it back down when his body flinched and he turned to stare at me.

I'd forgotten he might not be happy to see me.

Before I ran off, a smile lit his face. His eyes had this sparkle to them, like the reservoir has with a full moon and a nice breeze.

Then they stilled in their dance, focusing on details that had him holding his breath.

Flattery like that was a heady thing. It's funny how insecure you can get when people look at you too often and for too long. I don't think it's all that different from when no one looks at you at all.

When I got close enough, his eyes met mine. Whatever he thought he saw in me fluttered away and disappeared.

He wasn't seeing me; he was seeing Kori.

Sometimes even I forgot how much I looked like her.

A wing of black hair dropped over my face to shield me from his stare as I leaned down to rummage through my bag. I decided the best way to approach the situation was to continue the fantasy. Act like Kori. Flirt like Kori. I channeled some of her cocky confidence and smirked. "Take a picture."

"Huh?"

Okay, that was lame.

I covered by shaking my head playfully at him and laughing to myself. "You're like a total stalker, aren't you?"

"*Me?*"

"I saw you at the Mini Mart, you know." Guys loved it when Kori turned the tables on them.

"So I'm the stalker now, huh?" I glanced up at the playful expression on his face. There it was—the knowing grin. It was already working.

"Yeah. Are you following me? Should I get a restraining order? I'm awfully friendly with Kismet's finest this week."

He swallowed and shifted his stance, looking pretty guilty and like he was coming up with a plausible scenario. Which was kind of cute, but all he came up with was: "Yeah. I was there."

"Then the cops came and you ran."

"Yeah, well, I don't really get along with the law this week."

I regarded him with a laugh. "A sense of humor is good, a healthy distrust of the law is even better. I'll let you off this time, but if you start getting creepy, I'll have to hurt you."

The muscles in his stomach clutched as if bracing for impact. My eyes lighted on them. With a shrug of a smile, he stroked the trail of hairs on the hardened flesh, but his eyes didn't leave mine. In fact, he appeared utterly delighted in my distraction.

I twisted my lips into a devilish grin. "Wow, a six-pack. You must work out a lot."

"I try," he said tightly.

"Impressive."

"So, you still think you can hurt me?"

I dismissed him and all previous flattery with an arched eyebrow and a half-cocked shoulder. "Oh, I'm sure I can find a pair of body parts you can't protect with weight lifting."

He moved the rake in front of him, as if it might offer some protection.

I laughed and started digging through my bag, producing two apples, a peach, and several carrots. As I set them in the grass, the horses put their chests into the wire fence, stretching it as they tried to nab the treats.

Shay rested his weight against a wood fence post and watched me dole out equal shares.

"You're sure this is okay, right? I'd hate to get you in trouble with your long-lost uncle."

My tone was so obviously mocking that he laughed.

I finished feeding the horses and didn't have to turn around to know he watched me the entire time. "So, Shay Miller, do you ever get to ride?"

"I suppose I could."

"You never have?"

He hitched his thumb toward the tractor. "Too busy riding that thing. Not exactly turbo-charged. But I have a good imagination."

I glanced back at him and grinned. "That's too bad."

"And why's that?"

I tilted my chin and smiled up at him. This was almost too easy. "Because if you did, you could invite me."

"Uh . . . well, sure. If you want . . ."

"Yes. I. Want. What's your cell?"

"Cell?" I held mine up and waggled it in front of him. "Oh, cell phone. Actually, no. I don't have one."

"Geez, Shay Miller," I said as I scribbled my number down on a scrap of paper from my bag. "Where did you come from, anyway?"

"Nowhere you'd know," he muttered as he pulled his T-shirt over his head. It was inside out. He shoved his hands into his back pockets and shrugged, swallowed hard, and stared at his worn-out work boots. "So, maybe we can ride this weekend? Sunday?"

"Yeah, Sunday's perfect."

"Good. Okay, then."

"Okay, see ya later, Shay Miller."

I started to head home, but as I passed through the cold shade of a tall cedar, I heard him call to me. "Hey, Serena?"

I turned back. "Yeah?"

"Why do you keep saying my full name?"

I laughed and thought about Kori and what she might say. Thankful for the tree's shadow that concealed my blush, I told him, "Because, Shay Miller, it feels good on my tongue."

"Okay, then," he said stiffly.

eighteen

A s I got dressed for dinner with Doc, I briefly debated taking out my tongue ring, but then, right at seven, the doorbell rang. I sailed down the stairs looking my most innocent and daughterly.

"Destiny, you look . . . just lovely," Doc said, smiling from our doorway.

Just lovely? Heh.

Just lovely was the splatter of spaghetti sauce dribbled down the front of Mom's T-shirt. Her ripped Saturday sweatpants were moderately lovelier.

She locked her elbow straight, barring off the threshold as if Doc were going to barrel through uninvited. "Can I help you, Dr. Ramsey?"

"Sam, please call me Sam." He spoke the words very slowly, as if she were an animal about to charge and he didn't want to wave any sort of red flags. He was a smart man; I'd give him that. "Did Serena not mention inviting me to dinner tonight?"

Knowing my mother, she was making a list of all the things she would've done if she'd remembered: Washed hair. Vacuumed. Emptied sink. Emptied rank-smelling trash. Gone to grocery. Fixed dinner. Dressed in clothing that wasn't adorned in food stains. Made her trademark, disorient-them-into-thinking-you-are-the-best-mother-in-the-world 2X chocolate chip cookies. Put in a fresh Glade PlugIn.

"Hi, Doc," I said as I put my hand on Mom's arm. "I told you. Remember? In the car?"

She turned to me and looked like she was going to snap me in half, then she turned back to Doc. Through a tight-lipped smile, she said, "Now that you mention it, I do remember." The fake smile sounded in her voice as she opened the door wide for Doc Ramsey to enter. "A little too late, I'm afraid. We're not prepared for company. The fridge is empty. I was planning on ordering in."

All of our eyes went to the focal point of the room—the over-flowing trash, and more specifically last night's pizza box.

Mom's voice stayed even, cool. *Impressive.* "Maybe we should all go someplace nice? Serena, would you pick a restaurant while I change?"

"Sure, Mom." I gave Doc an apologetic glance. "Sorry, I thought since it was Saturday, she might've gone to the store. We've been out of food for a while now."

Out of the corner of my eye, I saw Mom's fists clenching as she restrained from storming back out to the living room to defend herself against these latest allegations.

"So, Serena, how are you doing?" Doc asked while we waited. I could tell by the question, he wasn't talking about the state of our town house.

Unless you count the pimp action I'd set up for him with my mother, I thought I was doing pretty well. I lifted my messenger bag to my shoulder, gave him a smile, and said, "I'm fine."

"Your bag looks like it weighs a ton," he said, eyeing it.

I'd already taken Baby Maru out in an attempt to prove to

Doc I was doing the assignment. I reached back and pulled out an apple as I gave him a weak smile. I'd actually taken it from our refrigerator, replenishing my supply for tomorrow, but I told him, "I take extras from the caf."

His forehead crinkled up and his eyes had this deeply concerned look. "Looks like you've got a lot of apples."

"Yeah, I guess."

I didn't explain about the horses. I don't know why. I guess I just liked the way having all that food in my bag made him worry over me, and if I told him the apples were for the horses, he wouldn't be worried about it anymore. Everyone should have someone who worries about her.

The restaurant I picked had starched white tablecloths, waiters who shaved, and a romantic view overlooking the reservoir. This time of year only a few sailboats slid across the surface. Just the diehards getting their last weekend runs in before winter started clamping down.

Mom had changed into a classic fall outfit—short-sleeved sweater, long skirt, and tall boots. Not exactly date wear, but as always, she looked perfect and together, and nothing like she had just moments before.

Her eyes kept cutting to the black flour bag with the pouting penguin face that sat in its own chair at the table. I could tell she wanted to ask about it. Like, why was it black? Was there any significance to that? But it would expose her ignorance about her daughter's school projects, and that wasn't something she would do—certainly not in front of the teacher who'd assigned the project.

After the waiter had come by and taken our order, Doc turned to Mom. "Serena tells me you work at the hospital. What is it you do?"

"I'm a nurse practitioner working with the hospitalist," she replied, her tone more job applicant than dinner companion.

"Say, you don't happen to work with Parker Walsh, do you?"

"Parker, yes," Mom replied with a smile.

I'd been thinking a lot about Parker. Wondering if he'd gotten any answers to all those tests yet. As much as I wanted to blame Parker for Kori's death, I couldn't. Not completely. If I hadn't been making out with Anthony, maybe I could've stopped her. In that regard, Parker and I were in this together. And a part of me wanted to see if he had improved. I wanted to mark my progress against his and determine what hope I had for a full recovery.

"Thank you," I said as I took a dinner roll from the basket Doc held out to me. "You've visited Parker, haven't you, Doc?"

"A couple of times, yes. I should stop by again soon. Tomorrow maybe."

"Do you think I could come with you? To see Parker?"

"That's a wonderful idea. I know Parker hasn't had many visits from people his own age."

Mom stiffened. She caught herself right as Doc did.

"I'm sorry, I spoke too soon. I can see you object, Destiny."

She avoided his eyes while concentrating on rearranging her napkin. "No, no, I don't object. Of course I don't object."

"We could all go together, maybe that would be better?"

I beamed at his totally brilliant suggestion. Perfect. The more time Mom spent with Doc, the better my chances were of getting her to fall for him. Except Mom looked like she wanted to scream as she, instead, grabbed a dinner roll, showing more interest in it than the conversation. My eyebrows knotted in shock at her lack of concern. Parker was one of her patients; if she would only start talking about him, then Doc could see how dedicated she was to her work, how compassionate she was about her patients. He would find that endearing. But noooo. Mom ripped apart the bread and dug a chunk of it straight into the communal butter.

One glance at Doc and I could tell he was as confused by her as I was, possibly even revolted at her behavior. It was the communal butter, after all.

"Mother?"

She slowed her chewing to a more respectable pace, fixed her eyes on me, and smiled as she dabbed at her mouth with her napkin. In her best placating mother voice, she replied, "Serena, honey, you can visit Parker anytime you want. Excuse me, please." Then she headed to the restroom.

I so didn't need Mom coming all undone here and now, not when I was trying to get Doc to actually want to date her. So she had some guy on the sly? It didn't mean she had to act all weirded out and rude with Doc.

Ever the gracious one, he pretended to be fascinated with the sailboats.

As I watched the bathroom door, I caught sight of the last two people in the world I'd wanted to see. Mr. and Mrs. Kitzler. Before I looked away, I couldn't help but notice how frail Mrs. K. looked in her designer dress. How fragile. Like the whisper-weight silk could break her if she didn't walk just right.

I turned away, following Doc's lead and looking out the window at the glistening waters, resigning myself to the fact that the date was a bust and I should forget it. But another part of me knew I needed to say something to my mother. Confrontation just wasn't something Mom and I did very well. It was more Kori's style. The part of me that envied her more than anything, admired her for it. Wished I could be more like that.

"We're more alike than you think."

How many times had I replayed those words, enjoying the implication that little ol' me was anything at all like someone so crazy brave.

Shared birthdays and faked hair color were about it, certainly not enough to warrant a friendship like we had. But now I'd never know. Never understand what she meant that day in eighth grade.

I looked across the lake at the beach where Kori had gone skinny-dipping, and then farther to the cutting rocks of the dam. Just remembering how it felt to stand on the crumbling ledge made my chair feel a little wobbly.

"Doc? Do you think Kori was a brave person?"

"Brave?"

"Yeah, you know, fearless?"

"Being brave doesn't mean you have no fears. It's having the ability to overcome your fears. So, yes, I think Kori was brave. But no, I wouldn't go so far as to suspect she was fearless."

I caught sight of Mom as she ducked outside. She was probably going to call her boy toy and tell him she would be late. "Excuse me."

I weaved my way through the tables, passing the hostess stand as I left the restaurant.

Mom gasped as I walked up beside her under the restaurant's deep green awning. "Serena!"

I didn't say anything as I retrieved a pack of cigarettes from my bag, tapped one out, and put it in my mouth. I fished out a lighter—the Zippo—as Mom's hand jerked in an attempt to snatch the cigarette from my lips. I yanked my head out of her range, my lips crushing down so fast and hard I was surprised the cigarette didn't snap in two.

"Serena! Smoking? No!"

I let the cigarette taunt her by bouncing loosely along with the words. "Serena. Smoking. Yes." I cupped my hands around the flame as I leaned into it. I kept eye contact with her as the cigarette lit.

It was no wonder she couldn't formulate a sentence, the way her face contorted, showing all of the thousand horrors swirling around in her brain. *My daughter is a smoker!* She couldn't figure out whether to rush down to the hospital and put my name on the lung transplant waiting list or to kill me herself.

She opted to bite her tongue for a change.

I snapped the Zippo shut victoriously and took a drag.

"You know, at least Doc's single." Mom's expression was a mixture of things, most of which were unreadable. But my smoking suddenly didn't seem to be her biggest concern anymore.

On Sunday, I stood in the barn's opening watching as Shay saddled the horses at the other end. I reminded myself for the millionth-point-five time this wasn't a date. I was here because of Kori and I should keep my focus on that. And maybe not so much on his abs.

Even from the distance, his movements appeared jerky and anxious. He kept holding out the leather straps dangling from the saddle and staring at them like he had no idea where they went.

I grinned, recognizing the behavior. This morning I had spilled coffee on myself. At breakfast my stomach had protested both eating and not eating. It'd been like that ever since he invited me to go riding. Like my mind was stuck on the spin cycle or something.

"Looks like you could use some help." My voice startled him and I grimaced apologetically. "Hey."

"Hey, didn't hear you come up." He rubbed his palms on his jeans, hunching his shoulders sheepishly. An endearing look on a guy whose chest strained his T-shirt. "So, yeah, I figured you'd want to ride Stargazer." He hooked his thumb toward the black horse.

"I'm not choosy, but yeah, he's perfect."

"Here, I'll let you do this . . . ," he said as he handed me a bridle. I pretended to ignore the way his fingers knocked gently with mine as the thin leather straps changed hands, even though my heart did fish-on-a-dock flip-flops as I fumbled with the buckles.

Outside the barn, the air was crisp. Refreshing, considering my body was sweating like a marathon runner's.

"Need a boost?" he asked, and all I could do was nod.

His chest pressed against my shoulder, rising and falling with each breath, as he maneuvered beside me. Sure enough, waves of warm electricity licked up my arm. *That* . . . I absolutely couldn't ignore.

An awkward moment ticked by when we both just looked at each other. Then one side of his mouth kicked up, showing off a deep, bracketing dimple. He probably thought he looked irresistible, and he wasn't far off. He cupped his hands for me to step into. "Ready?"

I swallowed and put a hand on his shoulder for balance—ironic because the closer I got to him, the more unbalanced I became. I quickly bounced on my booted toe to help lift me, and at the same exact time, he vaulted me up, nearly blasting me over Stargazer's back.

I grappled for the saddle horn just as Shay grabbed for my leg to keep me from sailing over. All well and good until I realized his hands were wrapped, rather intimately, around my thigh. An embarrassingly girlish squeal escaped me. Then awkward squirming began.

Yeah, real attractive.

"Here," he mumbled, shifting his hands to my ankle, helping my foot find the stirrup. "Got it?" he asked, looking up at me.

Again I felt the intense connection. I wanted to tug down the hem of my tank top, so that it tucked into my low-slung jeans. Even my shoulders felt too exposed. I hadn't really thought jeans and a tank top were all that sexy, certainly nothing like the skirts I usually wore, but in Shay's gaze I felt exposed.

I watched as he confidently mounted his horse, turning it toward mine. I had to get him to like me, trust me. Tell me things. Now was not the time to turn back into 'fraidy-cat Serena.

His eyebrows lowered as he caught my stare. "What?"

Then I blurted out, "I'm sorry, I know I sort of invited myself."

God, 'fraidy-cat Serena was an idiot.

"No problem," he said. "I would've invited you anyway."

As I turned to look at him, his eyes were perfectly aligned with mine. It should be illegal for guys to have eyes like his.

Assertive, Serena, assertive.

I flashed him a wicked grin Kori liked to use at times such as this. "Yeah. I know."

We rode in silence, enjoying the warm sun and the cool shadows. When I'd instigated this date/outing/whatever (I don't think we should try to label it), I'd hoped I could get him to talk about his relationship with Kori. Why she went to go see him in Golden. What she needed to work out with him. But I didn't know how to start that conversation. And he certainly wasn't volunteering any information.

Only the horse's soft footfalls over the rocky terrain filled the air as they picked their way from the flat pasture up a steep trail.

For the longest time we rode single file through a thick forest of evergreen trees. The sun beat down on their branches, releasing the heavy fragrance of spruce and pine. After we crested a small rocky peak and headed back down toward the ranch through the aspens, the trail widened and allowed us to ride side-by-side.

Whenever our eyes met, I had the oddest sensation that I was right next to Shay, curled against him, his summer-sky eyes looking into mine. The breeze could've been his fingertips trailing across my cheek, through my hair.

But it wasn't until we were heading back through the flat pasture toward Mr. Miller's barn that I found my voice.

"So, how do you like it here, anyway?"

"Hmm?"

"At Mr. Miller's." I bobbled as Stargazer kicked at a fly. "I mean—you aren't from around here, right?"

His expression was unreadable. "Well, it's better than the alternative."

"With your parents, you mean? You aren't close to them?"

"Of course I am—they're my parents," he said way too quick to be true. "Aren't you close to yours?"

"My mother and I used to be. Not so much now. Kinda sucks now."

I could sense him looking at me, but I avoided the contact by staring off at the mountain peaks that stretched north. I wanted to get information out of him, not the other way around. I braced for additional prodding, but it didn't come. Maybe he knew I'd just given him as much as I possibly could.

"So, what's living with Mr. Miller like? Does he have a lot of"—I turned back, catching his stare—"rules? Is he strict?"

"What do you mean strict?"

"You're living under his roof. Isn't that how the saying goes?"

"Actually, I'm living under the roof of the barn. There's an apartment in the loft, so I'm on my own."

"Oh? That's good." An image of how his apartment might look, his bed, flashed into my mind. When he caught my blush, I covered with: "I mean . . . that you don't have to answer to anyone."

"I'm eighteen," he bit off.

I flinched at the defensiveness in his tone. But damn it, I'd gotten lengthier and more reliable answers out of a Magic 8 Ball.

I tried a more subtle route. "I bet he's glad to have family."

"Miller's cool."

"Yeah? Except for sugar cubes, of course."

"Yeah, well, he's strict about the animals and all, but I think he likes having someone around." Shay's lip cocked. "You could say he was shocked to see me. But I guess having a long-lost nephew show up just when you need it isn't such a bad thing."

"Really?" An image flashed in my mind, a doorstep of a nice home. A man in the doorway. A confused smile that grew with understanding. A hug long overdue. Well, that was best-case scenario; there were other movie clips that played in my mind as well. "Was he excited? I mean . . . he wasn't upset?"

"I can tell what you're thinking, you know," he said as we stopped our horses in front of the barn. He caught the quick straightening of my features and quirked his lip.

"So, what am I thinking?" I said with a flirtatious tilt of my chin.

"You're thinking—what would happen if you showed up on your father's doorstep? Right?"

My spine went rigid. "I never said I didn't know my father. My father and I are very close. He's really great."

Shit. I wanted him to think I was like Kori, but that didn't mean I wanted to outright lie to him.

"When you mentioned just your mother, I assumed. My bad."

"It's okay." But it wasn't okay; I shouldn't have snapped at him. I just really didn't want him to know my neurosis over my nonexistent father.

He swung down from his horse and asked, "Want a soda?"

"Sure, I'll be right there."

"Take your time. Ride around."

I nodded, but I just wasn't into riding after that. And I really hated lying to Shay, but my MIA father was too deep a bruise to be poking at.

When I entered the tack room, I expected to find Shay bent over into the refrigerator, not rifling through my messenger bag.

"What are you doing?"

He jerked up. All of my bag's contents were scattered across the table, most notably both elaborately decorated flour bags. Shay's body blocked me from getting to them without causing a scene.

"I accidentally knocked it over."

"So you thought it would be okay to go digging through my stuff? Prying around?"

"No. Not like that." He sat with one hip on the table. Annoyingly cool. "Since when do girls carry bags of flour around?"

I swallowed, concentrated on not freaking out at the invasion, even as I snapped the words off. "You wouldn't get it."

His calm eyes took me in. They didn't seem to care about the panic thrashing about inside me. "Try me."

"It's a class project, okay?"

"So it's what? A project to see how much strain the human spine can endure?"

"No."

I looked for an opening to get to my things, to put them back in my bag, but he wasn't giving me one.

"They're supposed to be babies."

He picked up Baby Charms with one hand. "I don't get it."

"We have to be responsible for them like they're children or something. You know, make sure they're accounted for and taken care of."

He hitched his shoulder. "Can't a bag of flour take care of itself?"

"It's symbolic, okay?" I growled out in annoyance. "Gah. Why is this so hard for everyone to understand?"

"Because it's a bag of flour."

"Yeah, well, babies are heavy."

I made a move then, heading toward him. He crossed his arms over his chest, his elbow making the path around him even tighter. Too tight.

"So why do you have two? Did you get assigned twins?" He had both of them now. One in each hand.

"The white one was Kori's, okay?" I was breathing rapidly now, but Shay just stood his ground, not even aware of how rude he was being or the anxiety he was causing.

"And you're taking care of it for her, because . . . ?"

"I don't know!" Then, calmer: "Because, she didn't finish it. Because, if she had a child, I would take care of it. Okay?"

He reached over and picked up the sonogram picture I'd found in the bathroom. "Is this yours? Or Kori's?"

I swallowed and looked away. "It's neither. It's a friend's." When I looked back at him, I could tell he didn't believe me. "Well, she's not really even a friend. But it's not mine or Kori's. I swear."

As soon as he moved out of the way, relenting his interrogation, I started shoving my stuff back into the bag. I felt, of all things, ashamed.

"Hey, I wasn't making fun or anything, I was just curious." He reached out and lifted my chin with his finger to force me to make eye contact. "I'm curious . . . about you."

I jerked away. "Well, now you know."

I could hear the exasperated draw of his breath as he watched me close up my bag. Then: "I think it's really nice what you're doing . . . for her."

"You do?" I asked, not so sure.

"Yeah. I don't know too many people who would go to that kind of trouble. Even for a friend."

I shifted to lift my bag. "Yeah, well, she's . . . was a lot more to me than just a friend."

When his hand closed over mine, my eyes darted up. "I know," he said softly. Then a few beats later, with dimples flashing: "Let me walk you home, carry your bag. I'd really like to see your spine stay healthy, you know."

I narrowed my already suspicious gaze. "Sounds pretty stalkerish."

"Please. I just want to talk to you. You don't even have to talk back. But there's something I need to tell you."

nineteen

I'm not stalking you."

Shay swung my pack over his shoulder and started walking out of the barn. I had no choice but to follow.

"Actually, I should be running away from you. You've kind of been bad luck for me, you know?"

"Gee, thanks."

"I'm trying to explain something. It's not easy. I haven't been very . . . forthcoming."

"Just say it." My blasé tone masked my fear. He was about to tell me something I didn't want to know. Something about Kori being pregnant or that he'd sold her drugs.

"Earlier, when you were asking about Miller, I'm sorry I snapped at you. It's just that he wasn't happy to see me. I'm not here just to help him out. I'm not even here of my own accord. When the police hauled me in for"—he made finger quotes—"assaulting you, I was already on probation."

"Probation," I repeated. I hesitated at the end of Mr. Miller's driveway. Maybe I shouldn't be letting an ex-con walk me home.

"Relax. It was just petty stuff," he said tightly.

I glanced over at him, and figured if Kori trusted him, so

could I. "It's this way, not far," I said, pointing down the pine-lined street toward my town house. "So, what did you do?"

"I wish I could say wrong time, wrong place, but it was more a case of wrong girl, right reason. You know what they say, though, the road to hell is paved with good intentions."

"And Post-it notes," I muttered under my breath. I turned to watch a herd of shaved and spandexed cyclists pass us on the road.

"I've been in and out of juvie, among other things I'm not too proud of. So naturally the cops didn't buy my innocence."

"No, I guess they wouldn't. But I didn't press charges. I even told the officer that it was the guy in the Acura who Lexi called to tell them about, and that I didn't even know who you were, but I'd just panicked and overreacted."

He gave me a slight smile. "Yeah. Thanks for that. I still had to tell them the truth, and they still had to call my probation officer. He's a real prick nut job. Luckily, my uncle agreed to give me a job at his place. I guess there's a long-standing belief that working on a farm is good for a guy like me. So it smoothed things over," he said as he shifted his weight. "Anyway, I guess what I was trying to tell you was—I'm here because of you."

I glanced up, but he was looking away.

"Just kind of odd," he said absently. "Fate."

As we passed by an aspen grove, the wind teased the pale green leaves. I remembered playing among the skinny white trunks as a kid and thinking the noise—almost like the tinkle of bells—sounded magical.

We turned into the entrance of my complex and I held out my hand and took back my bag. Admittedly, it was nice not to have to lug it around. Even if it was just for five-point-five minutes.

"Well, since we're coming clean and all. You were right about my dad." I watched Shay for his reaction. "I've never even met him."

The corner of his lip quirked up as he said, "His loss."

In all of my father fantasies, I'd never thought of it that way. It probably wasn't such a bad way to look at it.

I arrived at the hospital well before I'd agreed to meet with Doc. In the hallway outside of Parker's room I heard his father talking with the doctors.

"We haven't found any physical justification for Parker's condition."

"He was in a car wreck. How much more justification do you need?"

"I understand. But there is nothing physically wrong with your son."

"He can't move his legs. Is that not physical enough for you? You just haven't tried the right test. Do I need to take him to Denver?"

"Dad," Parker said. It was the first I'd heard him speak. "I don't want any more tests."

"We need to know why you're paralyzed so we can fix it."

"I know why I'm paralyzed, Dad, I was in a car wreck."

"Parker, there is another avenue I think we should look down," the doctor said. "We think, perhaps, you're having what is called a hysterical conversion reaction. I'd like to bring someone in to evaluate your situation."

For a minute, the doctor was turned so I couldn't clearly hear his words. But then all of a sudden, Mr. Walsh was nearly shouting, "My son's not psycho. He was in a car wreck."

A few minutes after the doctor left, I heard Mr. Walsh softly begging Parker to try, just try to wiggle his toes.

"You can do it. You heard the doctor. There is nothing keeping you from moving your legs. All you have to do is try. Please try, son." The sound of Mr. Walsh's pleas wrapped around my heart and squeezed, and I couldn't stand there and listen to them.

A half hour later, I met Doc in the lobby and we went back upstairs.

Parker was under a blanket, his arms on top of the blue knit with one hand protectively over the remote control. His hair was matted from sleep on one side, and shaggy and long on the other. He had a hollow look that went beyond the atrophy. But he also looked better than I'd expected.

Shoving my hands into the pockets of my cut-off jean skirt, I nodded hello as I approached the foot of the hospital bed.

With brown wolfish eyes Parker watched me. I looked everywhere else. The taupe walls. The beeping machines. The television suspended in the corner. The clean, uncluttered surfaces where cards and flowers were meant to be displayed. It wasn't that no one had sent him stuff, I knew people who had. But the cheer they were meant to offer was nowhere to be seen. I knew why too. He didn't think he deserved it.

As he pushed down on the heels of his palms to position himself more upright in the bed, he looked to be in great pain. I watched closely for any motion from the bend of his hips to the soles of his feet—there wasn't any.

"Hey, Doc, mind grabbing me a Coke or Sprite from the vending machine?"

"Sounds good. Serena, you want one too?"

I shook my head. Doc waved off Parker's attempt to pay before heading down the hall.

Relief that we were alone spread over Parker's face, but I didn't understand why. It's not like we were friends.

"I think my mom's your nurse," I muttered when the silence stretched a little too thin.

"She's the best one." I wasn't expecting that, but I never doubted her professional abilities. "I was hoping you'd stop by. This morning when we were talking about you, she mentioned you might."

Mom had talked to him about me? I couldn't believe my yappy mother had been babbling to him. *God, what else had she said?* Had she talked to him about Kori? Told him, just like she had with Lexi and Cole, that I still hadn't talked to anybody about her death? Realizing what a bad idea it was to come here, I turned to leave. I'd figure out some excuse to tell Doc.

Parker called out, "Hey, wait. Stop." And I did, in the doorway. The empty hall waited patiently in front of me.

"Don't be upset with your mom. She wasn't, like, telling me a bunch of stuff about you or anything."

"I'm sure," I muttered.

"Kori talked about you, though. A lot."

Through my teeth, I asked, "When you were getting high with her?"

"Yeah, when we would get high together."

"Right. Whatever." Then, because I was there already and I wanted to know, I asked, "What were you doing that night? Where did you take her after the kegger?"

"You shouldn't be worried about that."

I realized that it might be his meds making him so annoying, but my patience wasn't going to hold out much longer. "Well, I am. It's important," I said as I walked back toward his bed.

"You've always been worried about her, she was always worried about you."

Clearly he had no intention of telling me where she'd gone, but he didn't need to be so obnoxious about it. I started to leave again and his voice reached out, scratching the edge of my soul. "You don't want to get better, do you?"

I turned back to him. His odd statement wouldn't settle in my mind. "I was going to say the same thing to you," I whispered.

"But I killed three people."

"Yeah. I know."

"Yeah?" he asked, looking a bit incredulous. "That's it? All you say is 'Yeah, I know'?"

"It's a fact. It isn't a judgment." Kori's words flicked off my tongue. "*It is what it is.* You were in an accident that killed three people. Of course you're going to blame yourself, you're still alive."

"Yeah, but alive isn't always living. Is it, Serena?" He lifted back his sheet and chills tore along my arms as my eyes took in the stockpile of pills he had wrapped in a washcloth. "Should I tell Kori hello for you?"

twenty

Parker's revelation disturbed me. I wondered why he told me about the pills, his plans. Did he want me to stop him? Tell my mother? Or maybe he just wanted me to know how sorry he was for killing Kori. No matter what his reasons were, I wished he hadn't. Now those pills were whispering about how quickly they could take me to her. How easy. How perfect. How painless.

After our visit, I ditched Doc Ramsey in the hospital parking lot, fully intending to return to Parker's room and see if he would share. As I headed for the hospital's back stairs, I ran into Marci Mancini—literally—knocking her pamphlets out of her hand. She scrambled to grab them up before I could read them.

"You know what the Monty Python boys say . . . ," I said.

"Huh? What?" She was too embarrassed and upset to answer right away, but quickly recovered. "Oh, from the Gwyneth movie, right? 'No one expects the Spanish Inquisition'? Who *are* the Monty Python boys anyway?"

I shrugged my shoulders. "So, are you going to have the baby?"

She glanced at me, looking a little scared and a little shocked. I fished the sonogram picture out of my bag and handed it to her.

Her eyes lit in a mixture of mortification and excitement.

"Um, yeah, I think I am." She stared at the sonogram. I couldn't even fathom the kind of a decision Marci had been wrestling with. To have her baby, she would have to give up everything she knew. A gentle smile spread over her lips. "No. I *know* I am."

That surprised me. Naturally my next thought was who's the daddy? But I knew better than to ask her that.

Then it hit me. It wasn't Chelsea's stupid question on the bathroom door; it was Marci's. The smeared stall door graffiti— *"Who Are You?"*—was really *"Whose Are You?"*

"So how far along are you?"

"A little over two months." She took a deep breath, and I kind of had the feeling she knew who the father was after all. But to me she said, "I guess I'll have to give up cheerleading." Then: "Chelsea is going to crucify me."

I had no idea what to say to her—she was a BB, after all. Well, a Blond Bitch with dark hair, but still. "I'm sure Chelsea thinks being pregnant is better than being fat, right?"

She caught my sarcastic grin, and laughed. "It's a toss-up." Then: "Prom's gonna totally suck."

My run-in with Marci in the parking lot had put just enough distance between Parker's pills and me to quiet their whispers. And I didn't want to be stuck anymore. I didn't want to be paralyzed in a hospital bed, hoarding my pills so that I could feel the pain that much sharper. Keeping them tucked close to my side for when the pain got to be too much. And then my feet were moving, and I was racing back up the hospital's stairs to Parker's room.

"I knew you'd be back," he said as he pulled out the washcloth full of pills. "Is this what you came for?"

I nodded.

"You know, it's kind of ironic, isn't it? A month ago, I would've done anything to get my hands on drugs like these. And now I have them and can't take them. A month ago you were shooting me death stares for lighting up, and now look at you. Visiting an invalid just to score some meds."

"I didn't come back to share them."

He raised an eyebrow. "You didn't?" His voice mocked me, and I know he'd caught the sparkle in my eye when he'd first shown them to me. "Are you sure about that?"

I directed my focus on the pills, wondering how to convince him to get rid of them. "I came back because I know you can walk."

"Wow. So are you, like, a doctor now?"

"You can walk," I accused again. "I saw you, you know. I saw you walk up to Brian and Curt's car."

He shifted more upright in the bed, as if preparing to watch something interesting play out in front of him. But I guess when you're stuck in a hospital bed, you take your entertainment where you can get it. "Why did you really come here?"

I swallowed. I hardly knew Parker. Was it safe to tell him the truth? But then I looked again at the drugs and realized we shared in something horrible together. Those pills bonded us.

"I needed to know why Kori died. Why I lived. And I think you need to know that too."

He looked away. The sadistic playfulness of a few minutes ago had slunk away. What was left was just a boy in a hospital bed.

"Parker, I don't believe in fate. But I can't help but think there is a reason you didn't die. And if you take those pills, you'll never have the answer."

I waited him out, and he reluctantly turned back to me. "Take them," he said, handing me the washcloth.

I walked into the bathroom and flushed the pills down the toilet. Silencing them.

Do not employ handsome servants.
    —Chinese proverb

twenty-one

No matter how many times I fantasized about it, in reality, watching a BB suffer was so pitiful I could barely watch. But it was also sort of like watching a train wreck, and when Chelsea confiscated food from Marci's lunch tray on Monday, I couldn't look away.

Marci let her do it too. The sad truth is, you just don't stand up to Chelsea Westad unless you're Kori Kitzler. And even then, nothing really changes.

I grabbed an extra muffin, thinking maybe I could somehow slip it to Marci on the sly.

As I approached our round table, I couldn't help but notice Poor Josh sitting in Kori's chair. I scowled at Lexi, knowing if anyone had invited him, it'd been her.

As I set my tray down, Lexi asked, "Isn't that Kori's shirt?"

I tugged at the tight fabric. "Yeah, I guess." All last week she'd been questioning me on my clothing choices. Which more and more were pulled from Kori's boxes.

"Where did you get all her clothes?"

"Kieren brought her stuff by." I left out the part about my asking Mrs. K. for them.

"I don't think I've ever seen you wear burgundy lipstick."

"What's your point, Lexi?" I asked, knowing full well what her point was. After all, she'd never entirely approved of Kori, even though she'd claimed to be friends with her.

"Nothing. No point," she said in a tone that had *I have a point* written all over it.

"Serena, let it go," Cole said. But I couldn't, not from Lexi, who just kept staring at me with those big eyes of hers. I couldn't believe I used to think her anime-looking features were so adorable.

It was a good thing that right before I did something crazy like stomp on Lexi, Anthony came up and asked, "You're not really going to eat this, are you?"

I jabbed a fork at the snot-green lasagna in front of me.

"Want to go out to lunch?" was what he'd said. What I heard was: *"Let's get you out of here."* How could I resist?

Ever since his *"Don't get mugged"* comment last week, I'd kind of been avoiding him. As soon as we got in his car, he called me on it. "I've been trying to catch you, but you always seem to be heading in the other direction."

"Yeah?"

"Yeah."

There wasn't much more to say on the subject. The whole drive to Wendy's in his Xterra I thought about Cole and Lexi and Josh sitting at the round table.

In the restaurant, I picked at my biggie fries. Comfort food, Anthony called it with a tired smile. I gave him a thin one back, but wasn't comforted. Even the Frosty wasn't doing much for me, and I live for those.

I looked across the table at him. His mouth pulled into a sheepish smile as his tongue cleared the ketchup from the corner.

"Let's go out this weekend."

I fidgeted. *A date?*

"Just something simple," he added, reading my apprehension. "A drive in the mountains. You don't even have to talk."

"I'm sorry," I said, realizing that I hadn't said a word since I ordered my food. "I'm just . . ."

He tried to get me to look him in the eye. But the connection scared me. I wasn't ready to get close to him, to let him inside, only to have my heart ripped apart whenever fate decided it was over. His hand dropped over mine. "I know. It's still hard. It can wait."

"No, it's not just that. My mom doesn't let me date." It was kind of an excuse. It was true, though.

"We don't have to call it a date. You can pay," he added with a grin.

A timid laugh rumbled in my chest. "I'll think about it."

I thought about how much I wanted to be with him. I just didn't know how to leap into the unknown.

In the Wendy's parking lot, I reached to open the car door. "Wait," Anthony said, and I turned to him. As he looked in my eyes, he reached out and touched my lips, his fingers stroking their fleshy surface with an oddly intense focus. He was ruining my lipstick, but I couldn't move or say anything. The kindness in his eyes broke my heart.

I watched, confused, as he put his thumb in his mouth, sucked on it for a second and then reached out. "Close your eyes," he whispered. As I did, he pressed the wet pad of his thumb to my eyelid. With extremely gentle strokes he wiped the makeup away.

My heart gripped, and I whispered, "What are you doing, Anthony?"

"I want to kiss you," he said simply. "And I want to know I'm kissing the right girl."

He repeated the process with my other eyelid. When he finished, his arms gathered me up and brought me against him as he pressed his lips to my forehead. "There, now you look like my Serena again."

I looked into his eyes, tears filling behind my lids. My teeth sank into my bottom lip to keep it from shaking. How could he know who his Serena really was, when I didn't even know her?

"Hey, hey," he said, wiping the tears away just as he'd done with my eye makeup. "No tears. Not about me."

He pulled me against him, bringing his lips to mine in a way that wrapped me with everything warm in the world. I'd hoped his fingers could replace Kori's, that his tongue would fill the void inside of me. That for five-point-five seconds I could forget. Forget that Kori was gone. Forget that my mom was never around and my father had never existed. Forget that I was lusting a little bit for my dead best friend's secret boyfriend. Forget about Kori's list and all the things I couldn't do for her.

It didn't make me forget anything.

I found Marci in the new bathroom next to Dick Click's classroom. Her white tennis shoes jerked up to the toilet seat just as I came through the door.

"It's just me."

She sniffed. "Serena?"

"Yeah."

Her feet dropped back down and she opened the door. Her eyes looked swollen and pink around the rims. "You're not going to light up in here, are you? It's bad for the baby."

"Naw. I'll be all right," I said, even though I was having a total nic-fit. "You know, not eating is bad for the baby too."

She nodded, leaned her weight against the wall. Sniffed again. "I eat at home."

"Here, I brought this for you." I fished out the blueberry muffin. "Sorry, it's a little squished."

"Oh, you're amazing!" She ripped the cellophane off and bit into it. A few minutes later, between mouthfuls, she said, "I'm going to tell them. Soon. I told my parents."

"Yeah? How'd that go?"

"Pretty good. Actually, your mom helped me out with that."

"Really? You talked with her?" She must've called Colorado Cares during the non-husband-stealin' hours. "She didn't suggest you tell them it was fate, did she?"

"No, she just said to be straight with them and they'll listen."

I nodded, but since my mother wasn't bothering to listen to me, I wasn't so sure she should be advising people about it.

"I have a feeling telling Chelsea and the squad will be a little more complicated than that."

"Yeah, I'm sure," I said as I turned to the mirror and reapplied Kori's burgundy lipstick. As I put it back into my bag, I pulled out the two apples I had stashed for the horses. "Here. I've got these too."

She brightened as she grabbed them up. "Oh, God, thank you! You're so my new BFF."

Right . . . "I better go."

BFFs? B freaking FFs? Okay, I was officially creeped out. No, not about having a cheerleader BFF, although that was pretty creepy too. But come on—this was eerily similar to my tempting fate list. Cheerleader best friend? Front page of the *Kismet Courier*? And I had Kori's fake ID burning a hole in my pocket.

Even a cynic like me couldn't come up with an easy explanation in the face of all this evidence. Yet, it wasn't my list I was thinking about; it was Kori's.

I don't want to leave anything undone.

I'd spent the rest of the afternoon trying to figure out how to ditch Mom or Mrs. Patterson, not realizing just how easy it was going to be.

Luckily, Mrs. Patterson was pretending to be at Whispering Aspens while her daughter "visited," aka checked up on her. And Mom left a note saying she was at a conference in Denver and wouldn't be home until late. Which left me, once again, all alone.

It was what I wanted, right? So why had the world stopped turning?

I sank down into the couch feeling paralyzed again. How many late nights, double shifts at the hospital, and last-minute conferences had there been? How many had been lies? How many times had my mom chosen to be with this guy over being with me?

If Kori were here, everything would be fine. We'd run away, cross state lines.

The metallic twist of a key in the lock made my heart jump.

"Serena! Come over and meet my daughter," Mrs. Patterson called through the open door.

I got up from the couch and followed her out the door. "You brought your daughter here? But I thought—" I clamped my mouth shut seeing the woman bent over and petting one of Mrs. Patterson's cats. She glanced our way with an awkward smile. I leaned in to whisper, "Weren't you keeping the town house a secret?"

"Oh, it's been fun, but it's time to tell them!" So much for keeping quiet. I'd forgotten how Mrs. Patterson had to shout to hear herself. "I'm not getting any younger, and if anything happens to me, I need to make sure the kittens are taken care of."

Her word choice gripped at my heart.

"Oh, honey, wipe that look off your face, I'm not dying! Not yet. But when I do, there's gonna be things left behind. Things that will need to be taken care of."

"Stop talking like that, Mom," her daughter said. She looked nice enough. For a sixty-year-old woman in metallic cropped cargo pants, that is. "You're not going anywhere anytime soon."

Big talk from the woman who dumped her mother in assisted living fifteen years ago. But whatever.

"We're just getting ready for dinner, want to join us?" Mrs. Patterson offered.

"I have study plans at the library," I said. I hated to lie to her, but one way or another I was going to find a way to finish things for Kori.

I rounded the barn looking for Shay, but he was nowhere to be found, the manure pile he typically cursed, removed.

"Shay!" I screamed, startling a flock of chickens.

I came full circle before I saw him. Well, saw him getting his groove on to his iPod. I tried to hold back from laughing, and snorted instead. Embarrassingly enough, he heard *that* and none of my earlier screaming. Not a stitch of humiliation about my catching him either. In fact, he kept right on dancing.

Unbelievable.

What is it about guys? They have no shame about dancing. They either dance or they don't dance; actual ability never plays a role in the decision.

He pulled the earplugs out. "Hey, you. Didn't hear you come up."

"Not with that thing cranked up." Seeing him dancing had caught me off guard. Laughing had dislodged my focus. "Good music?" I asked.

"Yeah, s'all legit."

I knew I was stalling. I was just scared I wouldn't be able to go through with it. But there was an even greater fear—that if I didn't do it now, I never would and I'd be stuck feeling hollow forever. It was that fear that shoved me from behind, knocking the words out, pushing me over the edge. "So, are you doing anything?"

His eyebrows gave a little hop. "Now?"

"Now." My own brazenness startled me. "Tonight."

"What have you got planned?"

"I want to get a tattoo," sprang to my lips. *If not now—when?* Right?

He grinned, casing my body for good spots to suggest, no doubt. "Something small and tasteful? Hidden where no one will see?"

Kori didn't do anything small, tasteful, or where no one could see. "Probably not."

He laughed and said, "So you need me to take you?"

I nodded, and said, "And after, we're going to dinner."

His eyebrows shot up, more surprised by this than my decision to get inked. "Like . . . a date?"

"Yeah, a date. I'm going to take you to the best pizza place in Colorado, and you're going to pay."

"M'kay." He rubbed his palm over his naked chest, disrupting the pattern of glistening sunlight and derailing my train of thought in one fatal swoop. "Mind if I shower first?"

Visions of waterfalls danced in my head.

"Not at all."

As I climbed into the truck, the smell of Shay's freshly shampooed hair filled my nostrils. Just a tad distracting. I turned my amorous eyes on the road, ensuring that I pointed out the correct turns. It wasn't nearly as riveting as the way his thigh swelled, straining against denim as he cajoled the old truck into shifting gears.

I was quite thankful to spot the exit sign, so I could point and babble and have something to do with my hands. "Here it is." I closed the phone book in my lap. "Just down that way, on the right."

The place looked clean and reputable—your basic strip-mall-type entrance. But as soon as I got out of the car, panic filled me. As Shay held the door open, I walked through it and tentatively asked, "It's not going to hurt, is it?"

Shay raised his eyebrows and bulged his eyes. "What if it does?"

I couldn't manage to smile at his sarcastic playfulness; I was too busy trying to figure a way out of this. "Well, what did yours feel like? A knife carving into you?"

He gave me a serious look. "No. More like a bee stinging me over and over."

"What?" I jerked to a stop. "Oh, no, that sounds . . . No."

"So, what? You're just going to chicken out? It can't be any more painful than that tongue ring."

"Yeah, well, that wasn't exactly pleasant either. But it was quick. This takes a little time, right?"

An amused grunt came out of the tattoo artist—a red-haired

guy who was coated with pumpkin-colored freckles. "Depends on what we're going to do," he said.

I glanced between him and Shay. Neither looked like they would be very understanding if I ran out of there.

"Let's see some ID first," he said, and I showed him the fake.

"Okay," the guy said as he handed it back. "So, what'll it be, Kori?"

I avoided Shay's glare as I slid the fake ID into my back pocket.

"This is what I was thinking of getting. A friend drew it," I said as I passed the guy the Chinese symbols and tribal cuff Kori had sketched in her *Doc Rocks!* notebook.

But when he quoted the price, it was way more than I could afford.

"Do you know what the symbols stand for?" I asked. "I think she said they were Chinese."

"No, they're Hiragana. Japanese. Most people come in with incorrect translations. But, judging from this, she knew what they were and what they meant. It's a quote from a movie."

"*I can't remember to forget you,*" I said.

"Yeah. I thought you didn't know what it meant."

Before I could answer, Shay cut in with, "I'm going for a smoke."

I glanced over and watched him walk out the door. I could tell he understood something about the tattoo. And while I understood what the symbols were, he understood what they meant. To Kori.

"*Memento* was her favorite movie," I said to cover.

Kori had lots of "boyfriends." None of them were a secret. And none of them were very hard for her to forget.

She was a total guy about sex. A slut. I don't think anyone, even Kori, would try to argue against the title. But she never used sex, like some girls at our school did. She never tried to get a guy or keep a guy or steal a guy with it. I think that's why other girls just didn't get her. For them, sex was always tied to something more.

I've done some things with guys. Things to get guys. And more things to keep guys. But the most extreme things I did weren't with guys and weren't about sex at all; they were the dares I did for Kori.

The very first dare—taking the cigarette Kori held out to me in eighth grade—I did to get her friendship. It could be argued that I did all the other dares to keep it. And it could also be argued that I was getting a tattoo for the very same reason.

But I preferred to think about it as filling the void without replacing it.

I picked out a pair of tattered black angel wings from the catalog and waited as the guy began preparing his workstation. He was wearing only a pair of jeans that hung on his very narrow hips with a wide black leather belt. His naked torso revealed a frail rib cage and skin covered in Seurat-like rust-toned tattoos. The dots making up his tatts matched the color of his freckles almost perfectly, so the artwork was thoroughly camouflaged unless you were close up.

An elaborate cross with angels and demons filling all the spaces decorated his back. If I blinked, it went back to being just freckles, like one of those crazy posters at the mall.

"Where do you want it?" he asked.

As furious as I was at my mother, I knew better than to come home with a tattoo on display. I unbuttoned my jeans and rolled down the denim to where the skin turned white.

"Just above the timber line?" he asked, and I nodded, grimacing at his cavalier description. "Lie back on here, then."

Looking very closely, I could make out a tattooed circle around the left side of his chest with a line slanting through his heart.

He caught me staring at it and said, "Just wanted to be up-front about it. You'd think it would scare girls off, but it's kind of a chick magnet." He laughed. Then: "Why do women always want what they can't have?"

I thought about it. Thought about why I was spending so much time with Shay and not with Anthony. Why I'd asked Shay out on a date, and not accepted when Anthony had asked me. Maybe before everything with Kori had happened, I would have answered differently. I would've told him, we always want to be The One that is different. But that wasn't what I felt with Shay. If anything, I wanted to be The One who wasn't different. Deep down I knew I wasn't Kori and that there wasn't any real future in Shay and me. And that was okay. The future was something I still didn't have much of a grip on.

What came out of my mouth was: "Because there's nothing to lose."

"Ah, but also nothing to gain," he said, cocking up one side of his mouth.

"Which begs the question, if you really feel that way, then why do you have a no-admittance policy on your heart?"

"I find it hurts everyone less this way."

"Is she still worried about getting hurt?" Shay asked, coming back inside. He had no idea what conversation he'd just walked in on or how appropriate his comment was.

Tattoo boy did, though, and grinned. "They always are."

I sucked in a breath feeling Shay's fingers link with mine. "You'll be fine."

I glanced up at him, but his eyes stayed trained on the guy's prep job. I was glad I couldn't really see what was going on. And

I was even more relieved that Shay was there with me and had a good solid grip.

After a few minutes Shay looked back at me. "How you doing?"

"I just wish he'd start with the painful stuff." So far I'd only felt the artist draw on the outline.

Shay smirked. "He has."

I let myself relax. "It doesn't hurt at—" I felt something like a cigarette burning me. "Shit."

"Oh, nope, you were right." He grinned down at me. "*Now* he's starting."

"That wasn't funny," I growled. And then it burned me again. "Shit!" And again. "Ow!" And then it got less intense.

"It's better if you're not all stiff and anticipating it," he said by way of apology. I noticed the shared grin between him and Pumpkin Boy and knew they were messing with me.

I kept hold of Shay's hand, not because it was too terribly painful, but because I wanted to stay connected to him.

Kori used to worry about floating away when she was high. Now I understood. She was worried that she was losing herself. And I started to wonder if I was doing the same thing by trying to fulfill someone else's last wishes.

twenty-two

Shay's gaze took in the exposed metal ductwork hanging from the high ceiling. The building looked more like a gutted mineshaft than a restaurant. As he held the chair out for me, his chin dropped and he gave me a mischievous smile. "So, this is the best pizza, huh?" he asked under his breath.

I looked around the restaurant. Despite the decor, it was packed with locals and tourists alike. "Yep. You order it by the pound."

I ordered for us, whisking through the seemingly complicated process of picking out dough, sauce, toppings, and of course weight.

"So this is a date, huh? I thought guys were supposed to ask girls out on those . . . do the ordering."

"It's a brave new world, Shay Miller. Welcome to it!"

His lips curved in a delicious grin. "I like it."

"You're still paying."

"Yeah, you mentioned that already. Is that why we're calling this a date? Because I'm paying?"

"No, we're calling this a date because I'm pissed at my mother."

He nodded. "Oh, well, that makes so much more sense."

"Yeah. See, she doesn't allow me to date, but I found out she's been leading this double life."

He choked. "Double life?"

"Yeah. She's been disappearing late at night. No telling where she goes. Some HoJo for hos or some other hypocritical bullshit place. The guy's married." I caught Shay's uncomfortable shift. "Sorry. I know, I'm ranting."

"No, no. Sounds bad."

When the pizza arrived, he dug in, obviously thankful for the diversion.

Several minutes later, he asked, "You know what pizza crust is made of, don't you?" I glanced up and caught his raised eyebrows. Then he ripped his teeth through an example.

I eyed him warily.

"Flour," he said, clamping his lips closed on a wide, very evil smile as he resumed chewing.

I crinkled my nose up at him before moving my messenger bag from the seat nearest him to between my boots.

"You're supposed to put honey on your crusts. Like this." I took the bear-shaped bottle and squeezed a squiggle of the golden goo across the soft twist of dough. "Mmm, good," I murmured to be extra-convincing. Shay watched as I pulled the lingering honey on my lips back into my mouth with the tip of my tongue.

I smacked my lips and smiled. "Your turn."

"Huh? Oh, yeah, right, the pizza crusts," he said, and busied himself with the process.

"Now tell me, is that not the best thing you've ever tasted?"

He glanced up, his eyes catching again on my mouth. "So far," he said under his breath. As his teeth scraped the remainder of honey from his lip, my stomach fluttered.

. . .

The air was cool with night as we emerged. If he'd worn a jacket, I would've borrowed it. Instead I rubbed my arms. He came up behind me and took over, briskly churning heat as he whisked his warm palms over me. Oh, so much better than a borrowed coat!

"So, home?" he asked, setting his jaw.

Kiss for the sake of kissing," Kori had told me. Why make it more than it is. And that's what I'd decided I needed to do with Shay. I wasn't going to worry about all those things niggling at my conscience. I just wanted to kiss him.

"Nope, one more stop. The quintessential date place."

One eyebrow curved up. "Just to get your mom back?"

"Of course."

He held the door open for me. "Okay, just so I know I'm being used here."

"Yeah, best keep that in mind, cowboy," I said with a wink.

We were quiet in the truck, until I pointed out the turn and he read the sign. "Landfill? Are you sure about this?"

During the summer, the dump was Kismet's notorious make-out place. "Yeah. Hopefully, it's not too late in the year."

"For trash?"

Just as he said the words, the truck bounced over the potholes of the last bend in the road. The dump appeared in front of us and the reason we were there became obvious.

Two rotund black bears were fighting over what appeared to be a container of Kraft Macaroni & Cheese.

"For bears."

My heart hammered in anticipation of our first kiss. It was like standing on the ledge of the dam again. But I wasn't exactly buzzing. With Shay, sometimes it felt like we were two bolts of tangled lightning. I waited for him to make his move. But he was sitting quietly, entranced by the comical antics of a chubby cub.

"He's cute, isn't he," I said. Then I got up the courage to turn to him and ask, "Remember how you told me you thought your being here was fate?"

"Yeah."

"Do you really believe that? I mean, in fate?"

"Yeah. Don't you?"

I shook my head.

"Why not?"

"Besides the fact that Destiny is my mother's name and that I live in a town named Kismet and every time I turn around someone is shoving it down my throat or copping out by using it as some lame excuse?"

"Yeah, that's not good enough. What's your real reason?"

"The real reason? Okay. The real reason is, if I believe in fate, then I have to accept that, well . . . that it was part of someone's great design that I lost my father, lost my grandparents all before I was old enough to even know what they looked like. Now I have to add my best friend to the list. And, oh yeah, my mom's having some sordid affair and lying to me. I want to believe there's more to life than just what I see. But how can I believe, how can I embrace something, someone who thinks that this is what's best for me? How can something I'm supposed to trust implicitly, to have faith in, treat me like this?"

His silence made me grimace. I'd said too much.

After a few moments, he said, "I guess you've just got to trust."

His words took me back to the dam, the last time I'd been there with Kori.

"You're scared to do. You're scared to be. You're scared to live. You're always scared, so you must like it, and you love the cozy, safe feeling of escaping reality even more."

"And doing a cartwheel on the dam will prove what?"

"It will prove you trust."

At the time I thought she meant it would prove I trusted her, but maybe she meant trusting fate.

If she only knew the crappy deal fate had dealt her, how short her time was, she wouldn't have said that, or maybe she would've just been thankful she'd never held back.

I thought about Kori's list. Maybe she did hold some things back. But somehow, that list had ended up in my hands. And somehow, I'd ended up here. When Shay's eyes met with mine, I smiled. "Yeah, maybe I will."

He leaned over, giving me an awkward half smile as he tucked a wayward strand of hair behind my ear. And even though I trembled at the small touch and moistened my lips, he only grimaced, blinked one extra blink, and returned to the entertainment of the bears.

He didn't kiss me.

He whipped the car in gear and took me home.

Who went to the landfill to actually watch the bears? It was a ploy . . . a gimmick . . . a grunion run, for crissakes.

I should've taken Shay to the dam to watch the submarine races. No guy would be thick enough to believe we were going there for that. He wouldn't have spent the evening laughing at the cub's awkward attempts at getting his snout into a soup can, because his teeth would've be nipping at my lower lip, my tongue would've be tracing his. But instead, I found myself thanking him for the pizza and giving him a clumsy smile as I let myself out.

As I slid across the seat, Shay reached over to stop me. "Wait."

My shoulder settled into the cup of his palm as I turned back toward him. Electric heat charged through me.

I sat back, my nerves charging. "Okay."

I took a deep breath and so did he.

"Right." He shifted uncomfortably, then turned toward me, facing me.

That wonderfully addictive buzzing of fear started raging inside of me. I nodded and gave him a little smile. "Yeah?"

"Okay."

I wet my lips. "Okay."

A small muscle in his jaw flexed. My heart fluttered. I wet my lips again. He pressed his together.

Then he looked away.

"The tattoo. I know what it meant."

It took me a minute to even comprehend his words.

When he looked at me, his eyes were creepily clear and unmoving. "I'm the person Kori wanted to forget but couldn't."

I turned to look out the windshield. Anywhere but in his eyes. Looking at them was like looking through a clear but impenetrable wall. It had been erected so fast, I felt sucker punched by its presence.

Not only did I feel deceived, naive, and ignorant of the depth of their relationship, I also felt angry. There had to be a good reason for Kori to not want to see, hell—remember, a person ever again. Clearly he had some kind of mysterious hold over her. And I wanted to know what it was.

"The motel in Golden." I couldn't keep the accusation out of my voice. My words were sharpened by pain. "Why did she want to meet you there?"

"Why do you think?" he returned with a tight upturn of his lips. It was not a smile.

I was pretty sure he was trying to intimidate me. But I didn't feel intimidated. What I felt was hurt. Pushed away.

twenty-three

I'd been pulling Kori's fake ID out and looking at it all week, knowing the clock was ticking down to decision time. On Thursday, the day she would've been using it to get into the club in LoDo, to sing with Bleeder Valve, I was still undecided.

I fidgeted through the lunch line. Ahead of me, Chelsea was again systematically removing everything from Marci's tray. I'd spent most of the week thinking about Marci and her decision to keep her baby despite everything. How she still needed to tell her teachers, her friends. And here all I was scared of was making a fool out of myself by singing in front of some strangers. I don't know if I just needed a break from my own problems, or if after all the tattoo-getting I'd become more like Kori than I was before. But I was just so freaking sick of Chelsea Westad and her bullshit.

I moved out of the line and set my full tray on top of Marci's now empty one.

"What the hell, Serena?" Chelsea screeched.

I ignored her. "Marci, eat whatever you want."

"Trust me, Marci, this is for your own good," Chelsea said as she started removing my items. "Fat is so not fabulous."

Tell her off, I could hear Kori saying.

"Leave her alone, Chelsea."

Chelsea spun on her Prada sport boot. "I'm sorry, are *you* talking to *me*?"

A hush filled the lunchroom with the speed of a tsunami wave making landfall. It was one thing for someone like me to steal a round table from the drill-me team, but to actually stand up to Chelsea Westad—mayor's daughter, head cheerleader, and all-around golden girl—it just didn't happen.

"She's not going to get fat."

"Look it, Serena!" She looked me up and down in challenge. "I think I know more about what it takes to stay healthy and beautiful than you."

I narrowed my eyes at her, and when I opened my mouth it was as if Kori had possessed me. "The only reason you're not fat is because you pop uppers like they're Tic Tacs and take so many laxatives you crap yourself when you sneeze."

Chelsea turned as red as the one remaining apple on my old tray as the lunchroom erupted in laughter. Her claws dug into it. Then, without warning, she pulled back and chucked it right at my face.

At the last second, I caught it. "That the best you got?"

But Chelsea wasn't dealing with me anymore; she'd turned her fury on Marci. "Don't even think of eating at our table! You can eat at the rectangles with all the other fat losers."

With a swing of her blond hair, Chelsea wheeled around and headed for the safety of her people.

"Sorry, Marci," I said, putting the food back on my tray.

She looked a little shell-shocked as she said, "It would've happened eventually."

I could see the worry seeping into her. Everything at school would be different, even things like being able to sit at the BBs' table. "Eat at our table; it's round. At least she won't get the satisfaction."

At our table no one said a word. Josh was back at his rectangular table, on Lexi's orders. Apparently I'd just screwed up the heart-to-heart they'd planned for me. *Oops.*

It waited until after lunch. As Cole and I headed toward Doc's class, she said, "You need to see something." One look at her face and I knew it was bad. "I don't want you to be alone when you do."

"Okay," I said, feeling a funny flutter in my gut as I trailed behind her, watching her golden highlights swing with the quick pace.

"Wait for me," Lexi called.

I glanced back and noticed Josh right behind her. God, I knew going to his house had sent the wrong message. Ever since I'd "called on him," he'd been trailing me with starry eyes and hope-filled smiles. Sitting at our round table all week long.

"I don't believe it," I muttered, and Cole turned to look.

"I'll tell you later," she whispered as she took my hand. I looked back at her, confused. What could *she* possibly have to tell *me*—about *my* crushy stalker boy—later? And that's when I saw Josh's sweaty palm on Lexi's back. It was so quick I convinced myself I'd imagined it.

Cole pulled me through the hall toward the entry of the new auditorium. As we rounded the corner, I lurched to a stop, anchoring my feet and yanking Cole to a halt. Right in front of me was Kori.

A sculptured clay bust of Korianne was more accurate. She looked exactly like the girl in the casket and nothing like the girl I remembered. I swallowed, shrugged off Cole's clasping fingers.

Alone, I approached the statue, creeping up on it as if it might start talking to me, which could very well happen, given the fragility of my sanity. "Please tell me I'm not seeing what I'm seeing."

Lexi shuddered and Josh—Josh!—put his arms around her.

"The Kitzlers are dedicating the new auditorium to her memory," Cole said from behind me. "Regina told me Mrs. Kitzler had an artist do a mold of Kori's face right before they did her makeup for the funeral."

I stepped closer, examining the oddly familiar and yet still so foreign eyes of the statue. They had the blank stare I expected from a girl who looked like that. Those damn dead eyes immortalized. Seeing them caused everything inside of me to shatter, falling in on itself like the frozen reservoir does at the start of the spring thaw.

Lexi begged me to breathe. Cole stroked my hair.

I told myself it was just a statue. It wasn't even anyone I remembered or knew. It was *Twilight Zone* humor at its finest and cruelest, and I wasn't about to stand and stare at it, give it credibility.

I dropped into my seat next to Cole's. I didn't really want to ask about Lexi and Poor Josh, but I was desperate to distract myself from what I'd just seen.

"So what's the story with Lex and Josh, anyways? When did that happen?"

"God, Ser, it's about time you noticed."

"I noticed," I snapped. How could I have missed it? Poor Josh got an RL girl. How could anyone not notice? Lexi and Josh. Josh and Lexi. I don't know why it bothered me—it wasn't like I wanted to date Josh or anything, but still.

"You know, Lexi's been so excited about him and you didn't

even acknowledge him at our table. Haven't you noticed Lexi smiling all of a sudden?"

"Sorry, geez, he's always been . . . Well, whatever, it's just weird. What was I supposed to do?"

"I don't know, Ser, maybe be happy for her?"

"I am happy for her. I just didn't know she liked him." He was *my* crushy stalker boy, after all. "I mean, I just find it odd that she's, like, going after a guy so soon after Kori." That meek and mild, scared-of-boys Lexi was getting on with her life before me. And here I could barely bring myself to talk to Anthony and had basically been lusting after the one guy I couldn't have—my best friend's "need to work things out with" guy.

"Did you ever think that maybe that's exactly why she is? You know, Kori's death hit her hard too. She's going through this whole I-can't-waste-one-second-of-precious-life thing right now."

I should know that. That's what Cole was really saying. But I wasn't ready to think about how Kori's death was affecting them. I just couldn't add any more guilt on top of what I already felt.

And even if I could, I wouldn't know where to begin. The list of secrets I was keeping from them was out of control. I hadn't told them about Shay or my tattoo; about Mom's crazed outburst over "The Mini Mart Mugging," her sordid affair, or my botched attempt at setting her up with Doc Ramsey; I hadn't told them about how I'd visited Parker, or the latest gossip on Marci.

Problem was I was heaping secret upon secret. And it was going to take way too many postcards to be free of them all.

Cole wasn't kidding about Lexi's new take-life-by-the-horns attitude. But Lexi might as well have been waving a red flag in the face of a bull as she confronted me at my locker after school.

"Okay, Serena. Tonight. We are going out like we used to."

The tacit understanding being it was time for me to start acting like a normal friend. Thing was, that was exactly what I had planned, just not with them.

Ever since I'd seen the statue of Kori, I knew what I had to do. Kori'd always wanted to be immortalized. But not their way. Not frozen in hardness, in wavy hair and apple cheeks and pearls and everything she wasn't. She wanted to be immortalized with her music.

The statue was a crock. Kori's family didn't really give a crap about her, not before she died and certainly not after. I knew that more than anybody outside of her family.

When you're best friends with someone, sometimes you see a private moment meant for family, a vulnerable moment too intimate to be shared with outsiders, and there you are like a fly on the wall wishing someone would smack you with a rolled-up newspaper.

The first time, Kori and I had only been friends for a month. We'd snuck down to the hot tub during some important business dinner her father was having. It wasn't like we were interrupting their party or anything, but through the dining room windows some of the guests could sort of see us.

All of a sudden, in the middle of dessert, Kori stood up and flashed them, *Girls Gone Wild* style. And that's when all hell broke loose.

Kori's brother Kyle, who had just started college and was working for their dad, came rushing over. He dragged Kori out and started shouting. If you ask me, he made a much bigger scene than she had, with all of his, "What the fuck are you trying to pull? Don't you understand how important this dinner is?"

"Oh, I know exactly how important it is," she said, tight-jawed.

Kyle was in her face, livid. "You have no respect for Dad's business. Hell, you have no respect for your own goddamn body."

"Fuck you. You really think Dad gives a damn about me or my body? Why should I?"

Kyle looked her up and down like he might spit on her. "Why do you have to be so fucking insane all the time? Always trying to one-up yourself. You think you're cool? You're a fucking embarrassment."

It stung. Not just his words, which were as harsh as any I'd ever heard one person speak to another, but because he'd said them in front of me. It was as close to getting a "truth" out of Kori as I ever came, but it was one she'd never intended to share. It was a violation.

Just like the memorial statue was.

"Sorry, Lex," I said as I shoved my books in. "I've got plans."

If the simple act of wearing Kori's makeup got Lexi all bent, I wondered what she'd think of my singing with Bleeder Valve.

"No, Ser," Cole said, trapping me on the other side. "No more hiding in your room, avoiding our calls."

"We're going for pizza and to the movies. I know it doesn't sound like much, but we'll have fun, lots of fun. Promise." Lexi's eyes were pleading, trying to pull something out of me, but I wasn't sure what.

Cole had a wide smile plastered on, too many teeth showing. "Doesn't that sound fun?"

Lexi's head bobbed along, nodding in my direction. *Yes, Serena, come with us!* She spoke in big bubbly words. "You love pizza!"

My questioning gaze bounced between them. What the hell was going on? Did someone put magic mushrooms in the lunch? And did Cole and Lex eat them or did I?

"Ser, listen to us." Cole spoke calmly and evenly, squeezed

my elbow to get my full attention. "It's time. Time to do the things we used to do."

"It's a school night. Mom's been up my ass ever since the Mini Mart Mugger thing. We can go this weekend, maybe," I said.

Lexi brightened. "It's okay. I'm sure your mom won't mind. I'll call her. I'll ask."

It bothered me to hear Lexi suggesting she could ask my mother, but there was something else about their behavior that concerned me. Their voices sounded perky, their eyes encouraging, their words insisting I go to the movies. On a school night? This screamed of Mom. All week she'd been prodding me to take their calls, to talk to them. Which really meant talk about Kori's death.

I knew what this was . . . This was an intervention!

I gritted my teeth. But before I unleashed, I realized they'd just given me the opportunity to kill two birds with one stone. Get out of this movie-intervention and have an alibi so I could go down to LoDo with Kori's fake ID and finish what she'd started.

But I couldn't tell them that. They were walking on eggshells around me as it was and this would definitely qualify as padded helmet behavior.

"Actually, I can't. The real reason is I have a date." I shut my locker door. "With Anthony. And Mom doesn't know, so I need you guys to cover for me, okay?" I looked directly at Lexi and asked, "I can count on you, right?"

"Yeah, sure, of course," Cole assured me.

I looked at Lexi and she gave a tiny nod. The way I see it, they forced me to lie to them. And Lexi owed me. Big.

twenty-four

K orianne," the Duke Nukem clone bouncer exaggerated sarcastically. With one eye pinched for greater scrutiny, he glanced at the ID and then at me. I feigned what I hoped would pass for Kori's sleepy-eyed sexpot look. "Kori-anne? Korean? Kory-en?"

I scowled, mimicking her, as if it would make a difference. "Corian is a countertop. Everyone calls me Kori."

"What's your address?"

"Nineteen oh one Aspen Run," I spouted back.

"Your eyes aren't brown," he said.

My heart thumped hard. "The DMV guy screwed up. I wrote *b-l-u* not *b-r-n*. I think he was on something."

The bouncer looked at me. For a moment I knew it was over and wasn't sure what to do. Grovel? Run? He shook his head, disgusted. Apologize? Then he said, "I *know* the DMV guy I had was on something. Do I look like I'm three twenty-five?"

I gulped. He looked 500 pounds to me. "Um, no?"

"I'm three oh five. I put down a zero, not a two. A zero."

"I would've guessed two seventy-five," I said earnestly.

"You think?"

"Two eighty, tops."

"Thanks. You're all right." But then he dropped his smile and returned to scrutinizing my license.

And so we went line by line, and I laughed even though I was nervous as all hell. I mean, I'd never had trouble convincing men I was older before, and now trunk-neck was playing twenty questions with a real ID. Okay, so I was usually only going for eighteen, and, yeah, the ID belonged to a dead girl . . . who had obtained it questionably from an even more questionable DMV employee. Wait. Did he have the DMV chatting with him through that high-tech little ear device?

"Go ahead," he muttered, handing the card back.

He nodded Shay through without so much as a glance at his ID. How annoying is that?

"Your brother's inside, by the way," the bouncer said as Shay held the door open for me.

Kori's brother?

I whirled back and got tangled in Shay's outstretched arm. My nose went straight into his pit, and it smelled pretty damn good, if you want to know the truth. All Tide and Downy goodness.

"Kieren's here?" I asked the bouncer, praying it wasn't Kyle.

"I guess it is you. Thought it was a fake. You look too damn young. Wait, I know, Kori's your older sister? Right?"

"Kieren's inside? Here? In LoDo?"

"Yep, same last name, same address. He's been here a while. If that was your older sister's ID, you better watch out," he said with a wink.

Shay dropped his hand to my shoulder and turned me around, propelling me inside before the guy changed his mind.

"I'll get us some drinks, find a table?"

I nodded at Shay, but went off looking for Kieren instead.

Something told me he wouldn't be in very good shape. I searched the dark crowd, but he ended up being the one who found me.

"Serena? That you?" Kieren's words didn't slur, but his eyes might as well have been swimming in amber and froth.

"Kieren. Hey."

He plopped onto a barstool and fisted some mixed nuts into his mouth all casual-like. "So, what are you doing down here, anyway?"

I swallowed, figured I should just come clean. "Singing." Quickly I reverted to lying. "Yeah, the band called. Without Kori, they needed someone." Lying was much better. No sense alerting him to my Kori obsession. "Yeah. So, they called me."

"Really?" Kieren nodded, then finished off his drink while simultaneously motioning for the waitress to bring another. "Well, I guess they needed a female voice for the audition. Some producer's here trying to hook 'em up with a front girl or something. Wants to hear them before getting her involved. She's some reality show diva. Who knows."

"Yeah, who knows. Well, that's pretty much what they told me too," I fudged.

I'd thought Kieren looked pretty good, a little drunk, but handling the situation well, and then his face crumbled. His voice went up in pitch as he told me, "You're a good friend, ya know that?"

He pulled me into a sloppy, overly dramatic hug. I didn't fight it.

"Kori loved you. And you probably don't know this, but you saved her," he said into my ear.

I jerked out of his embrace. "I didn't save her, Kieren. I didn't."

He took hold of my wrist and tried to look me in the eyes, but he was starting to have trouble focusing. "Listen, you did. She was in bad shape. Before she met you. She met you and everything changed." His words were slurring into one another, making it hard to hear over the music and the noise of the crowded bar.

I leaned in closer, barely catching his last words. "She told me you were her protection. You protected her. Tha's what she said."

He patted my arm. Hard. Then he was heading toward the restrooms, and I stood there a little stunned.

"There you are," Shay said from behind me. "Who was that drunk guy?"

"Hey. Um, that was Kori's brother. I better get backstage and let the band know I'm here."

The black walls at the back of the club were plastered with the band's flyers. "Bleeder Valve? That's the band?" Shay pulled one off and looked closer at it. "Are those metal spikes pierced to the drummer's skull?

"They really called you?" Shay paused to give me a once over. I was dressed in Kori's clothes, but there are just some things you can't fake. "To sing with them?"

He so wasn't helping my nerves.

"Um, maybe it's better for me to talk to them alone. I'll be right back." No need for him to see me grovel.

I found the band easily—just followed Mary Jane's perfume; and while they welcomed my groupie-like approach of crashing their dressing room with my shirt unbuttoned, they weren't exactly welcoming of my plan to sing with them.

"Where've you been? When you missed all the rehearsals, we sort of wrote you off." The lead guitarist—Marc, I think—stroked his black goatee into a devilish point. It didn't dissuade me.

"Yeah, I know. Look, here's the thing, I'm not Kori."

"You're not Kori?"

One of the guitarists looked up from where he'd been half-asleep on the couch. "Whoa man, that must be some wicked shit I took."

"Kori died a few weeks ago. We were best friends. This meant a lot to her. I just, I don't know . . . I want to finish this. For her."

It came out so much easier with strangers, and it felt good to say it aloud. Share it with someone, even if it was Bleeder Valve.

"Can you fucking sing?" This came from the other guitarist, the pudgy one. Kohl eyeliner circled his eyes by a good inch, more drooping down and contrasting with the polar-white skin of his round face, making him look sort of panda-ish and sad. The plug piercings wedged in his lobes looked more like something the zoo had tagged him with to track his movements than jewelry.

"Well . . . never in front of anyone, you know, in the shower and stuff, but yeah I think I sing okay."

"Fuck that then," Marc said, even though he looked like he might suggest a shower audition.

Ling-Ling Panda-boy all of a sudden developed a major case of fleas and rubbed his face with both hands—for a moment all I could see were his full-sleeve tattoos. Impressively, he didn't smear his eye makeup.

"Dude, just let her sing. It's one song. What the hell, right?" Ah, my sole supporter, the drummer, Derek, whose face looked like a giant magnet that had been run between a seamstress's couch cushions. No one ever needed to ask if he had a safety pin.

"This isn't fucking *American Idol*; you know who's here. Hell, that's the only reason we agreed to Kori coming in the first place."

"So what? He'll still hear all our shit, what's one song? We'll squeeze her in when he goes for a piss or something."

Panda-boy started acting very panda-noid—pacing and shaking his pawlike hands in jerky, random convulsions. "Look, I'm not making the decision. I'm not going down like that. If she does this, it's on everyone."

"Just let her sing, man, her friend died."

"Yeah, what the fuck, dude." Marc slicked back his black hair with ring-covered fingers. He had that whole Dave Navarro thing going on. I bet Kori crushed hard on him.

"Fuck. Fine. Fuck," Panda-man growled, welcoming me into their band.

Marc nodded to me, and I mouthed a thank you. "S'all good. You've got spooky cool eyes, you know? Blue with black hair, that's damn sexy."

"Thanks," I mumbled, making a hasty retreat to wait with Shay.

From the back of the stage, the crowd mashing in the pit looked hostile. One level higher, a few people mingled at tables, but most leaned on railings.

I easily picked the producer out of the crowd. He had a table all to himself and filled it just fine. No suit or tie, but he had an all-business look about him. No, not intimidating or anything. I made a silent prayer of thanks that he would be taking a piss while I sang. *While I sang?* I barely knew the song she'd prepared, barely knew how to hold a mike. People would be watching. These people. *All* of these restless, drunk people. What was I thinking, anyway? I can't sing.

An image of Kori flashed in my head. She winked one heavily shadowed lid at me. *"Picture them naked. That's what I like to do."*

And I did my best to do that, I really did. But . . . then I turned around and looked at Shay, who was sitting on the stage behind the speakers.

"Oh, shit."

"What?" Shay asked. "Gotta go pee?"

"No. But thanks, I probably will now. No. I can't do this. I . . . I can't do anything right. I'm trying to picture the audience naked, but I keep picturing myself naked."

Shay's eyes shot up. His gaze locked on something in the crowd behind me. "Shit is right."

"What? What now?" I craned my head around, expecting to see Denver's finest parting the crowd looking for underage drinkers. Thank God I didn't have an alcoholic drink on me—Shay had only bought us Cokes. The judge would have to take that into account, wouldn't he?

But I didn't see anyone. "Shit is right *what*, Shay?"

"Now *I'm* picturing you naked."

twenty-five

When the man at the solo table got up and headed with his cell phone to his ear for the door, Marc gave me the nod.

Time was of the essence, so I rushed to the stage. "So, um . . . Kori was going to sing Alicia Keys's 'Fallin,' right?"

"Right. Start out trad but build lots of anger into it. Whenever you're ready."

"Right. Are you going to, like, introduce me—no? Okay."

I strangled the microphone stand with sweaty hands. The naked audience and a way too pleased Shay stared back at me. I closed my eyes. The guys started in, but I had no idea when to start singing.

They repeated the initial rift twice before I managed to stumble in. My throat clenched tight against the words, speaking them poorly, rather than singing them traditional or angry or any other way. Every word sounded like it had to hack through my tongue in order to escape my mouth. My throat closed. I couldn't continue; it was literally too painful to try.

My eyes popped opened and I saw a guy in a Hollister tee; the collar was frayed and separating from the shirt. His eyes were dark, but I could see them as if I were right next to him, as if I were letting him in. I looked quickly somewhere else, but again I found myself looking at some girl I didn't know. Her head cocked angularly to the side and her elbow bent holding up her palm, like a waiter with a tray, as she huffed. Again I averted my eyes, my gaze landing on an overweight guy with a shaved head. He shot a blast of cigarette smoke out the side of his mouth— *Come on, princess,* he was thinking. I scanned the crowd, my focus acute on each and every person.

How could I let all these angry people in?

"What's the matter, kitten? Scared?"

I'd closed my eyes, thinking how many times Kori'd said it to me. How many times she pushed me to do just one more thing.

"I'm sorry. Sorry," I croaked. I dropped my grasp on the mike stand, wheeling out of the spotlight. The edge of the stage was mere inches away when Marc caught my arm.

"Hey, don't," he said in my ear. "That's a really tough song, just try something else."

"But that's what she was going to sing."

"So? We can play something else. Just name something."

I didn't want to sing, I wanted to crawl beneath the seats in Mr. Miller's truck and have Shay drive as fast as he could away from there.

"So what's it going to be?"

Marc wasn't asking me if I was going to be able to sing, to which my response would have been no. He was asking me what song I wanted to sing.

Ling-Ling sneered at me, but it was Kori's words I heard. *"'Fraidy cat, are you useless or what?"*

And I wanted to prove she was wrong, prove I wasn't the doormat or wuss-girl she'd always accused me of being. That I could be just as fearless as she was. That we were more alike than *she* thought.

"We need a song," Ling-Ling growled.

Right then, only one song came to mind, the one that had rocked me through my grief. "Pearl Jam? 'Black'?"

"Not exactly easy," Marc said. "But, fuck, whatever. Got it? Guys?"

I walked back to the mike and took it out of the stand. I needed to get out of the spotlight; I needed to be alone. Channeling Eddie Vedder and picturing Kori, I sank to the floor at Marc's feet and pulled my knees into my chest. My voice trembled as I started, but soon it found its pace and settled in deep and tight.

Even when Marc rocked out the guitar inches above my head. Even when I glimpsed the mashing horde as they pulsed up, up, up. Nothing but the scream of the song registered in my heart.

As I pushed the last sound from my throat, I understood why Kori had to do this. It was a freaking rush! Looking at the crowd, I realized they were cheering. For me. Me! The intense connection that had terrified me was still there; it hadn't broken. Only now there weren't any hostile eyes challenging me. I'd changed them all. And something more. When I looked closer, I realized I'd made them feel what I was feeling. I'd shared something I'd been unable to put into my own words. And they'd actually listened.

I'd never felt so understood in all my life. No wonder Kori sang for people any chance she got. It was because they truly heard her.

"That was amazing!" I screamed at the night as another rogue wave of ecstasy overtook me.

Even an hour later, the calm of the parking lot and fresh air did nothing to quell my post-performance high. Neither did the dead-drunk body of Kieren tossed over Shay's shoulder. He was adamant about making sure Kieren got home safe, but when he unceremoniously dumped him into the truck bed, I started to doubt his compassion.

"No offense or anything," Shay said, "but you can't sing."

"You are so missing the point. But since you brought it up—people clapped. You don't see any rotten tomato stains, do you?" I twirled my body around, twisting on the gravel, showing him all of it. Probably a mistake. His eyes licked over me like he was picturing me naked again, this time covered in delicious tomato sauce.

He made an awkward grab for the door handle, his fingers slipping once before he managed to open it.

"I didn't say it was awful," he continued as he got behind the wheel. "Besides, they were clapping for you, not for your singing."

"I don't think it was *that* bad. The band said I did really well." Marc's actual words might've been, *"Ya know, it's fucking hot hearing a girl sing about another girl,"* but I was so not telling Shay that! "They took my name and number and everything."

He grunted and shot me a knowing look, probably already aware of what Marc really wanted it for.

I squished my face at him. "Can't let me just enjoy it, can you? It's not the most feminine of songs, you know."

"Just saying, if this was like some dream of yours or something, I really think you should reconsider."

I realized he had no idea why we were there, so of course he assumed this was about me.

"It's not my dream. It is . . . was Kori's. She was really amped about it and I just wanted to do it for her. Sounds stupid, huh?"

He hesitated, taking me in with a long look before starting the car and turning his attention to the road. "No, not stupid."

When we were back on I-70, I settled deeper into my seat. "I wasn't that bad. Was I?"

"It wasn't great."

"Have you heard the song before?" I said with a playful grimace.

"I haven't heard it, no."

"Oh, well here." I rooted out my iPod and cued up the song. As I leaned across the center console my arm brushed the hard planes of his chest; my fingertips grazing his jaw, his ear, his hair as I put the earphones on him. I couldn't help but notice his eyes fighting to stay focused on the road; I had to pry mine away and remind myself to pull in some air.

After a few minutes, he took the earphones out. "You did really well. Your version even had a certain . . . quality. Sorry."

"Apology accepted, jerk. So, what kind of music *do* you listen to?"

The noises he sputtered out in an attempt to sing made me laugh so hard I almost peed a little. I could barely make out the lyrics through his pathetic screeching howls.

"Okay, that wasn't singing. You sounded like you were skinning a cat. The really mean way. Did you do that at your niece's party? 'Cuz that's not right, dude."

"What? It was good." He looked way too proud of his Eminem rendition.

"You honestly think you can sing better than me?"

He nodded.

"You're delusional. Cute, but delusional."

We were quiet again. I kept thinking about how scared I'd been up on the stage with all those people just staring at me, like *who the hell are you?* For the crowd at the bar—I was nobody. And it scared the shit out of me. But then something had changed; I knew Kori wouldn't have given a crap if they thought she was a hack, because the only person she ever answered to was herself. And then it didn't matter to me if I was a horrible singer, because that wasn't the point.

The point was I fought through my fear and I did it. I was unable to suppress another grin. *I did it.*

As we left the city, I saw the exit sign for Golden. The last place Kori went. Reality hit me hard.

I thought again about what Kori had been doing with Shay in the first place. Why did he think she'd want to forget him? Was he some drug dealer, like Brittney had proposed? Did he get Kori pregnant? No, that was impossible, and I didn't want to think about that . . . No matter how things might've started, what I was feeling for him now had very little to do with Kori. I didn't really even want to think about who he was to her, because part of me wanted him all for myself.

"Shay?"

When he didn't respond, I looked over at him; he was deep in thought. "Earth to Shay, wake up, Shay." I laughed, poking a finger in his ribs. He jolted, swerving the truck. A thunk sounded as Kieren's body rolled hard into the truck bed's wall.

"Where'd you just go?"

"Sorry, nowhere. Just thinking. So what else did Kori have planned?"

I thought about Kori's list. *Work things out with Shay.* For all I knew, that's what they did in the motel room in Golden. But since Shay seemed to think Kori's tattoo referred to him, that she'd want to forget him, I wondered if they'd ever really worked those things, whatever they were, out.

"Don't you think getting up in front of all those people and singing was enough?"

A few moments passed before he said, "You did pretty good."

"You said I sucked."

"I said you shouldn't strive for a career in it. For what it's worth, it's not everyone's fate to be a famous singer. More people need to realize that."

"Yeah, well, what purpose in life would Simon Cowell have, then?"

He grinned. "What purpose, indeed." He cleared his throat. Then: "You miss her more than you let on, don't you?"

"Don't think that qualifies you as some sort of Dr. Phil or anything."

He continued, undeterred by my snippiness. "What do you miss most?"

"We're really going to do this?"

"It's a long drive back. We've got to talk about something."

And here I'd thought I'd dodged the whole Kori-convo when I'd ditched the movie intervention. I looked out at the mega stores that lined the highway, watched a car pass alongside us. "I was kind of planning on sleeping."

He waited a beat and then repeated his question. "What do you miss most?"

I shifted in the seat, giving him a cursory glare. I couldn't believe he was actually pressing me to talk. But I relented, because it felt good to talk to someone who actually seemed interested. And in the dark truck, heading up the highway, it was surprisingly easy to talk about Kori with him. Like letting out a breath I hadn't even realized I'd been holding.

"I don't know; she made me feel safe. Protected." I swallowed. The words sounded so selfish. Was that really what I missed most? Was that why the thought of moving forward without her terrified me? Because I didn't feel safe enough to take one step on my own?

"You can look out for yourself, can't you?"

I let out a challenging huff, but considering our first encounter had him doubled over and wailing in pain, I didn't think he was going to buy my denials. "It's just that she was always looking out for me."

"You seem pretty tough to me."

I didn't want to tell him that the toughness was all Kori's influence, because I didn't want him to know I'd been pretending to be something I wasn't around him. That all this time, I'd been lying to him. And I didn't exactly see him reaching across the console and wiping off my heavy makeup and understanding when there was someone else beneath it all.

I flicked a glance over at him before turning my eyes out the window at the hard panels of rock jutting up where the dynamite had blasted through to make room for the road. They looked close enough to reach my hand out and touch.

But just like with people, I knew they weren't nearly as close as they appeared.

twenty-six

*W*hy *haven't you done it yet?"* Lexi used to ask me. She loved to ask personal questions of people, even though she herself couldn't seem to muster the courage to say the word *sex*.

"Just haven't," I'd say, and it was a lie. Every girl has a reason—why they have or why they haven't.

Cole's was because Nickelback was playing and Ty Carter has eyes like Orlando Bloom's. Lexi's reason was no one had asked her, and as soon as some guy did, she'd probably have a new reason. Like the car wasn't very romantic or her underwear wasn't sexy or there weren't enough rose petals on the bed. Kori had already lost her virginity before we became friends, and there had been so many guys since then I don't think she'd even remember why. But I'm certain she had a reason.

I had a reason too. My reason was I'd never trusted a guy to stick around long enough for there to be an after.

That's what Lexi called it. She always wanted to know what it was like *after*.

The big, vast dark hole of after. The great unknown. Menopausal women had "The Change." And teenage girls had "After."

I didn't have answers for Lexi. I didn't know what after was like. But Kori knew all about *after*.

She once told me that she liked to have sex because after, it made her forget. And I asked her, "Forget what? Your panties?"

She laughed and almost like she couldn't believe it herself, she'd say, "No, forget the person I used to be."

It was hard for me to reconcile the Kori I was friends with against the Kori who used to wear her hair in a ponytail, giggle with Chelsea Westad, and worry about boys seeing her underwear when she did cartwheels on the playground.

She hated that old version of herself. I could hear it in her laugh. I could see it in her eyes when she mocked the BBs. When we went through old yearbooks, that Kori was crossed out with deep cutting strokes.

Shay might've had reason to believe the tattoo was about him, but I knew it wasn't. It was for the old Kori, the one she wanted so much to forget.

After getting the tattoo, singing at the club, and hanging out with Shay, I knew why Kori enjoyed being the new version of herself. I just didn't know what had made her change in the first place. I gathered somehow Shay might've had something to do with it, though.

The more I thought about the night of our date, the more convinced I was that he had wanted to kiss me. But I didn't understand what had made him change his mind, what had made him put that wall up between us.

The old Serena would have just gotten out of the truck, but instead I leaned quickly over, giving him a hug. I tucked my nose into his neck and I could feel his heart beating through the warm skin of his throat. The sound of his breathing magnified, filling the warm air between us.

Hoping maybe he would get the hint and kiss me, I whispered, "Thanks for being there with me."

Silence.

My heart rate surged as the quiet stretched. Everything hinged on what I'd do next. My stomach clenched as if I were standing on the ledge of the dam. And I knew falling . . . no, crashing was a certainty.

I jerked back and quickly grabbed up my bag. This time Shay didn't stop me from leaving.

He waited while I walked to the door. I tugged the key at my neck and put it in the lock. With a wave of my hand, I heard Shay put the truck in gear. I turned to watch him leave and caught a shifting in the shadows. A dark image by the hedges in front of my door moved. Stood.

"How was our date?"

My breath caught in my lungs. Anthony Beck.

"Anthony? What are you doing here?"

He shoved his hands into his front pockets, his mouth turned downward.

"I guess Lexi?" I nervously flicked my eyes to him.

"Yep."

"Great. Just great." I couldn't believe she was checking up on me.

"Don't worry, I covered for you. This time," he said, then: "Where'd you go?"

"To Denver."

"Why?"

"To do something for Kori. She had an obligation and I didn't want them to think she flaked on it."

"Why didn't you—" Even in the minimal light of the slim moon, I could see his face, and in it see how hurt he was because

I hadn't asked him to go with me. But instead of saying that, he changed his question to: "Who drove you?" And from the way he snapped off the words, I knew he saw the lingering hug I'd given Shay before getting out. Seeing it had stung.

I averted my eyes. "He's just a friend."

"Right. Look, I've been trying to give you space. I know how upset you've been about Kori. But I can't do this," Anthony said, pacing. "Not like this. You have to start—" He exhaled, not finishing his thought.

What we had with each other was so fragile. I held it in the palm of my hand as it struggled for life. But I knew from experience I wouldn't be able to save it.

"You don't have to do this," I said quickly.

"Do what, Serena?" he asked as he stepped closer to me. "I'm just trying to . . . to make you understand."

I forced myself to be cool, detached. Bulletproof. Just like Kori. I had to be. If I didn't, I'd come to a screeching halt. I'd be paralyzed. Stuck. "We both knew that first night was just . . ." I waved my hand around in a dismissive circle. "Whatever."

His green eyes stared through me. "Is that how you want it to be?"

As much as I wished things were different, I also knew that if I didn't do it to him, he'd most certainly be doing it to me. I unbuckled his watch and handed it back to him. Then, perhaps to save some face: "I knew this wouldn't work."

He turned to the street and a shadow dropped across his face. "Well, you seem set on that, don't you?" He shook his head like he couldn't believe he'd even bothered coming over when a simple text message would've done just as well. "I've got to go."

As he made his way to his Xterra, I watched the blades of his shoulders working rhythmically against the cotton of his

T-shirt. As he disappeared inside his car, my heart slipped and fell. Hard.

When I walked into the living room, Mom looked up from the romance novel she'd been reading. "I was expecting you hours ago. How was the movie?"

"The movie was fine. Sorry I'm late. We had a lot to talk about."

She tilted her head, her eyes full of sympathy as she misread the weary tone of my voice and pink-rimmed eyes. The way my black fingernails kept scratching at my watchless wrist. "Oh, honey, I'm so glad you went with your friends tonight. You need to talk about this." *This* meaning Kori's death.

"Right." I couldn't believe she was so happy to see me feeling like shit. But then again, the sooner I was over Kori, the sooner she could forget my friendship with Kori had ever happened. "Well, I better get to bed. 'Night."

" 'Night."

Not even ten minutes later, I heard the water in her bathtub running. From my window I watched her Jeep Cherokee drive out of our complex. Pressure built behind my eyes. My lungs clenched so tight they started shaking. I swallowed back the tears.

"I'm sorry I kept you waiting," I whispered to the disappearing red glow of her taillights. Then I crawled out my window.

I hardly realized I'd been running or crying until I found myself inside Mr. Miller's barn in front of Shay's door. I knocked loud and hard. When he appeared, I was struck speechless.

So I threw myself at him. Lips first.

A lie runs until it is overtaken by truth.
—Cuban proverb

twenty-seven

Shay's mouth took over, crushing hungrily into mine. Things went dark for a moment as I moved in response. Low-slung heat churned deep inside, seeking out his taste. Finding it dark and thick and better than honey, I wanted more. Everything pounded with one overwhelming need.

His words were muffled with panting attempts at breathing between kisses. So quiet, I convinced myself I hadn't heard a thing. But when his body yanked sharply back and cold reality shocked through me, I knew I'd heard correctly.

"God, you remind me so much of her."

He stared down at me, his fingers gripping my wrists like I was hanging off a cliff and was slipping away. My own eyes felt stretched wide and out of control. His hands jerked to my shoulders, locking me away from his body as he caught his breath. Then: "What are you doing here?"

I tried to breathe my sanity back. I had to convince him that I wasn't looking for forever. That, like Kori, I was just looking for the next step, not the thousand that would be following it.

"It's okay. We can, you know . . ." I reached my fingers across the cold air between us and stroked at his naked belly. Through tear-thickened lashes, my eyes made promises.

I could see the wheels turning in his head slam to a stop. Smell the smoke of the brakes. "No. No no no."

He shook his head as he pulled away. The hard look on his face broke my heart in the cruelest of ways. Then, almost to himself, he said, "You're fifteen."

He said it like it was a disease, and right then it really felt like one. "And I have a probation officer and a rehabilitated conscience. So we're friends. That's what we are. Friends. Us. Friends."

"Yeah, I got it," I snapped. I don't think anyone had ever dropped more F-bombs in one sentence. He was practically semi-automatic with his spray of the obscene word. Friends. Friends. Friends. Friends. F-f-f-f-friends.

"Ser, I don't want to be making promises I can't keep. I don't even know how long I'll be here for. I care about you too much to do that to you."

Care? That was right up there with "friends" in the things you never want to hear a guy say to you.

No matter how devastated I was about the f'ed up "us," I tried to play it cool. "I shouldn't have kissed you. I totally overstepped. I freaked you out, didn't I?" I caught the sad conflict in his eyes as they studied my face. "Oh, no, please don't give me some bullshit line about giving me mixed signals."

"No, I wasn't—"

"Not the it's-not-you-it's-me line." I tried to smile. "I've got my pride." *Well, what's left of it.*

"No, just you *and* me. You know, you've never really asked me about Kori." His eyes wouldn't meet mine all of a sudden. "Did she ever say anything about me?"

I could hear the warning in his tone. I wouldn't like what he was about to tell me. "No."

He stepped out of the doorway and sat on a stack of hay

bales in the aisle. He focused on his hands. "I met her two years ago at this program. It was an alternative to juvie. A brat camp."

My brows squeezed in confusion. "What?"

"She never told you?"

I thought back to that summer before eighth grade. I remembered the rumors about her being a slut, dropping E, cracking a Tiffany lamp over Chelsea Westad's brother's skull, getting arrested, spending the summer in rehab. "There might've been some rumors. That's all they were, though. I don't understand. Why would she have been there?"

"Officially, I think they diagnosed her with"—he made finger quotes—"rage control issues. But it was all bullshit. Self-defense was what it was and the guy was lucky all he needed was a couple of stitches. He tried to rape her and she beat the shit out of him."

I looked down at my hands, took a steadying breath. Someone had tried to rape Kori? "I had no idea."

"She hit the guy over the head with some heirloom lamp and put him in the hospital. I guess he's the son of someone pretty important. When Kori's father found out what happened, he was pissed. Not at the kid, but at Kori. The whole thing put some big land deal in jeopardy. So to smooth things over with the guy, her father chose to believe their side of the story—that Kori had attacked the kid for no reason. He sent her to brat camp to prove it."

"Shit," I said, knowing that the asshole kid must've been Chelsea's older brother. He was now at Harvard. It explained why she and Chelsea stopped being friends. But I couldn't understand how Kori's family could've turned on her like that. Her own father.

All these years Kori had put up with my father fetish, she listened to me ramble and drone on and never once told me what really happened with hers. She kept it all locked away, hidden from me. Never choosing truth.

And now I understood about all the crazy things Kori did. Kyle was wrong, it wasn't because she thought it was cool; it was because it kept her from feeling the pain, the same way screaming while skinny-dipping in the freezing reservoir did.

"Look, there's a reason I'm telling you this now. I pushed you away for two reasons. One was because I'm on probation, and you're very illegal to have around that way. And the other—"

"Was Kori," I said, cutting him off. "I know. I just forgot for a minute. But I get it now, why you look at me the way you do. I'm sorry I put you in an awkward position . . ."

"It's okay. I know that if everything in your life was going great, you wouldn't have shown up on my doorstep tonight. You wouldn't have offered to have sex with me, no strings attached. You wouldn't be pretending to be something you aren't. And I just didn't want history to repeat itself."

"By history you mean Kori?"

"Kori wanted her first time to be her decision. On her own terms."

"Oh," I said, just to say something. "And you know this . . ."

"Because I was her first." He reached out then, touching my arm in a painfully delicate way. "But I shouldn't have. That's why she wanted to forget me."

I swallowed, pulled back from him. "I think you'd better explain."

"The whole summer we'd been close, and I knew how young she was, but . . . then there she was—coming on to me. I think we both were so messed up." He dropped his eyes, unable to look at me as he said the rest. "We understood each other; we were friends. I should've realized, known what she was thinking. But by the time I understood, it was too late. It just really freaked me out. I'd crossed a line."

"What do you mean—*you crossed a line*?"

"The guy who attacked Kori didn't just get all handsy; he really did a number on her. It scared her pretty bad that another person could have that much power over her. She couldn't let something like that ever happen to her again. So she decided to never give someone else the chance. When she was with me, it wasn't because she was ready or even because she wanted to. She felt she had to do it to protect herself." He shoved his hands through his hair, still upset at himself. "God . . . I'd like to think I wouldn't have gone there with her if I'd known her reasoning. But, fuck, I was a just a punk kid."

His eyes darted to mine. Sadness obscured their denim color. His jaw had this odd, wired-shut look to it, and I wanted to reach out and run my fingers along its strong edge. But he seemed so distant, so remote. When I looked into his eyes, I couldn't feel that lightning anymore. And I knew that on some level, I'd imagined it all along. He wasn't here for me, he was here for Kori.

"Before, when you said you were here because of me, because of fate . . . I don't understand."

Shay stood up. "Serena, Kori didn't want to meet me at the motel in Golden for sex."

I took a steadying breath. The barn's dark interior shadowed his eyes, but there was pain there. At least they didn't look like walls this time.

"I think one day very soon, you're going to ask me to take you there too."

twenty-eight

"Okay," Doc said after the bell rang. "It's been one month since we tried to tempt fate. Raise your hand if one of the things on your list has happened."

I looked around the classroom and every hand was raised.

"Two things?"

Almost everybody still had their hand up.

"So can anybody explain it? No? Well, let's see what some of the great thinkers of our time say on the subject, shall we?"

Doc began writing quotes on the dry erase board. When he was finished he had no more white board and everything from *It is choice, not chance, that determines your destiny* to some long diatribe about seafarers and stars.

Standing back, he scanned our faces. "What do you guys think? Is it really fate if you chose the things on your list?"

As always people raised their hands and offered their thoughts. And I thought about what Shay had said about fate bringing him to Kismet. About taking me to Golden. I'd been so caught up in something I'd thought we had together, I still didn't know why Kori had needed to meet him there. Or why I would want to.

What was so important about the Sleep Inn if it wasn't about secret babies, drugs, or sex?

After the bell rang, I gathered up my bag and headed out the door with Cole. She caught the hell-freezing look Anthony shot me as he walked past Doc's doorway. "I thought you guys were dating," she said with a smirk. "You didn't have to lie, Serena."

She moved past me, heading quickly out of the classroom. The chill coming off of her was more biting than Anthony's.

"Serena?" Doc said from behind me. "Everything all right?" He looked at me with that soft gaze of his. The type of look a father might give a daughter. And I wanted to wrap it around me like a blanket.

I returned to my seat. "I think I really screwed up."

"What happened?"

I shook my head. "I can't even begin to try and explain."

"Have you ever?" he asked softly. "Tried to explain?"

Under my breath, I muttered, "Who would hear it?"

Doc sat in the seat next to me. "You know that saying?" He waited until my eyes met his to continue. "If a tree falls in the forest and there's no one there to hear it, then it doesn't make a sound?"

"Yeah?"

He grinned. "It's bullshit."

"Huh?"

"Just because no one hears it doesn't mean it doesn't make a sound, it just means nothing was around to process the noise it did make. Which, if you think about it, is also bullshit, because of all the living organisms in a forest. I mean, unless they're talking about some testing ground in a bubble completely void of life, but they aren't. They're talking about a forest. But my point is this: you aren't alone, Serena, you are very much in a forest."

I smirked. "The forest must be in Nutsville."

Doc gave a slight chuckle. "Well, that's entirely possible."

· · ·

When I got home, I started digging through Kori's boxes, looking for anything at all that might point to the Sleep Inn. As I flipped through her notebook again, I stopped on a verse she'd written. *The more I pretend to be shiny and bright, the darker I feel inside.*

Now that I understood what had turned Kori so dark, the envy I felt for her became something else. Sadness. I closed her notebook. Maybe the last of her secrets should stay buried with her.

As I shoved her notebook back into the box, a photo fell out of it and flickered to the floor. It was the original from her Postcard Secret. Looking at the picture again, I couldn't believe I'd missed it the first time. I guess her handwriting had obscured it. But right there behind the happy couple was a sign for the Sleep Inn.

I ditched Mrs. Patterson, telling her I was going over to Lexi's, and headed immediately for Mr. Miller's. Shay was quiet most of the drive to Golden.

"We're here," was all he said as he turned into the motel parking lot. He backed into an empty space so that we were facing the rows of red doors and box windows and turned the ignition off.

"The night I came here with her, all we did was this—wait in the parking lot, watching a room door. She came here to confront her father and she didn't want to be alone. That's it."

"What do you mean, that's it? What happened with her father?"

"Nothing. Kori couldn't bring herself to get out of the car. She'd been so angry. The entire time we were at that camp together, she just kept waiting for the day she'd be able to tell him off. She kept hoping to find the right time and place, and we followed him around for an hour. She didn't know he was having an affair. It just added fuel to the fire. And she went into a big down-ward spiral afterward."

Confront D.

He pointed to a man who was walking across the lot toward a room. Mr. Kitzler. I watched as he put his cell phone to his ear. For a minute he looked upset, agitated, and then he turned back and got in his car. Drove off.

"Looks like she stood him up," Shay said, turning toward me.

"She?" I rocked forward, my hands gripping the edge of the seat. I started to feel a little sick. "Oh, right."

"I'm sorry. I didn't say anything. I put two and two together when you told me your mom was leading a double life. The night I was here a woman with blond hair came out and got in an SUV. Just like the one in front of your house."

"The night Kori died," I said under my breath.

"No. I never showed. I couldn't come here and go through that with Kori again. It's . . . complicated."

"What do you . . ." I started to speak, and scarcely managed to get the words out. "What night were you here with her, then?"

"It was about two years ago. Right after we'd gotten out of that brat camp. Like I said, she went into this downward spiral. She was using drugs heavily and I was struggling to stay sober. I had to . . . I had to stop talking to her. It's been harder than I ever thought it would be. When I saw your picture a few weeks ago, I thought it was her. I thought she'd cleaned up, but then she wanted to meet me here again and I just couldn't go through that with her. I couldn't see her like that. I couldn't be a part of her life that way. I didn't meet her. And now I wish like hell I could go back. Maybe if I had been here . . ."

"Did you say two years ago?" I closed my eyes, feeling a little dizzy. "I think we'd better go."

For two years, for our entire friendship, Kori'd known my mother was having an affair with her father.

I knew and I didn't tell you . . .

My mom and Kori's father. It explained a lot. Why Kori became friends with me. The way she'd questioned Mom on spring break. Why Mom banned her from our house and me from hers. Why we had to leave the hospital so the family could have some privacy. The way she acted at Kori's funeral—sitting in the back, not going through the receiving line. The dinner with Doc Ramsey when the Kitzlers came in. Wow.

I'd blamed myself for Kori getting into Parker's car and leaving the party. I blamed myself for letting Kori go, letting her die. And all this time it was my mother she'd gone to see.

"Where have you been?" Mom demanded before I was even through the doorway.

"Funny, I was going to ask you the same thing." I pushed past her and headed down the hall toward my room.

She caught my arm and stopped me. "I've been worried sick. I called your friends. Lexi didn't know where you were."

I tossed my bag into my room. "That's 'cuz I wasn't with her."

"Who were you with? That guy?"

"Nope," I said, knowing she meant Anthony. Knowing Lexi couldn't hold it together and had tucked tail. Which was exactly why I didn't tell Lexi about Shay.

"Tell me the truth, Serena. Where have you been? Who have you been with?"

"Just out," I said as I leaned against the doorframe.

"Lexi told me you didn't go to the movies with them last night.

She told me you were seeing a guy. I know it all, so you better just come clean."

Then I figured, what the hell, what did I have to lose? There wasn't much left to protect between us anyway. And besides, I wasn't the one who should've been on trial, she was.

"You want me to come clean? Okay. Last night I was in Denver."

"Denver?" she screeched.

"LoDo. At a club."

"What?" Her hand reached behind her for the wall. She couldn't believe it. It was kind of humorous to watch her try to figure out how on earth I could have managed that. She had no idea just how easy it'd been. "Who took you? Who were you with?"

"You don't know him."

"Him? Who is he?"

I shook my head at her constant need to know such insignificant details. Always asking the wrong questions, caring about the wrong angle. *Why*. *Why* was a far more interesting question. *Why* did I go to Denver? But she didn't want to know that. Apparently all she cared about was *who*. So I told her, and in that moment, I felt like I was Cole, sliding over the console of her father's car and taking the wheel. "The guy from the Mini Mart."

"The guy . . . The guy . . ." She was screeching again. She looked like one of those squawking birds trying to get its baby to fly. Her mouth opening and shutting, nothing but noise coming out. No wonder that little bird never got back up in the nest.

"You mean you were *with* the guy who attacked you?"

"Yeah. Well, actually I attacked him, but the whole thing was just a misunderstanding."

"No. No. I don't want you seeing him again."

I laughed. "Sure, Mom, okay." Like she could police me—she was never even here.

"I mean it, Ser."

I rolled my eyes. But she was still trying to figure it all out.

"What were you doing? In Denver?"

Ah, now she was getting somewhere.

"Singing in a band. For Kori."

"Kori?" She rubbed her face. I don't know what she thought that would accomplish. "I don't understand."

"Don't you get it? Kori wasn't supposed to die. She had things to finish, Mom. I'm finishing them. Now, is it finally my turn to ask the questions?"

I glimpsed the worry in her eyes. Nervousness in the gripping of her fingers. *No. We aren't going to turn this around on me.* That's what she was thinking. Her eyes narrowed at the carpet as she gathered her resolve to say just that. Looking for anything to distract me. Anything to keep me from asking the big—Where was she? Why was she? Who was she with?—questions. The questions that would prove it was because of her Kori had gone to the motel in Golden. It was because of her Kori needed to catch a ride with Parker Walsh. It was because of her Kori was dead.

"This is not about me, Serena."

"Oh, Mother, you have no idea how much it really is." And with that, I was out. So freaking out. I stormed into my room and slammed my door.

She was quickly pounding at it. "Serena!"

I grabbed up a pair of jeans. T-shirts.

"Serena! I wasn't done talking to you!"

"Talk, talk, talk, talk, talk! That's all you ever do!" I screamed.

Then I grabbed a fistful of the "Let's talk" notes from my wall, opened my door, and threw them at her.

"That's it, Serena! You're grounded."

I shot her a big fake smile. "Great, fine. Super!" I said, then shut my door and locked it. When I heard her turn up her meditation music a few minutes later, I ducked out my window.

twenty-nine

The surface of the reservoir sparkled. From my spot on the retaining wall it looked like a thousand stars had come down to soak in the cold water. The air stirred and I took a deep breath.

In my pocket my cell phone buzzed. I pulled it out and looked at the screen. *Mom.*

I turned the phone off and dropped it in the grass. I tried to picture her at our house, standing and listening to the sound of my phone going to voicemail. I couldn't see her face, couldn't imagine what she might look like. I didn't even know her anymore. A dark part of me didn't care if I ever saw her again. Another part was terrified of what I'd just allowed to happen to us.

"Serena!"

I turned to see Lexi running toward me.

"Get down. You're going to kill yourself!"

"Not unless I bomb the dismount," I said with a grin. "Hand, hand, foot, foot. Easy."

"Serena, don't. Please."

"Don't what? I'm not jumping." I looked down at the cutting rock, felt a quiver in my stomach.

"Get down. Please!" When she got close enough, she made a grab for my hand.

I pulled it away. "It's just a cartwheel, Lex."

"No, it's not. None of this has been *just* anything. It's not just a pair of jeans or just some lipstick. It's not just one lie about a date. And it's not *just* a cartwheel."

I turned toward her. "I swear I'm not jumping," I said, hopping down so she'd stop grabbing at me. "I just wanted to do a cartwheel. Kori did them all the time."

"Serena, why are you trying to be like Kori?"

"I'm not. I'm just . . ." I sat on the retaining wall, unable to finish the sentence. I wasn't even sure how to explain, and I really didn't feel like trying with Lexi of all people. "How did you know where to find me?"

"Your mom called earlier looking for you. She sounded really worried. I knew Kori came here a lot, so I took a chance. What's this?" Lexi looked at my camping pack. "Did you run away? What happened?"

"Are you going to go running back to my mom and tell her?" I said through my teeth.

Her eyes widened. "Serena, I'm just trying to help. Your mom is worried."

"Give it a rest, Lex. You don't have any idea what she's been trying to pull with me."

"She cares. She wants to make sure you're all right. I told her you probably just needed some space."

I needed space from Lexi, that's who I needed space from. "Just leave me alone. Please."

"I'm not going anywhere," she said, sitting down in the gravel. "You can push me all you want, but I'm staying." She didn't cower at my glare. "You want me to be on your side? Give me a reason. What did your mother do that was so horrible?"

I laughed. "Where do I begin?"

"Wherever you want." Her simple, calm words gave me pause.

I took a deep breath, not sure if I could say the words but speaking them anyway. "Mom's having an affair with Kori's father. Kori wouldn't have been in Golden that night if it weren't for her." I watched Lexi closely, waiting for the shock and outrage to spring to her face. But it never did. I spelled it out for her: "If it weren't for her, Kori would be alive."

"You don't know that," she said.

"See, I told you. You're always taking her side. She's been leaving me at night to go and be with him. She's lied about conferences and double shifts. She wasn't with me because she was with someone else. Someone more important."

"You're more important to your mom than he is," she said.

I don't even know why I bothered trying to explain it to Lexi. "Whatever. You don't understand."

"You're right, I don't understand. I *know*." Lexi sat down next to me on the retaining wall and turned, looking in my eyes. "I know you are more important to your mother than he is. I know because I know what it's like when you're not. In the house in Aspen Grove, I couldn't step foot in the media room because that's where Don kept his state-of-the-art sound system. And, well, you know how kids are always pulling out cables. There was one guy who wouldn't let me eat peanut butter and jelly sandwiches because he hated the way they smelled. One who wouldn't let me eat anywhere but the kitchen counter because kids leave crumbs. I never once heard my mother say, *She's just a kid. Kids leave crumbs. Deal with it.*"

She paused to take a breath. "When I was seven, my mother met a man who didn't see kids in his future. For three years I lived with my grandmother in Idaho, and my mother claimed to be childless."

My heart felt like it was an empty beer can in Adrian17's drunken fist. Shame ate at it like acid. "I had no idea, Lex. I'm sorry."

"When I see the way your mother looks at you, I know with every cell in my body she'd never allow those things to happen to you. So if she's making a mistake with this man, maybe she just doesn't want to drag you into it alongside her. But you'll have to ask her or you'll never know for sure."

"I've asked her things before. How many times have I asked her about my father? Why would she tell me the truth about this?"

"Did you ever think maybe she wasn't keeping your father a secret from you, but maybe she was keeping you a secret from him? There are a lot of men out there who don't deserve to know their children. To know you. I know you think I always take her side, but quite frankly the odds are in her favor on this one. Besides, when it comes right down to it, you're right, I am always on your mother's side, because your mother is always on your side."

The first words that sprang to my mouth were arguments. But I swallowed them back, realizing they weren't facts. I didn't know why Mom had kept so many secrets from me.

"Even if your mom was the reason Kori went to Golden, Kori might've still been with Parker that morning. It wouldn't have been the first time she caught a ride with him. I know you want a reason. But if you had one, would that change the fact that she's gone?"

"She wasn't your best friend," I said quickly. "She wasn't ripped from you."

"I miss Kori too. I can't believe she's gone," Lexi said softly. "Sometimes my mind refuses to accept it."

I cut my eyes to her, hoping she'd see the warning and back

off. But just to be sure, I added, "You never even wanted me to be friends with her."

"Where did you get that idea? Serena, I loved everything about Kori. Even the bad things. What I didn't like was how you stopped loving anything that wasn't her." She put her hand on my leg and said, "Like me."

I stood up and moved away from her. "You have Cole. Who do I have?" My chin started quivering. I swallowed, feeling a knot forming in my throat. "You want to know why I'm trying to be like Kori? Because she was never afraid to be alone."

She snorted in disbelief. "Serena, you're not scared to be alone. If you were, you wouldn't do such a great job of pushing people away, now, would you?"

I turned to stare at her. I'd never heard her sound so matter-of-fact. It was the kind of thing Kori would have said.

Maybe because of that I gave it some thought.

I spent the weekend at Lexi's house. I just wasn't ready to talk with Mom. Not yet. But I let Lexi call her to let her know I was fine and where I'd be. I'd been thinking about what I would say to her, when right before lunch on Monday I got a message from Parker Walsh.

Want 2 c a miracle?—park

When I got to the hospital, I was nearly out of breath. Parker was in the same exact position as the last time I'd seen him, and for a split second I feared he hadn't moved at all.

"Ready?" he asked in that sadistically playful tone of his.

I took a deep breath and nodded.

The blue knit blanket, where it peaked over his toes, began to wiggle.

"Parker!" I screeched.

"That's not all," he said with a wink. He maneuvered, using his arms to help lift his legs as he swung them off the side of the bed. With a little effort he stood up. After another long minute, he shuffled one step.

"You can walk!" I screamed.

"I can walk," he said with a grin, then he collapsed back down on the bed.

I scrambled toward him before he fell to the floor. "I gotcha," I said, grabbing a leg and lifting it back up on the mattress. "There ya go."

"Well, I'll have to do some physical therapy, I'm sure."

I helped him get his blanket untangled. "What did the doctor say?"

"I haven't shown him. You're the first."

I jerked back. "You haven't shown anybody?"

He shook his head, still grinning, even though he looked like he was about to pass out. "I killed three people. You're kind of the only friend I have."

"What about Doc Ramsey?"

"He came to see me, yes. But when you didn't judge me, you gave me hope. Doc's a good person, Ser, but he's just doing what he thinks is right. He's a servant to society, just like everybody else. That's why he came to visit me; it was the right thing to do. The first time you came to visit me, you didn't really come to see me, did you?"

I glanced at him, remembering how I needed to see him, not because I cared about him, but because I needed to know if I was going to get better. "I don't know."

"Yeah, you do. But it's okay. You made me realize something. You didn't judge what I did. You didn't hate me for it. I thought everyone did. You especially."

"I didn't want to blame you, because I didn't want to blame myself."

"Why would you blame yourself?"

"Because I should've stopped her. And I didn't do anything."

Parker looked at me for a long time, then: "You couldn't have stopped Kori. Since when did she ever do anything she didn't want to?"

I grimaced, remembering what Shay had told me. I'd always mistook her independence for bravery, but now I think it was just another way she protected herself.

"You haven't asked me again about the night Kori died. Do you still want to know what happened?"

Kori had gone to Golden to confront her father, or my mother, or both of them. Shay never showed. Without Shay she'd never gotten the courage up to go through with it. Parker brought her home. End of story. Lexi was right, it didn't change anything.

"I think I know everything I need to," I said softly.

"You know those flour babies everybody's got?"

I nodded, feeling their collective weight in my bag. How could I forget?

"You know, Doc never did say what we were supposed to do with them. He just said we'd discuss it later. Everybody assumed they were supposed to do the right thing and take care of it. You want to know what Curt and Brian did with theirs?"

I nodded, feeling a little sick about getting yet another one of Doc's assignments screwed up.

"They had their flour babies on the hood of the car. They must've gotten to school early, because they were coming toward us. Curt gunned it to hit one of the new speed bumps and the flour went everywhere, all over the windshield. He swerved right into my lane. I was going too fast, didn't realize they had put the speed bumps in. They hadn't even put signs up. They should've put signs up. Yeah, I'd been a little high, but I saw what happened. They hit me."

I reeled from the image, more so because I knew that Doc must've known about the flour. That he probably blamed himself. But that was crazy. How could he have foreseen something like that happening? How could he have stopped it? And in thinking those words, I forgave myself.

As I exited the stair door at the hospital, I took a deep breath and looked up. The yellow aspen groves surrounding Kismet shocked me. Their leaves had turned overnight, making the world so different and yet so much the same.

My steps were slow as I returned to school. In addition to figuring out how to confront Mr. K., I had to figure out what to say to Mom.

I'd overcome almost all of my fears and after all of it—singing with Bleeder Valve, the tattoo, telling Chelsea off—I knew I'd be able to handle whatever happened next.

As I turned onto Lakeshore Drive, a car pulled up alongside me and slowed down.

I glanced up, half expecting to see a black Acura with tinted windows or maybe even the lawn-mower guy's truck, but it was a silver Xterra with none other than Anthony Beck at the wheel.

"Beautiful girl like you shouldn't have to walk anywhere. Get in" is what he said; what I heard was, *"Let's get you out of here."*

"Dude, you didn't just say that." Correction: Anthony Beck and three junior guys.

I was sure he was just being nice in front of his friends, so I let him off the hook. "Looks like you have a full load."

"She can sit back here, Becks. I'll make room," one of the guys shouted over the stereo as he patted his thigh.

"Schmitty, backseat," Anthony said.

Steve Schmitt glared from the shotgun seat. "I'm six two, dude. No fucking way."

I couldn't believe Anthony was making an issue out of this. Especially for me. I looked down at my boots, then up toward Kismet High. "It's okay; I'm fine walking, really. It's not far. I'll catch you at school."

"Schmitty, backseat or your damn-ass long legs can walk," Anthony barked.

"Dude!"

"Dude! Serena's not sitting in the backseat of my car." He didn't sound pissed or anything, but his tone and the look he gave Steve didn't leave any room for argument. I never guessed Anthony was so, well, commanding.

Steve opened the door, got out, and held it for me as I reluctantly climbed in. I really wasn't the kind of girl who liked guys making such a fuss over them, but it was kind of cool. It made me regret how I treated him even more.

I glanced back at his friends. From the collective looks on their faces, you might've thought Anthony had signed them up for *Brokeback Mountain, the Musical*. Although, I suppose to a junior guy, pressing thighs with another guy pretty much qualified as homosexual activity. After all, these were the very same guys who required an empty buffer seat between them at the movie theater. I grimaced apologetically at them.

Before Anthony even had the SUV in park at the school lot, the guys shot out. Laughing, I put my hand on the door handle. Anthony took hold of my other hand, weaving his fingers between mine. My breath caught as a dangerous and exciting hum spread up my arm. "Stay for a minute, we have a few."

"Okay." I settled back in the seat, but didn't exactly feel settled inside.

"So, how was your weekend?" Talk about a loaded question. Some things were just too complicated to explain when you only had a few.

"Things have been kinda crazy. I've had some stuff to deal with. I think it's going to work out, though. I hope so."

"Good, because I want to see you this weekend."

My heart fluttered. "But? I thought . . ." My voice sounded breathless. One look in those eyes of his and I felt exactly like I had the first time I'd looked into them. Excited and nervous. Scared and happy. And I felt a click inside of me. All these days I'd felt incomplete, this is what was missing. A path. *My* path. The one I'd lost sight of when I thought I needed to have Kori there to lead me. The one that included cute guys with green eyes and irresistibly spiky lashes.

Oh, yeah. I was so into him. Such a loser for letting him go. No, not letting—I pushed. Lexi was right, I wasn't afraid of being alone, I was afraid of opening myself up. I lifted my eyes to his and let him see everything. "I thought you didn't want to see me again."

"I don't know." He gave a small laugh. "I felt . . . jealous and used. But, Ser, I wouldn't forgive myself if I let one bad thing weigh more than all the good."

"We haven't had much good either," I whispered. I looked at his face, his soft lips. Regretted again the drunken hookup at the park and wishing like hell for a clean slate and a real first kiss.

He tilted his forehead, tapping it against mine. "We have potential for mad amounts of good. That's got to count for something. We can trade on our future," he said with a curvy grin. Then, more serious: "Your friend Lexi told me if I didn't give you a second chance, I'd be making the biggest mistake of my life."

"She told you that? Lexi?"

"Yeah. She also said if I hurt you, she'd make sure I regretted it. She's kind of scary."

"Lexi?" I said with a laugh. "Scary?"

Anthony reached out and brushed his fingers over my lips. There wasn't anything to wipe off this time. "It didn't help that my watch smelled just like you. I kept bringing it to my face and all I wanted was the real thing."

The air in the car suddenly got very thick and still. I searched his eyes and let my heart take a leap. We traded silly smiles, my eyes sneaking peeks at his lips. His seemed to graze along the curve of my neck.

"If I took you to the landfill, what would you do?" I asked.

He leaned over and his lips answered. We'd kissed before. The embarrassing public mauling at the park certainly had its moments, but this kiss swelled with unknown pleasures, nervousness of exploration, embarkation. This was a first kiss. The best first kiss of my life.

My body hummed with tension. He stroked his hand through my hair, raining tingles down my scalp, my shoulders, my entire body. I'd woken up covered in his scent with no greater priority than washing it off; now I savored it like a new favorite, pulling it in and spreading it thick across my soul.

My voice trembled. "So, does that mean you wouldn't watch the bears?"

"I don't know," he said with a wicked smile as his fingers

drew my shirt open just enough to reveal my skin, "I've seen better . . . bares skinny-dipping at the reservoir."

He leaned over and kissed me again. Everything pulled me
closer to him, needing to touch him. My blood pulsed faster,
faster, faster, as it revved wild through my veins. Lightning
licked across my skin. And this time I knew it was real, because
this time I felt it returned.

Even as his lips broke from mine, his arms drew me in closer.
Our exhales mingled together as we caught our breaths, staring
at each other.

A car whipped into the parking space next to us, breaking
our goofy trance. "It's late," I muttered.

"Yeah, who do you have this hour? Doc Ramsey, right?" he
asked.

"Huh?"

"I know," he whispered, brushing my hair out of my eyes. He
looked as disoriented as I felt. He kissed me again and quickly
once more. "I'll wait for you after school, take you home."

Take care of her, Becks. Get my kitten home okay.

Home.

No matter what had happened, the town house with Mom
and take-out Chinese was home. That's where I wanted to go.
That was where he would take me.

Cole turned to me as I slipped into class late and mouthed,
Where've you been?

Later, I mouthed back, smiling, both because of Anthony and
because Cole was still talking to me. But I was figuring out that
friends didn't abandon each other. They give each other chances,
many more than they deserved.

I couldn't help but notice Adrian sitting on the other side of the room scowling. As soon as we broke into groups of two to discuss the various aspects of self-fulfilling prophecies, I asked Cole what had happened.

"You missed *everything*! Marci Mancini is pregnant."

I tried to look surprised. "Yeah? And?"

"And she claims jerkwad Adrian's the daddy, but he says she's lying."

"I don't think she's lying," I said, glancing over at Adrian. "I'm sorry, Cole."

"Don't be sorry, he's a loser. You should've seen the way he acted when she told him. Even if he wasn't the one who got her pregnant, he shouldn't have talked to her that way. He doesn't deserve her. Or me."

I felt horrible for not being there for Marci. "How's she doing? Is she okay?"

"I think she's fine. I mean, the BBs aren't talking to her, but that's, like, a perk if you ask me. She ate with us at lunch. She told us that you've known."

"Oh, look, about that . . ."

"It's okay, it wasn't your secret to tell."

"Speaking of secrets . . . ," I said, and spilled everything to Cole. When I was done, I felt about a thousand times lighter.

After class, Doc called me up to his desk. "You were five minutes late to class, Serena. If you want me to excuse it, I'll need a reason."

"You don't need to excuse it," I said.

He pressed his lips together and nodded. "Okay. Fair enough."

"I went to see Parker at lunch, but I was late because I was kissing Anthony Beck in the parking lot."

Doc's eyebrows shot up. He clearly hadn't expected me to be

so forthcoming. Just a few days ago, I probably would've lied to him or tried to turn my visit with Parker into some kind of humanitarian outreach. But that was when I thought secrets were protection. Now I knew secrets were really just Band-Aids that never allowed the cuts beneath them to heal.

"I'm afraid kissing isn't excusable. Fun, though," he said with a grin.

Since I was being honest, I figured it would be a good time to get everything out on the table. Literally. I pulled Baby Charms out and placed it on his desk.

"This is Kori's," Doc said more than asked, but I nodded anyway.

"She wouldn't have kept it this long," I said in way of explanation.

"Hmm. Maybe you're right." Then he looked back at the flour sack. "Do you know what this project was really about?"

"I thought I did, but to be honest, I really don't. I'm guessing it wasn't supposed to teach us the responsibility of childbearing."

"No. It's a flour sack—who would I be kidding? But I'd hoped at some point you'd ask yourselves—why am I lugging this burden around? Is it just because someone else told me I had to? How much else am I lugging around for someone else? Just because?"

I looked down. Here I was carrying two of the damn things—how stupid was I?

"You know, we carry around burdens for other people all the time, and we give people our burdens to carry around for us. We do it for many reasons—for friends, for family, for school, for religion. But very rarely do we ask—why am I doing this? I bet you'll find you weren't alone in not knowing why you hung on to your flour bag. Most people don't ever question it; they just do it. Maybe they feel guilty, or like they owe it to you, or maybe they just don't like confrontation."

I'd carried around Kori's, no one even had to ask me, but I also realized I'd been dumping my burdens on others.

I let out a sigh; it was time for that to be over.

"Doc, I am officially turning in my assignment. I got it."

He nodded, taking Baby Maru, and then he held up Baby Charms. "So what would Kori have done with hers?" His expression beckoned me to conspire with him. "She would've done something crazy, don't you think?" he asked.

I smiled as his eyes encouraged me to share in the excitement. Was I really ready to let go of the last tie I had to Kori?

"Well, come on. What would she have done?"

I laughed trying to think of all the options. I thought of all the fates of flour babies everywhere. There were the ones that had been forgotten in the shopping mall, or dumped with paid-off nannies, or dropped off tall buildings, or left on the roof of a car, or worse. But only one right answer existed for Kori's.

"I think I know. But I need to do this myself."

A camel never sees its own hump.
—African proverb

thirty

I walked down the hallway past Dick Click's classroom; Kori's bust watched me with a naive calm the entire way. Oh, yeah, this was definitely what she would've done. I set down my messenger bag and lifted out Baby Charms. I pressed my lips to it and apologized, then stretched back and let her fly.

It sailed through the air in a graceful arc before smacking straight into the pretty and perfect Korianne's face. I'd assumed the memorial statue was bolted to the pedestal, and the bust would be solid and able to handle the impact with the grace of someone taking a pie in the face. But when the hallway filled with noise and an explosion of white flour, I knew my fate had been sealed; there was no wussing out now.

One confrontation with Dad coming up, Kor.

When the cloud of white flour cleared, it revealed the damage. Chunky pieces of Korianne's bust lay at my feet in ruins.

Oops.

The wheezing, huffing bellow of an out-of-shape history teacher making his approach filled the hallway. The crash must have interrupted his sacred lecture. The one I was supposed to be listening intently to right at that very moment.

"Miss Moore!" Dick Click managed between gasps. His

beady eyes bugged out at me. Not only was I not in his precious class, I'd just destroyed school property.

Oprah was right, I got my whisper, got my pebble upside the head, got my brick, and now I was about to hit my brick wall.

It was just as well; it'd only make the inevitable happen faster. And I was ready. "I know, I know. Principal's office."

Dick was still barking lectures at me as I walked past him. I couldn't hear him, though. In the movie of my life his sound was turned off and the Foo Fighters were cranked.

For the fourth time in as many weeks, I found myself waiting in Principal Teasley's office. When the door opened, I expected Catherine Giles to come in with some advice about how using physical release to achieve emotional release doesn't mean to destroy school property.

But the person who followed Principal Teasley brought chills to my arms.

In his dark gray suit and shiny black shoes, Mr. Kitzler had that straight-from-the-office look. I knew Teasley had to call him and let him know what I'd done to his expensive memorial. I just hadn't expected Mr. K. to drop everything and come rushing over.

"Serena, this is Keith Kitzler. I believe you owe him an apology."

Mr. K.'s salt-and-pepper movie-star hair danced atop his deeply-tanned-by-many-rounds-of-golf face. He looked me over, in the same regretful way he had at the funeral. "I never saw it before," he said.

"I'm sorry I broke the statue. I'll pay for it. I just . . ." I started into my little speech, but Mr. K. held up his hand and gave a small shake of his head.

"Stan, would it be possible for me to have a word in private with Serena?"

Principal Teasley's face wrinkled as he balked at the idea, but I guess when the guy who'd paid for nearly every wall in the school asks for a favor, you comply. "Um, well, Serena, are you comfortable with this?"

"Yes," I said, because I really didn't think Mr. Kitzler would do anything crazy with all these witnesses, and besides, I needed to say some things to him that were none of Principal Teasley's business.

"Okay, I'll be just outside the door," he said with a nervous smile.

After the door latched shut, Mr. Kitzler walked in front of me. I stayed in my chair. For some reason it felt a little safer.

"I can't believe how much you look like her." He looked over my face framed with the same black hair as his daughter's. "You really do."

I could hear a spark in his voice, like he was giving in to the illusion that he'd been given a second chance with her. But it was the other way around. Through me, Kori had a second chance with him, a chance to tell him what she hadn't been able to when she was alive.

"Kori trusted you," I said quickly. I steeled myself against his reactions and kept talking. "You were wrong to send her away. To believe Mr. Westad and his disgusting son over her."

The pained look on his face stopped me. His eyes were shut tight and tears seeped out of the wrinkled seams.

Suddenly Mr. Teasley's office felt very small and I didn't want to be with Mr. Kitzler and his tears. I didn't want to feel bad that he'd never have a chance to make things right with his daughter. I wanted to stay mad at him and carry out Kori's wish.

But now I realized I should have just sent him a letter or something.

"I'm sorry about the statue."

There was a low quiver to his voice. "I should've seen it."

"I *will* pay for it." And just to be certain he understood I meant it, that I was sorry, I looked him in the eye. Pale blue eyes, same as mine. My heart stuttered like Mr. Miller's truck engine as it tried hard to turn over. Then suddenly it roared hard and fast. And I knew.

The picture Kori had sent me wasn't the secret she couldn't tell me. This was.

Mr. K. had to sit down. I needed to stand up, but my legs wouldn't budge.

"I should have seen it," he repeated, and I knew this time he wasn't speaking of the statue. "I never knew. I asked, of course, at the time, but she told me you weren't mine. And I wanted to believe. And so I did."

You don't know it now, but we're more alike than you think. We're connected in ways you don't understand.

I nodded, slipped my hands under my thighs, and rocked forward. "Kori was my sister," I whispered. "I'm your daughter." I wasn't sure if those things would ever truly settle in my mind.

All these years I'd wanted a father I could look up to, someone who was capable of love. This man was not it. I'd been in his house. I'd been friends with his daughter. He knew it was possible and never even looked. Never wanted to know.

The tears that came flowed so heavy, they couldn't be stopped, not even with both my hands. And when Mr. K.'s arms came around me, I didn't shake them off.

He smelled like the interior of a Lexus. The silky fabric of his suit, where my nose mashed against his shoulder, felt like cool liquid. The words *"I hate you"* crashed through my lips. But his hold only got tighter.

Tentatively, I let my arms wrap around him. And I hugged him back. "I'm just complicated."

"So was Kori," he whispered into my hair, sending tingles across my scalp.

I waited in the school office while Mom talked privately with Principal Teasley. She didn't have bulletproof hair this time. I couldn't tell if that was a good sign or a bad sign, though. Luckily Mr. K. had already left before she'd gotten there, because now was not the time for a family reunion.

In fact, I thought, seeing Mom's face when she exited the principal's office, now seemed like a good time to get the hell out of Dodge.

Oprah might have thought this was the moment when my brick wall was going to crash down around me. And in a way, I was glad it was. There are just some walls that need to come down if you want to be able to see beyond them.

When I got into the Jeep Cherokee, I turned to her. "I know everything. I know about the affair and I know Keith Kitzler is my father," I said calmly. "But I want to hear your version. Why did you get involved with him at all?"

She reached her hand out to turn the ignition on and stopped. After she took a deep breath, she said, "When we first met, I was sixteen. Dad was sick and Mom couldn't work full-time. I heard about a job that paid well, but I had to be eighteen. So I got a fake ID. Everyone I worked with thought I was nineteen, and I played it up. I liked pretending I was older and wiser, worldy and womanly. Everything I thought a nineteen-year-old was," she said with a laugh. "When I met Keith and started seeing him, I was already in way over my head. He told me he loved me and I believed him. I didn't know he was married, not at first, and when I found out, it was too late. I was already pregnant. But I wasn't the only pregnant one, and because of that he broke things off with me. I was shocked, hurt. I pretended to date lots of guys, and when I started showing, he didn't even question if you were his. He was sure you weren't."

I closed my eyes, not wanting to hear any more lies. "He told me he asked you."

"In his mind, I'm sure he did. *It's not mine. If it were, we'd take care of it.* That's the way he asked, Serena. It wasn't a question. He didn't want to take care of you. He wanted to make his problem go away."

I thought about Marci and Adrian, and I trusted what my mom was telling me. I'd been so convinced my mom had never really wanted me. But now I finally understood. It wasn't that Mom hadn't wanted me; it was that, just like Marci, she chose to have me over everything else.

Mom was right, something like that doesn't happen by accident. But it didn't happen because of fate either. It happens because you embrace it with all your heart and hope.

It didn't excuse everything, though. "So why are you with him now?"

"I can't explain it. It's not always easy when your heart's involved."

"Kori knew. You knew she did. And you forbade me to see her. She was my best friend. My sister! Were you so scared she'd tell me that you couldn't risk my being friends with her?" I ignored the pained look on my mother's face. "That you couldn't even let her in our house?"

"I was wrong. And yes, I was scared. Serena, all your life you've wanted to know who your father was. You built him up in your head as this wonderful person who could come in and make everything better. And I'm sorry to disappoint you, but he's just not capable of being that. I knew if I told you who he was, you'd want to meet him. You'd find a way. And then you'd be crushed."

"You don't think he deserved to know?"

"No. I don't. He made his choice that day sixteen years ago. He gave you up. If he had his way then, there wouldn't even be an opportunity now. So no, I didn't think he deserved to know."

"But still you took him back."

"Serena, I know how this must look. But we haven't been together this whole time. Not by a long shot. We were apart until about two years ago. He sent Kori away and realized he'd made a mistake. He hated himself for it and he turned to me. And after losing Kori, he's needed someone who would listen and be there for him."

"You were more than just friends," I said, pushing the words through my teeth, hating the way they tasted. "You were having an affair."

"It's not so black-and-white. Things aren't as perfect as they seem on the outside."

I shook my head. Did she really think I didn't know that? I'd been raised by a woman who transformed herself every time she went out the front door. "He was still married. No matter how imperfect a marriage it was."

"I knew it was wrong. That's why I didn't want to bring you into it."

"But you did. Don't you see that, Mom? We're a package deal." I tried to keep my voice even. I wanted to stay calm. "When he gave me up, he gave you up too."

She looked at me, and what I saw in her face wasn't concern about her love life, but something else. "Serena, I'll back away. I won't complicate this. Whatever this is."

"You couldn't stay away from him before. What makes you think you can now?"

"Before I was trying to do it for me. Now I'll be doing it for you."

I looked into her eyes, and I believed her.

"I want you to understand something, Serena. You don't owe him anything. You don't have to be anything you don't want to be, just because you share some of the same biology. It's not your responsibility to make him a better father. Okay? That's his burden, not yours."

I couldn't help but smile. One less flour sack to carry around sounded damn good to me.

"So, you're grounded for life, huh?" Shay asked, glancing over at my mom's car.

To be perfectly honest, I didn't think she'd actually stop when I told her I needed to talk to Shay, aka Mini Mart Mugger, aka Internet predator. But she did. Of course, she was also prepared to gun the Jeep Cherokee straight at Shay if he made one wrong move.

"I just wanted to thank you for everything. Especially for telling me about Kori."

"You know, when you IM'ed me to meet you at the Mini Mart, I almost didn't go. I didn't really think meeting Kori in Kismet was any different than meeting her at the motel would've been. I'm glad I did. I mean, I wish your friend hadn't called the cops. But I'm glad you and I became friends."

"You remember when you wanted to know if there was anything else I planned to do for Kori? There was one thing. When I first told her you had mistaken me for her and IM'ed me, I asked her what she wanted me to tell you if you wrote again."

"Yeah?"

"She said, *'Tell him I want to run away, cross state lines.'* It's kind of an inside joke. But it's not the kind of thing she would say about someone she wanted to forget. She wanted to work things out with you, Shay. Not forget you. She trusted you with her deepest, darkest secrets. For her to trust anyone after what had happened to her, well, it must've been real. She felt safe with you. So whatever you think her reasons were, I know what happened between you both was also about love. She'd want you to stop beating yourself up over it."

Shay looked down at the ground, then squinted up at the sun. "So, I guess this is good-bye for a while, huh?"

I glanced over at Mom and knew her patience for this was thinning. "For a long while, I'm afraid." I leaned over to give Shay a hug good-bye and heard the Jeep Cherokee roar to life.

"Did she just rev the engine?" Shay asked, moving a step behind me.

"I'm the dangerous one, remember?"

"Right," he said with a grin. "So, yeah, I'll probably be free before you are."

"Probably. I don't think your parole officer has anything on my mom."

When we got home, Mom didn't even mention the suspension. She seemed thankful just to have me home. She did, however, subject me to her attempt at home cooking and a Mandy Moore movie, which she mistakenly thought I liked now.

As we headed for bed, she turned the dishwasher on. The shushing noise of the water kicked in as I walked down the hall toward my room. I looked at the photos of Mom and me framed on the wall and it felt good to be home. To be together.

I hesitated in my doorway; there was something more I needed. I just didn't know how to ask for it. I thought about Lexi and how easy it always seemed to be for her, the way she'd lope down the hall and glomp on my mom like a kid. It didn't mean anything. But for me, it had just been so long.

Too long.

"Mom?"

She turned, and she looked tired. And I knew it was partly my fault. I walked over to her and put my arms around her. "I'm sorry. For everything."

"Me too," she whispered into my hair.

The principal, on Mr. K.'s appeal, had let me off easy. *Easy* being a three-day suspension. The best part about it was getting to sleep in.

Except for that horrific noise that jerked me out of my precious slumber.

Whap. Whap. Whap.

It sounded suspiciously like a cane being whacked repeatedly against my door.

"Get up, you little vandal!" Mrs. Patterson started screeching.

I pulled my pillow over my eyes and prayed it was just a nightmare.

Whap. Whap. Whap.

"Get up or I'm coming in after ya!"

I jumped out of bed. "I'm up, I'm up!" I swung the door open. Nothing like waking up to your ninety-five-year-old babysitter in a T-shirt with a picture of a Bundt cake and the saying I LIKE BIG BUNDTS AND I CANNOT LIE.

"How does some hashy-brownies for breakfast sound?"

"Perfect," I said with a grin. "Thanks."

"Don't thank me, you little hoodlum, you're the one who's gonna be fixin' 'em. Now get yourself in the shower and get dressed, we've got a big day. Oh, what? You thought you could go around wreaking havoc and you were going to get to sleep in and watch TV all day? Your mom's got floors that need scrubbing, and those litter boxes of mine don't clean themselves."

Note to self: three-day suspension equals three days of Mrs. Patterson's idea of boot camp.

"I'm going, I'm going," I said, heading toward the bathroom. I couldn't help but smile, thinking things were looking up. Well, except for that business about the litter boxes.

Everything I knew had been turned inside out. Kori had died, but in a way she was and always would be with me.

Mrs. Patterson was right; people didn't leave us. Because no matter how short their time on Earth is, they've impacted someone else's soul. Kori's fingerprints were all over mine. With every dare she put me through, I'd gotten stronger.

I finally knew why Kori had sought out our friendship and why she kept our bond a secret. And I knew what Kori had meant when she'd told Kieren that I protected her. All this time I'd thought she was protecting me, but now I understood that it also worked the other way around. I was her ace in the hole if her father ever hurt her again.

On the dam when she talked about my needing to trust, she wasn't talking about fate. She wanted me to trust in myself.

And now that I knew her secret, I knew why. All the crazy dares were just her way of preparing me for the truth. Making sure I wouldn't need him if that time ever came.

And I didn't need him. I had Mom, and Cole and Lexi, Marci, Parker, Shay, Anthony, Mrs. Patterson, and at least a hundred cats. Like Doc said—I did live in a forest; problem was, I had been cutting down all of the trees.

But that was all going to change. It was a lot easier to cut a tree down than it was to grow one. I wondered if that was going to be Doc's next proverb. It should be.

I even made a new list to tempt fate with:

1. Try sushi with Lexi. *Without puking.*
2. Go to a football game with Cole. *And decorate Adrian17's truck with condoms.*
3. Trust people more. *Especially ones with irresistibly spiky lashes.*
4. Stop smoking. *Not so hard . . .*
5. Make it to Dick Click's class on time. *If I can only manage to pass by Anthony Beck's locker without kissing him . . . Yeah, that's never gonna happen.*

I still didn't believe I could control fate. Not really. Fate presents you with opportunities. That's all. You control how you react to it.

To think just a month ago my biggest problem had been not telling Mom when I took the last of her tampons. Wait . . . a month?

Crap.

I rushed back to my room and grabbed up my cell phone. Anthony would already be in class and phones were supposed to be shut off. I took a chance he would check his messages before lunch and texted him.

Five minutes later my phone rang.

"Anthony?"

"Yeah? That you, Ser?"

"Hey. Sorry about yesterday, Mom had to pick me up."

"I heard. Suspended. Ouch. Should I ditch class and come over? Rescue you from boredom?" *Let's get you out of here.* Ah, best six words a guy could say to me.

Once upon a time.

"I'm in enough trouble already, thanks. Can you pick me up something while you're at lunch?"

"Sure, french fries, a Frosty?"

God, could he be more wonderful?

"No, um . . . tampons."

"What?"

"Tampons."

"Is this like a test?"

"A test?" I asked, curling a strand of hair around my finger.

"I mean—only a guy who's really into a girl will humiliate himself by going and buying feminine needs products."

"Feminine needs?" I asked as I held back a chuckle. "Is that like some charitable cause?"

He groaned. "You know what I mean."

"Seriously, it's not a test. It's a favor. And it will definitely earn you major bonus points."

"Since we're working on the point system, I want some credit for yesterday."

"Yesterday?"

"Yeah, my friends have been calling me Swayze ever since."

"I don't get it."

"Like from the movie *Dirty Dancing*."

"Still drawing a blank."

"God, I don't want to say it—okay, they're comparing my making Schmitty get in the backseat to the famous 'Nobody puts Baby in a corner' speech."

"Okay, funny as that may be if I weren't involved and weren't 'Baby' in this little scenario, I think the bigger problem here is what it says about your friends. Now about those tampons."

"I'll do it. Just stop saying that word."

"Tampons?" I managed, through a barrage of sound deflecting la-las.

"Right. Whatever. Just tell me exactly what kind so I won't be standing there like an idiot longer than absolutely necessary."

A goofy smile crept to my lips. It had every time I thought about him, which had been freakishly often for a girl who was suspended and in a world of trouble.

"I'll do you one better. Call me when you get there and I'll talk you through it." I smiled as I rolled my eyes. "You can ask really loudly what kind I need so no one will mistakenly believe they are for you."

"They'll know they're for my . . . girlfriend?"

"Girlfriend, huh? Think I can still get that Frosty too? A good boyfriend would make it a Biggie."

"You're such a Frosty slut."

"Now, now, I think that's Chelsea Westad's title."

He chuckled.

I said good-bye and flipped the phone shut as I padded barefoot to the kitchen.

The color of blue jerked me back. On the refrigerator was one of Mom's sticky notes. Things hadn't changed that much after all. A suspension for vandalizing school property certainly warranted one.

I plucked it off with annoyance and then smiled. In my mother's perky handwriting, it said,

"I'll listen."

Acknowledgments

There are so many people I'd like to thank for making this dream possible.

Thanks to those who were there from the beginning: Aunt Bic, for having floor-to-ceiling bookshelves and an unlimited imagination; Grammy, for always smiling, even though you must have been worried about some of my interests; Sandy, for always listening, even to my crappy angst-ridden poetry; Granny, for having a map of the world and lots and lots of pushpins; my teachers, for all those wonderful writing assignments; and my friends and family, for always asking to read more.

Thanks to those who helped me do it for real: the OKRWA Outlaws, for training me in all things writerly; the Why?Eh?-Errrrs (Teri Brown, Cyn Balog, Cheryl Mansfield, and Heather Harper), for their constant encouragement, insightful critiques, and the occasional dose of edgy chocolate; and Jordan Dane (who knows Shay's real identity), for recognizing what was right and what was wrong with this story—thank you for not blowing sunshine up my skirt—every writer needs a reader like you!

Thanks to those who made it happen: Kristin Nelson, for believing in it; Emily Easton, for not only getting it but for also knowing how to make it better; and everyone at Walker, for taking such great care of it every step of the way!

Thanks to BBS for being proud even though you don't read these bound paper things.

And last but certainly not least, to my mother—thank you for always knowing this day would come, even when I wasn't so sure.